Angels' KISSES

CONNOR RANCH SERIES

NIKKI ASHTON

acknowledgments

This book was difficult to write in so far as I needed to be sure I got it right. The subject matter is heartbreaking for many families, and I needed to do their courage justice. I hope I've achieved it and if I have then I have Cath Williams to thank.

Cath, you gave me an insight into how a terrible disease can devastate a family and not simply through coping with the loss. You never flinched at any question I asked of you and yet I know it must have been hard. You're an amazing woman, from a brave tribe of women.

dedication

For the Williams sisters
Your grief is profound and your courage is epic

playlist

Make you miss me - Sam Hunt

Heartbeat - Carrie Underwood

Love me now - John Legend

Call on Me - Starley

Gorilla - Bruno Mars

Came Here for Love – Ella Eyre

How Will I Know - Sam Smith

Superman - Rachel Platten

Everglow (radio edit) – Coldplay

Stay With Me - Sam Smith

Impossible Year - Panic at the Disco

Tear in My Heart - Twenty One Pilots

All Night - The Vamps

I Feel It Coming - The Weekend

Just the Way You Are - Bruno Mars

Can't Stop the Feeling - Justin Timberlake

Be the One - Dua Lipa

Faded - Alan Walker

Catapult - John Savoretti

You and Me Song - The Wannadies

Don't Go Away - Oasis

prologue

Jemma

A s I watched him sleeping, I knew that I was done for. Garratt Connor was the most beautiful boy I had ever had the pleasure of feasting my eyes on; and he was all mine. That's what he'd whispered to me the night before, when he was slowly thrusting in and out of me.

"You have me, Jemma, every damn piece of me."

His words and his bright eyes told me that, while it definitely wasn't love…it was deeper than just sex.

I leaned forward and dropped a gentle kiss to his perfect, deep pink lips and let out a quiet sigh. Garratt's long lashes fluttered against my cheek, and I felt his face break into a smile. I moved back to look at him, and was greeted with cornflower blue eyes, full of sparkle.

"Morning gorgeous," he said as he stretched his arms above his head. "How are you this morning?"

I looked at him from under my lashes, allowing a shy grin to break.

How was I?

Happy, sated, damn well shagged to perfection; that's how I was.

"I'm fine thanks," I replied, resting my chin on his hard, naked chest.

"Just fine?" Garratt's brow furrowed as his fingers started to comb through my messy blonde curls. "You sounded a lot more than fine last night."

Garratt craned his neck and reached up to kiss me softly.

"I think the words were 'oh fuck Garratt, baby, that is so good'."

I started to giggle and buried my face against his chest, trying to hide my embarrassment. The next thing I knew, Garratt had pushed me onto my back and was on top of me, holding my hands loosely at the side of my head.

"Don't be embarrassed, Jemma with a J," he whispered, nibbling at my jaw. "It was the best night ever and you were amazing."

I smiled at his joke about my name. When I'd first met Garratt, in our English Literature class, he'd asked my name and I'd been quick to point out I was Jemma, with a J. Garratt had laughed, flopped down into the seat next to me and told me that he was "Garratt with a magic dick". Corny and crass as his line was, I couldn't help but smile. And yep, he was right.

We'd had sex together for the first time the night before, a month into our relationship, and it had been amazing; and amazing was an overused word that I personally didn't use lightly.

"Garratt," I whispered, trying to ignore the fire that was starting in the pit of my stomach. "We need to get up. I have to get to my tutorial with Professor Jacoby, and you've got to study for your Physics test tomorrow."

"Don't be such a spoilsport," he said against my sensitive skin. "We have plenty of time for a quickie. It's only ten after seven."

He stopped kissing me and flashed his perfectly straight, brilliantly white teeth at me. What was it about American's teeth, that they were just so flawless? We Brits were not so hot on the old dentistry front, it had to be said.

American teeth were just one of the things I loved about the place, and as an overseas student, there were lots of differences between here and the UK. The guys were hotter than at my old school for one - Garratt being a case in point. But, it wasn't just because of Garratt that I loved it here. The education I was getting was second to none. So much more superior than what I was getting back home. While everyone here partied a lot, they all studied really hard, too. At my university in the UK, the most important thing on everyone's mind was where they could either score some cheap drugs, or who was going clubbing at the weekend. I was therefore often referred to as the "nerdy, arse licking, creep", by many of my peers. I was the one that they begged lecture notes from while they stayed in bed with a hangover. So, when the opportunity to study in the US came along, I applied and was lucky enough to get the scholarship; much to my parents dismay. They got over it, thanks to my older sister, Lauren, who fought my corner with me. Now, here I was, two months into my first semester and enjoying some seriously good sex, with a seriously hot guy.

I groaned as Garratt's mouth moved down my neck, dropping kisses on the path to my nipple. As he took it into his mouth, I arched my back and grabbed a handful of his hair.

"I take it you've changed your mind about that quickie," Garratt said, moving a hand down the side of my body.

As he pushed my legs open, I couldn't speak but nodded and let out a breathy sigh.

"Good decision, baby."

It was just as Garratt was reaching for a condom that my phone shrilled out with Land of Hope and Glory; my mum was calling.

"Oh, shit," I grumbled. "I need to take that."

'Really?" Garratt asked, kneeling in front of me with the condom poised, ready to roll on to his impressive erection.

"I'm sorry, but it must be urgent, she usually only calls in the evening."

My heart was pounding as that thought registered. Mum had never called this early, we'd always agreed that evening, my time, was better. I quickly snatched up my phone and answered.

"Hey, Mum. Is everything okay?"

"Oh Jemma, sweetie, I'm sorry. I just had to call you."

Her voice was nasally and she was sniffing, but not like she had a cold, as though she'd been crying.

"M-mum," I stammered. "What's wrong?"

"It's Lauren," she said, her voice breaking on my sister's name. "She's ill, Jemma."

"What do you mean? What's wrong with her?" I scrambled out from under the covers, pushed up from the bed and started to walk away, but Garratt caught hold of my hand. "Mum, please."

"She's got breast cancer, sweetie."

I almost collapsed to the floor as my knees buckled, but Garratt must have sensed it, and his arm came around my waist, holding me up.

"But she's going to be okay?" I asked, my voice full of desperation. "She's too young. There must be a mistake."

Mum was silent for too long.

"Mum? She's going to be okay, they've caught it early haven't they?"

As tears flowed down my cheeks, Garratt gently dragged me back to the bed. He sat down and pulled me onto his lap, his arms coming around me; holding me tightly.

"I'm sorry, Jemma, but I think you should come home."

My mum's words were like jagged pieces of broken glass, digging into my heart. Lauren, my beautiful, twenty-five year old sister, had breast cancer and I needed to go home. I knew then that this was going to be the worst thing to ever happen and the pain was only going to get worse.

one

Garratt

Seven Years Later

As we waved away the last car, Mom let out a long sigh.

"Well that's it, it's over."

Dad pulled her to his side and kissed the top of her head. "Come on, honey, let's get those dishes cleared up and then you can rest up."

"No way," Millie, my brother's wife, protested. "Garratt can help me while Jesse goes and gets the kids."

She flashed me a huge smile that said "you're helping", and I couldn't say no.

"Yeah, you get on home, Mom. Millie and I will sort the dishes."

"Yeah, Mom," Jesse said, wrapping her in a hug. "I'm going to stable the horses, and then I'll go and pick up the kids from Zak and Sarah."

"If you're all sure."

The three of us nodded and watched as she walked wearily, with Dad, back to their house across the pasture from Millie and Jesse's.

Today had been our great auntie Ruby's funeral, and it had been hard for Mom. Auntie Ruby had lived with our parents for the last six months, as she couldn't cope on her own after a stroke, and while she was always cussing and being cantankerous, Mom loved her. We all did really, she just scared the shit out of me. Right up to the day before she passed away, she was yanking my chain and asked me whether I ever got scared my girlfriend would melt if she was too near heat, or did I just deflate her when I wasn't home. She didn't seem to understand that just because Jesse was married to his soulmate, it didn't mean I had to settle down, too. I was more than happy with my life.

My home in the city was six hours away from the ranch, and was where I worked as a loans manager for a bank. It was where I had a few regular "girlfriends" who could scratch an itch for me when required. There just wasn't anyone special. Okay, at twenty-eight, maybe I should be thinking of settling down, but I was only *just* twenty-eight, so there was plenty of time.

"Have you done anything about your dating site yet?"

I shook my head and groaned. This was Millie's question every time I came home to visit. Just because I'd told her once that I wanted to set up a dating website for college students, she now wouldn't let it lie. It wasn't that I was being lazy about doing something about it, but I was kind of enjoying the money and lifestyle that I had. Plus, setting up a dating website wasn't actually my dream these days. I'd been tutoring kids on math and I loved it. It had started when a colleague at the bank was telling me how their kid was struggling; so being a math genius, I offered to help out. After that, another three colleagues asked for help for their kids, too.

It was the best feeling ever watching their faces as they suddenly understood something, simply because of the way I'd explained it to them; it was awesome. The pride that it instilled in me was immense, and so the idea of becoming a teacher had been nagging at me for a while. That nagging had led me to start a teaching degree online and I was now almost finished. I just hadn't told anyone else about it yet. I think I'd kept it quiet in case I fucked up, which was what I'd been known to do on many occasions. After all, I'd fucked up my education in epic style at college.

To be fair, my dating agency for my fellow students had been totally misunderstood; I was not a pimp and was not running an escort agency. Well, I guess I was of sorts, but no sex was involved, or paid for. I simply provided a service for the nerds, geeks, and shy people who didn't have the nerve, or the looks in some cases, to get themselves a date. That, however, was in the past and because of it I'd had to go down the online degree route. What my family also didn't know, was that I'd managed to get myself some teaching practice, covering for a teacher at my old high school. He'd gone on a teaching sabbatical to Africa. One of my best friends, Benjie Stewart, was the gym teacher and he'd put a good word in for me with the Principal, Miss Turnbull. I had a feeling that he was boning her, but who was I to question his means? I hadn't taken many vacation days in the last two years, so in two weeks I was taking three weeks to teach math and I couldn't wait.

"Okay, I'll tell you my secret," I sighed, taking a dish from Millie and starting to dry it. "Because if I don't you're just going keep bugging me, aren't you?"

"Secret," she hissed. "What secret? Did you meet someone?"

I rolled my eyes. "No, I didn't."

"Oh God, you're so boring," she groaned, washing another dish. "So, what is this great secret?"

I told her everything and low and behold, she actually kept her mouth shut and listened.

"I had no idea," she finally said.

"No one did. I wanted to be sure it was going to work out, so I kept it to myself."

"When do you start?" she asked, her eyes bright with excitement. "Are you going to stay here while you're there?"

"I start in two weeks and will be there for three weeks of the last semester before summer break. I might take an extra week beforehand just so I can relax first, but no, I'm going to stay at Mom and Dad's. They're off on their cruise then, so it'll fit right in."

Millie screwed her nose up. "Oh, Addy will be really disappointed."

I smiled softly at the thought of my beautiful niece. She was my buddy and we were real close; it would be great to spend some time with her, especially as she was going to be going away to school next semester – a thought that Jesse was not coping with at all. Maybe she could bunk with me for three weeks. Then I thought of Hunter, Millie and Jesse's youngest child, and I knew that if I had Addy stay he'd want to come, too. He adored Addy and followed her everywhere. Unfortunately, that kid was wild and noisy, not like his sisters Addy and little Clemmie who were both fairly quiet and studious.

"She could stay with me, but," I said, "that would mean having Hunter, too, and I don't relish the idea of him climbing all over me and waking me up at the crack of dawn every day."

Millie giggled and looked out through the window into the yard where all the girl's toys were piled neatly, but those belonging to Hunter were strewn around the lawn.

"Yeah, I guess you're right." Millie turned to me and gave me a soft smile. "Whatever, it'll be lovely to have you home, Garratt."

I returned the smile with one of my own, because she was right, it would be good and I was ready for it.

two

Jemma

It had been over seven years since I'd seen Hannah, and I was feeling a mixture of nervousness and excitement at seeing her again. We'd kept in touch via social media, emails, and Christmas cards over the years, but nothing more. We'd only been roommates for a couple of months at college before I'd had to go home, so I was really surprised to receive an invitation to her wedding.

At first I'd thought about politely declining, but it fitted in with the plans I'd made to get away and leave my messy divorce behind me for a while. That and my shit of an ex-husband and his slut of a new girlfriend. I say *new* girlfriend, but they'd been together for the last eighteen months and as we'd only been married for two years; I'd say me calling him a shit was far too tame.

After I'd booked into the hotel and freshened up, I decided to have a look around; see if I could get a peak of where the ceremony was being held. It was as I was passing the bar I saw a couple of girls that I recognized from college, so went over to say hello. I wasn't confident that they'd recognize me, as I was the English girl that'd had a couple of classes with them for the sum total of two months, but thankfully, when we reacquainted ourselves with each other, both Krystal and Eden remembered me. It was probably my accent that prompted their memories, but I was grateful nonetheless.

"So, you know she's pretty much invited the whole graduating class," a wide eyed Krystal said, as she slurped on her strawberry mojito.

That thought had my heart hammering in my chest. "Just the graduating class?" I asked, trying to sound calm.

"More or less, sugar," Eden replied in her southern drawl. "She has no family, except her daddy and brother, so anyone she studied with is here; well they've been invited at least."

I swallowed my Tequila Sunrise past the huge lump in my throat. Pictures of a beautiful boy with dark hair and bright blue eyes danced through my memory banks. Damn, who was I kidding, visions of him had never left my head, there was no memory bank that needed to be raided for hazy recollections. Every minute I'd spent with Garratt was like a fresh, sharp image that had only been created yesterday.

If I was honest, I'd only been attracted to Ollie because he'd looked a little like Garratt. It was a pity he hadn't been as sweet and loyal as him. Garratt had tried to reach out to me for almost six months after I left, Ollie had only kept his dick in his boxers a little longer than that once we were married.

How I wished I'd answered just one of those first texts or emails from Garratt, but things were too difficult; Lauren had to be my priority then. By the time I had the opportunity to sit down and read his emails, it seemed too late to contact him. Almost a year had gone by and the messages had stopped months before, so I wasn't sure he'd be interested. I did write one email, explaining everything and telling him how sorry I was that Tyler had ratted him out and got him kicked out of college, but I never sent it. The words seemed so hollow and inadequate and I imagined he was already enrolled somewhere else by then; me and his previous college a distant memory. It wasn't long after that I re-enrolled at University in the UK, and my life became full of other things, but Garratt and Lauren were never far from my mind. Until Ollie came along and he asked me out on a date, and the rest, as they say, is a shit story.

"Will Tyler Davis be coming?" I asked, the need to throw a drink in his stupid face was strong.

Even though he was Garratt's best friend, I never really felt comfortable around him, and for him to then do what he did to Garratt, just proved I was right about him.

Krystal shrugged. "I'm not sure, although I doubt anyone would speak to him. After what he did to Garratt. You heard about that, right?"

I nodded. "Yes, I did."

"Douchebag," Eden grumbled. "Everyone loved Garratt."

She then pulled her straw from her mouth and looked up at me, a smile lighting up her face.

"Oh lord, I remember now. Y'all were hot for each other before you left, weren't you?"

I knew that I was blushing as I felt the heat creep up my neck to my face. Nodding, I lowered my gaze to my own drink.

"Sheesh, I remember," Krystal almost screamed. "You were always kissing and whispering and Garratt used to look at you like you'd hung the damn moon, the stars, and every other damn galaxy. We were all jealous," she added.

"We were just kids," I said with a nervous smile.

"Kids who were horny as hell." Eden fanned herself and then nudged me. "Maybe at the wedding y'all will get to start up where you left off."

That thought had me crossing my legs. We'd only had one night of sex, but it had been the best I'd ever had, and there'd been a couple before Garratt and one before Ollie. None since Ollie admittedly, but that wasn't because he'd ruined me for anyone else, that was because I didn't want a relationship with anyone.

"I don't know about that," I said. "He's probably married himself by now."

"Nuh uh," Eden said around her drinking straw. "He's single, and looking hotter than a Savannah night."

My head shot up as I stared at her with saucer like eyes.

"H-how do you know that?"

"I know he's single, sugar, because Hannah told me."

"So Hannah kept in touch with him?" I asked, pushing the sickly drink away from me.

Krystal nodded as Eden carried on drinking. "Of course she does," Krystal said. "Mikey is one of his best friends from back home."

I gulped. "Mikey, who she's marrying?"

"Yes," Krystal replied. "It was so strange, she was here on vacation, in Hawaii, with her girlfriends, and Garratt and his friends were here, too, in the same hotel would you believe."

"And they hit it off," Eden added.

"So Garratt is going to be here," I stated quietly.

"Oh, didn't we say?" Eden replied. "He's the best man."

"You'll see him before tomorrow," Krystal added. "Hannah has invited any wedding guests, who have already checked in, to come to the rehearsal dinner tonight."

My heart started to thump wildly and my palms got sweaty at the thought of seeing Garratt. Maybe I could lose myself in the crowd of people, because I wasn't sure I could cope. I'd held the fantasy of him, of us, for so long that I felt sure I'd faint if he even looked at me.

"You'll be able to catch up," Krystal said, with a grin and a wink. "Maybe rekindle that fire that you two had."

"Oh no," I replied, shaking my head. "He'll be too busy and there'll be too many people around that he'll have to talk to."

Eden shook her head. "No there won't. Apart from Mikey's parents and sister, and Hannah's daddy and brother, we're it, sugar. No one else is getting here until tomorrow morning, with the wedding being in the evening and all."

"Oh, okay." I twisted my fingers together and thought about how I could get out of the dinner. "But I'm sure he won't remember me."

Krystal grinned and nudged me with her knee. "Well, we'll soon find out because he's coming this way."

I swiveled around on my stool to see that Krystal was exactly right. Dressed in faded jeans, a white tee shirt, and an equally faded denim jacket, walking towards us with the graceful and confident strides he had even seven years ago, was my beautiful boy, now a beautiful man. My Garratt Connor.

three

Garratt

From the doorway of the bar, I could see Krystal and Eden quite clearly, and as soon as my eyes landed on the cascade of honey blonde curls, I knew it was her. To be honest, my heart knew it was her before I did - it was trying to beat its way out of my chest to try and get to her it was so damn sure.

I had to take a couple of deep breaths before I made my way over to them, but as soon as she turned around to face me, I knew that she had to be mine, just one more time.

Her girlish figure had changed to womanly curves and peeking out from the neckline of her plain red tee, was the most amazing cleavage. She still had those fantastic tits that showed off her small waist, and her hair was longer and more lustrous than I remembered, but she looked just the same as she did at twenty years of age. There was no word for her other than beautiful. As I got closer, I could see just how beautiful she was, so much more than my wet dreams remembered.

Her hazel eyes were framed with long, dark lashes that could easily have been false, they were so long, but I knew they weren't. There was nothing false about Jemma Stevens, from her forthright personality to her amazing rack; all of her was real.

I'd pretty much fallen in lust with her from the minute I'd seen her in a lit class the first day of the semester; her English rose complexion was highlighted by pink cheeks, heart shaped lips, and a pile of messy curls on top of her head. When she spoke, in what I now knew was a Manchester accent, I felt my dick stir. Jemma with a J was hot and most of the guys wanted her, but I was the lucky bastard who got her. Yeah, it cost me my friendship with Tyler, and in turn my education, but I figured I didn't miss either of those things. The only thing I had missed over the last seven years had been her. Yes, with time those feelings had diminished, after all we'd had just one month together, but in that one month I'd fallen hard. Now she was here in front of me again, and all those feelings came flooding back.

"Ladies," I said, giving them my best smile. "It's great to see you all."

Krystal and Eden pushed up from their stools to hug me, Eden's lasting a few seconds too long, but Jemma stayed where she was, playing with the black drinking straw in her glass.

"Oh, Garratt, it's so fantastic that you're here," Krystal gushed, brushing her hand against my chest.

"You, too." Not wanting to be rude, but desperate to speak to Jemma, I moved aside to get a good view of her. "Well if it isn't Jemma with a J."

Jemma slowly lifted her head to look at me, and as soon as her pretty hazel eyes locked with mine – bam, I was a goner. The intensity in them bore into my heart, making it wince with need. While they were bright, they looked a little lost, and sad, too, and all I wanted to do was lift her up and carry her off to my room.

"Hey, Garratt," she said quietly, her eyelashes fluttering in time with her heavy breaths. "Good to see you."

"You, too," I replied, gripping on to the back of one of the bar stools for support. "How've you been?"

"Okay. You?"

"Not bad."

Eden let out a quiet snort beside me. "Oh y'all still have it bad," she drawled.

"Sorry?" Jemma's eyes widened as she looked from Eden to me and then back to Eden.

"Oh, don't give me that," Eden giggled. "Y'all have it so bad I can smell the sexual tension."

"Eden!" Jemma protested but then looked back at me.

The way her eyes raked down my body, had my dick on high alert. Seven years it might have been, but I still wanted her like it had only been yesterday that I'd made her scream my name.

"Can we talk?" I said, reaching a hand out to her.

Krystal and Eden both gasped, but Jemma simply took my hand.

"Okay," she said, almost in a whisper.

I didn't waste any time in pulling her to her feet and dragging her from the bar to my room.

four

Jemma

As Garratt pulled me through the hotel lobby towards the
elevators, all sorts of things were going through my head.

God, he's still so beautiful.

Will we have sex?

Do I want to have sex with him?

Should I refuse to go with him?

Will the sex be good?

God, he really is still so bloody beautiful.

"Garratt, just stop," I cried as he pushed me inside the waiting elevator.
"What are we doing here?"

Garratt pushed me against the elevator wall, caging me with his hands
on either side of my head. My heart thudded as his face got close to mine
and his tongue flicked out to lick his bottom lip.

"I have no damn idea," he breathed out. "I just know I need to be alone
with you."

"It's been seven years, Garratt," I said, stumbling over my heaving breaths.

"I know, and I didn't realize how much I've fucking missed you until I saw you."

His face dipped even closer, and just when I thought he was going to kiss me, the elevator shuddered to a halt and the doors opened. Garratt glanced over his shoulder, grabbed my hand, and led the way out and down the corridor to his room.

When we reached the door, he put in his key card and stood back, allowing me past. Once we were both inside the room, Garratt slammed the door and moved into the main part of the room where there was a huge bed, a sofa, a TV, and desk.

"Take a seat." He pointed at the sofa and slipped off his jacket, hanging it on the back of a chair at the desk. "You want a drink?" he asked, moving over to the mini bar next to the desk. "White wine, right?"

I nodded and, twisting my hands on my lap, looked around the room; moreover the huge bed. The pillows were pushed up against the headboard, as though someone, namely Garratt, had been leaning against them, and on the pale grey comforter was the TV remote. His case was on the floor, next to the bed, clothes spilling out where he'd obviously been rifling through it.

"Here you go."

I turned to a smiling Garratt who was handing me a glass of white wine. His gorgeous eyes were bright and I let out an involuntary sigh.

"Thank you."

Garratt turned and snagged a bottle of beer from the desk and then pulled the chair out to sit on it. My stomach dropped, wanting him to sit next to me, but also glad that he'd put some distance between us.

This was all too weird. We'd dated for a month, had one night of brilliant sex, and just him being here, sitting watching me, was making my heart pound and my knickers wet.

"Why didn't you reply to any of my contact?" he asked, typically Garratt – straight in at the crux of the matter.

My eyes dropped to my glass as I thought about his question. There'd been lots of reasons and they were all to do with my sister and her illness.

Did I feel comfortable enough to tell Garratt, a man who I hadn't seen for seven years? We were practically strangers.

"My sister," I finally said. "You know that she was ill." Garratt nodded. "I had to make her my priority for a while."

Garratt nodded again and took a swig of his beer. "I get that," he sighed. "Sometimes family need you more than anyone or anything else. So, what happened, is she okay now?"

Tears pricked my eyes as a scratchy lump formed in my throat. Biting down on my lip, I shook my head.

"Lauren passed away, about eight months after I got home."

"Oh shit." Garratt put his bottle down, and in a flash, was sitting next to me on the sofa, pulling me into a tight hug. "Jemma, I'm so damn sorry."

He rested his chin on the top of my head and slowly rubbed his hand up and down my arm. I felt as though I should pull out of his embrace, but it was nice there. He smelled delicious, he was warm and he was strong; and at the moment, strong was just what I needed.

'She…" I took a deep breath. 'She had breast cancer, I think I told you that at the time."

"Yeah, baby, you did."

My stomach flipped at his term of endearment, and seven years disappeared with that one word. We were back at college, in his bed, in his dorm room, the door locked against the world and against Tyler, his shitty roommate.

"I guess they didn't get it soon enough?"

"No," I replied. "It was a high grade tumor and had already spread to her lymph nodes. She had surgery and then treatment, but it didn't work. It was quick towards the end."

Garratt's arms tightened around me and I wondered how I could feel so at ease, so comfortable with him, after all this time. But this was Garratt Connor, he made everyone feel like that - everyone loved him.

"I have no idea what you must have gone through," he whispered against my hair. "Or what you must still be going through."

"You're right, it still hurts, a lot. My mum had it, too, three years after Lauren."

Garratt pulled back and looked at me with wide eyes.

"She's okay, she got the all clear."

Anguish washed over me as memories came flooding back. Shit, why had I told him that and why had I reminded myself of the pain?

"Fuck, Jemma." His eyes dropped down to my chest and then back to my face. Pity was in his eyes, pity and, I think, fear.

I didn't want to talk about it, or be questioned about it. Enough was enough, and I was supposed to be using this time to forget.

"I really should go," I said, pushing away from him. I couldn't have the inevitable conversation with him. "We have this rehearsal dinner to go to apparently. I had no idea, so I need to call Hannah and find out what the plan is."

"It's not until seven-thirty. It's only just after one, you have plenty of time." He reached up and caught one of my curls between his fingers. "You've still got that wild and sexy thing going on I see."

My cheeks burned as his lips parted slightly and images of the magic he could perform with them flashed before my eyes.

"Never could get it under control." I laughed and shrugged.

"Wouldn't be you without it. I like it longer," he said with a grin. "It's very Kate Hudson."

"Argh," I groaned. "You and your obsession with Kate Hudson. She's too old for you, you know that don't you?"

"Hey, ten years is nothing, and I'm sure that there are lots of things that Kate and I could teach each other."

I wrinkled my nose and slapped at Garratt's chest.

"Please don't."

He smiled and ran a finger down my cheek. "You do know that my obsession with Kate only started after I met you, don't you?"

I shook my head and laughed. He'd always insisted that I looked like her. The only resemblance that I could see was that we had similar hair.

"I know what you're thinking," Garratt said, reading my mind. "But it's not just the hair. Same eye color and same pointy little chin."

He took my chin between his thumb and forefinger and gently rubbed his thumb across it. My whole body came alive at the tenderness and sensuality of his touch.

I had to get out of there.

I wanted Garratt so much, but you didn't always get what you wanted.

"Well, I really should go," I said, clearing my throat. "I haven't even unpacked properly."

Garratt sighed resignedly and nodded.

"Okay, I guess I'll see you at dinner."

"Yes, you will." I leaned forward and kissed his cheek. Wrong thing to do because the want for him increased ten-fold. "Great to see you again, Garratt."

I quickly pushed up from the sofa and made my way to the door. Garratt followed me and reached around me to open it. His arm brushed the side of my breast and I almost jumped ten feet in the air. Oh my God, this was torture.

"See you later."

"Yeah, Jemma, see you later."

When I got to the elevator, I turned to see that Garratt was watching me from his doorway, and he stayed watching until the elevator door closed in front of me.

five

Garratt

When Jemma left my room, it took every bit of strength in me not to chase after her and drag her back inside. The feelings and ideas that were buzzing around in my heart and my head were crazy. I hadn't seen her for seven years, yet my affection for her had gripped hold of me and was squeezing tight.

I just wanted to hold her for the rest of the day, and night, especially after that all too brief hug after she'd told me about her sister, Lauren. That must have been the worst time of Jemma's life, then to have her mom get the same damn awful disease; I know I'd be a fucking wreck. I also know she must be petrified that she was going to get it, too. I'd read somewhere that it can be hereditary, that the gene can be passed on. She must be scared shitless. I want to be sure that she's okay, but how do you raise a subject like that with someone you haven't seen for seven years?

Looking at my watch, I saw that I had plenty of time before I had to head down to the rehearsal dinner and typed out a text to Jesse. Thinking about Jemma losing her sister had me missing my big bro.

Me: *Hey Jess how's things?*

I didn't get a response straight away; I should have realized that it was bedtime for the kids, so he was probably reading them a story. Something he insisted on doing every night. I'd even known him do it over Skype if he'd been away from home on ranch business; so different than the brother who merely existed before Millie came along.

After five minutes my phone buzzed with a reply.

Jesse: *Hey Garr – sorry it was story time…*

I grinned. He was so gone for those kids it was worthy of a Hallmark card in his honor "Happy Soppy Dad's day" or something like that.

…We're all good here. Mom & Dad excited about cruise, kids excited about you coming to stay – me not so much!!

Me: *Why the fuck not?*

Jesse: *You lead my eldest daughter and my wife astray. I still haven't forgotten on your last visit how you got her so drunk she climbed the flag pole outside the Civic Hall – Millie that is not Addy!*

Me: *Lol yep she was really wasted but she was the one who insisted on Tequila not me.*

Jesse: *Whatever. Actually will be good to have you home for a while*

I sighed and my heart swelled. God, I loved my family and hadn't realized how much I'd missed them with living six hours away. The sooner I got home the better.

Me: *Love you bro*

Jesse: *Pussy!*

I was laughing to myself when another text came in.

Jesse: *Love you too*

I looked at my watch again and decided to hit the gym before for dinner, where I was going to make sure that I seated myself next to Jemma. I was determined that over the next couple of days, we would get to know each other again - intimately if I had my way.

When I got down to the restaurant, only Hannah and Mikey were there, wrapped in each other's arms, oblivious to everything and everyone around them. It was hard to believe that I was friends with them both, but they'd met by accident. Fate certainly played its part when we all booked separate vacations in this very hotel four years ago. They'd done the long distance thing for a while, seeing as Hannah was a midwife in Minneapolis and Mikey worked at a design studio in New York, but for the past two years they'd lived together. Both of them transferring to jobs in Chicago had seen them move in together and then get engaged within six months; and now here we were, in the very hotel where they'd met, for their wedding.

"Hey guys," I greeted them as I pulled them into a group hug. "Let's leave the foreplay to the bedroom shall we?"

Hannah blushed behind her freckles and gave me a shy smile.

"I was just getting my hands on her one last time," Mikey sighed. "She's insisting we spend the night apart."

"You've booked a separate room for one night?" I scoffed, looking at Hannah. "Seriously, Han", you don't really believe all that superstitious crap, do you?"

"No!" she exclaimed. "But it's tradition. Anyhow, we haven't booked a room."

Mikey rubbed a hand down his face. "That's where you come in," he said, with a grimace. "I was hoping I could bunk in with you."

My heart dropped. For some stupid reason I was hoping I'd be bunking with Jemma tonight. Yeah, like that was going to happen. At that moment, I really wanted to punch our high school buddy, Benjie, in the face. He should be here - he could have had Mikey in his room. But no, his damn sister had to be getting married the same weekend. I guess that meant that Mikey was my roomie for the night.

"Yeah, no problem, buddy. So, what about you, Han?"

"I'm going to be fine. I spoke to Jemma earlier and we're going to have a sleepover with Krystal and Eden, seeing as my best friend, who also happens to be my Maid of Honor, isn't coming until the morning." She was pouting and had a deep furrowed brow.

Mikey laughed and pulled her to him. "Babe, you know Shannon couldn't get out of work." He turned to me. "Shannon, her best friend from home, runs a Bed & Breakfast, so had to wait until her help could take over."

I nodded in understanding, but grinned as Hannah pouted a little more.

"I just wanted her here for every bit of this," she said. "I'm only doing this once, and want the people I love to experience it with me."

Hannah let out a little sob and Mikey pulled her against his chest, rubbing his hands down her back and whispering soothing murmurings against her hair. A wedding is a joyful time, but it was probably sad for Hannah, too, not having her mom around.

"Well, you got all of us," I said, trying to lighten the mood. "What more could you want?"

Hannah pulled away from Mikey and gave me a watery smile.

"Thanks, Garratt." She turned and reached up to kiss my cheek. "Oh, hey," she then cried down my ear. "Here's the girls."

As Hannah ran off, my heart jacked knowing that meant Jemma was here. I turned and drew in a breath.

"Fuck me," I muttered. She looked even more beautiful than she had earlier. She was wearing a skin tight, royal blue dress and high silver sandals, and all her gorgeously wild curls were piled up on her head.

"Yep, I knew it," Mikey said on a laugh. "I knew you'd still have fucking feelings for her. Every damn phone call we had for six months was about her."

I turned to him and frowned. "Fuck off, they were not."

"Yes they were. First it was, 'Oh, Mikey, I've got this real cool, English girl in some of my classes'," he said, mocking me in a doofus voice. "Then it was, 'Oh, Mikey, I've asked her out, she's so fucking cute', and let's not forget, 'Oh Mikey, she's amazing', or, 'Fuck, Mikey, she makes me so damn hard'."

I started to laugh, until he continued.

"'Oh, Mikey, she's gone and won't return my calls', 'Oh, Mikey, I can't contact her, man, and it's killing me', 'Oh…'"

"Okay," I said, holding up a hand to cut him off. "I get the picture."

"Yeah, well," he replied, nudging me hard in the ribs. "If you still have feelings, take it from someone who had to live apart from the love of his life; tell her and make it work."

"I never said she was the love of my life."

Mikey waved me off and started to walk towards the girls. "Whatever, douchebag, whatever."

"I never said that," I whispered to myself, and with a shake of the head, followed him.

six

Jemma

Yep, I knew it, he looked near perfect in his suit. If the vision of him now in a navy suit and pale blue shirt wasn't hot enough, Hannah had told me the guys were wearing a tux for the wedding…with open neck shirts. How on earth was I supposed to remain sane and not dribble throughout the ceremony?

"Well, I'll be damned," Eden whispered into my ear. "He's looking mighty fine tonight, sugar."

"He looks nice," I replied, only to have Eden slap my back – hard.

"Damn girl, if you don't want him just say and I will definitely see if he wants to share some lovin' with me for the next couple of days."

My heart slammed hard against my breast bone as I inhaled sharply.

"Nope, didn't think so," she said with a laugh, and sauntered away.

I hung back as Krystal and Eden said hello to Hannah, Mikey, and Garratt, watching them as they all interacted with the ease of people who'd spent some of their formative years together. I felt like a fraud and totally out of place. I'd only known them all for a matter of weeks, and while I'd always kept in contact with Hannah, we obviously weren't that close otherwise I'd have known that she was marrying one of Garratt's best friends.

"Hey," a voice said, close to my ear after a couple of minutes of me daydreaming. "You not coming over to join us?"

It was Garratt. I'd been so busy in my own head, I hadn't even notice him approach.

"Yes, sorry. I was just giving you all some time."

He frowned at me. "Time for what?"

"To say hello, you've all been friends for a long time. I barely know you all."

He laughed and shook his head, his gaze capturing me intently.

"I've seen you bare, is that what you meant? Because if it was, then we know each other quite well."

My nose twitched as I tried not to giggle. Garratt had always been so good at making people feel comfortable with his easy going nature, and his corny lines.

"I suppose we do," I replied.

"Well then, come on and join us."

He linked his fingers with mine and led the way to the small group. His touch felt good; it felt safe and familiar.

After a few minutes, Mikey and Hannah's families joined us and we were ushered to our table. Garratt never let go of my hand, and when Hannah's brother, Deacon, tried to sit next to me at the table, Garratt practically pushed him away.

"Sorry, man," Garratt said, putting a hand on Deacon's shoulder. "We have a lot of catching up to do."

Deacon grinned and winked. "No problem, I do believe Eden is currently single, maybe I'll sit next to her."

Garratt let out a loud laugh as we both watched Deacon rush to Eden's side.

"God, I feel so used," I joked with a pout.

"Yep, he's a player alright. He was two years ahead of us at college and was an absolute legend amongst the guys."

I looked over to see Deacon already had his arm around Eden, and was rubbing his thumb over her shoulder.

"He's a quick worker, I'll say that for him."

"So," Garratt said as we sat down. "What about you, are you single?"

"Get right to the point, Garratt," I laughed out.

He grinned and shrugged.

"Need to know what I'm up against," he replied.

My stomach fluttered at his words and the intensity in his bright eyes.

"I'm single, but that's the way I like it."

Garratt's jaw tightened momentarily and then he nodded. "Okay, well I guess it's up to me to convince you otherwise. Maybe I need to remind you how fucking hot we were together."

The bloody butterflies started again as I drew in a breath and my bra tightened as my nipples grew harder. I felt myself get wet and wondered how he could have such an effect on me with a few words.

"Garratt," I protested quietly.

Garratt reached for my napkin, shook it out and placed it on my knee. His hand trailing along my thigh.

"Don't pretend you don't remember, Jemma," he whispered close to my ear. "You can't have forgotten how I made you scream when I fucked you to oblivion."

I chewed on my bottom lip to stop the moan of desire escaping. As the throb between my thighs increased, I shifted on my seat to try and alleviate it. Garratt grinned at me.

"Yep, you remember." With that, he turned to Mikey's mum and started a conversation with her.

After dinner, and a speech from Mikey about how much he loved Hannah, everyone started to make mutterings about what they were going to do next.

Hannah and Mikey disappeared to 'make a couple of final checks on the ceremony', but we all saw them disappear into the elevator locked in an embrace. Mikey's sister also went back to her room. She was engaged to a serving soldier and she was expecting a Skype call from him. I felt for her, he was due home from his final tour in three weeks, and she told me that she was counting every minute and praying every day that nothing happened to him in his remaining time there. The parents had all decided to have a last drink in the bar, while Deacon, Krystal, and Eden decided to visit the hotel's casino and try their luck for a couple of hours before the sleepover in Hannah's room.

Throughout dinner, Garratt had been extremely attentive to both me and Mikey's mum; making sure our glasses were always full, or that we were enjoying our food. The conversation was light, and with Hannah's dad on my other side, I felt totally relaxed, forgetting everything else that was going on in my life. It had been a lovely evening, and now it was just Garratt and myself, nursing our coffee.

"You look beautiful tonight," Garratt said before taking a sip of his coffee.

"You're such a flirt." I smiled at Garratt and radiated in the warm glow of the one that he returned.

"It's not flirting if it's simply telling the truth," he replied.

"It's most definitely flirting, but then you could never help yourself, could you?" Garratt had always been a huge flirt at college; even when we were together he never missed an opportunity to flirt with me. I didn't embarrass easily in those days, but Garratt always managed to bring a tinge of pink to my cheeks.

"Once you came along, I only ever flirted with you."

He was right. I never once saw him look at another girl, unlike Ollie. Right from the beginning of our relationship, I'd often caught him eyeing up other girls. He said there was no harm in looking, it meant he still had flowing blood in his veins; pity he didn't just keep it to looking.

"I fell real hard for you, you know," Garratt said quietly, running a finger around the rim of his cup. "I was pretty fucked up about you leaving. I understood why, but I just wished you'd have kept in touch."

I let out a long sigh. "I know, I'm sorry, but after Lauren died and I finally started to pick up my life again, I just thought you'd have moved on."

Garratt's gaze on me was intense, his eyes now the color of a stormy sea and I felt captured - unable to move.

"You were pretty difficult to move on from, Jemma," he replied. "We might only have been together a short time, but it was a real intense month. That night we spent together changed things, you know they did."

Garratt shifted his chair closer and linked his fingers with my hand that was resting on the table. His other hand came to my face and he rubbed his thumb gently over my bottom lip. Breathing became difficult as his touch lit up all my senses.

"Those damn sexy lips of yours," he said in a hushed voice. "I dreamt about those fucking lips for months."

I held my breath as Garratt's head moved closer and his lips moved softly over mine.

"So beautiful and perfect." He kissed me again and then very slowly pulled away. "I don't want to disrespect you, Jemma, but we probably have a couple of hours before Mikey arrives at my room for our damn pajama party, so let's spend those two hours together."

With my heart hammering and adrenalin rushing through my veins, I slowly nodded. Maybe I was being stupid, but the need for him was palpable. But, would a couple of hours with this man be enough? No, probably not, but that was all I could give him.

"Okay," I whispered.

Garratt's eye's closed as he let out a breath. "Thank you, God," he whispered.

Standing up, he pulled me up with him and drew me into his arms to kiss me.

"You won't regret this, I can promise you that," he said seductively. "Not one damn minute of it."

seven

Garratt

oing up to my room, I made sure that the only contact I had with Jemma was our fingers touching. I knew if I kissed her I wouldn't stop, and there was no way I was disrespecting her with a quick fuck against the elevator wall.

I had no idea what the hell was going on with my body and my heart. Yeah, my body I could kind of explain; I'm a man and she's a damn beautiful woman, why wouldn't my dick want in on the action? As for my heart, I had no damn clue. Just the thought of her leaving me again in a couple of days was making my chest ache. I was missing her already, and the weekend wasn't even over yet. A few hours in seven years was all it had taken. The problem was, I knew exactly how good it was being with her, talking and laughing with her. We might have been young when we were together, but shit, I'd fallen real hard for her. The night we'd spent having sex had just been the icing on the proverbial cake. She was as perfect in bed as she was out of it, and her being here had reminded my heart how good that felt.

As soon as we got to my room, I pulled Jemma inside and had her against the wall before the door had even clicked shut.

"You have no damn idea what you do to me, do you?" I asked breathlessly, as I trailed kisses down her long, elegant neck.

Jemma's hands came down to the waistband of my trousers and started to fumble with my belt.

"I do," she gasped. "Because you do the same to me. Always did."

As my belt came undone, Jemma's delicate fingers pulled at the button of my pants, then the zipper, before she pushed her hand inside my boxer briefs.

"Fuck," I groaned, as she wrapped her hand around me, giving my dick a gentle tug.

My hand trailed down her thigh until I found the edge of her dress. I lifted it up, bunching it around her waist, and almost blew my load as my fingers pushed aside her panties to find her hot and wet pussy. I coated my fingers with her wetness before pushing them inside her and cursed as she let out a moan.

"Baby," I whispered against the curve of her breast that showed at her low neckline. "Had no idea how much I fucking missed you."

"Garratt," Jemma gasped, as I pulled my fingers out and rubbed at her hard, little bud.

As I played with Jemma's clit, her hands pushed down my pants and boxers, giving her more room to touch me. She gently held my balls, and my head fell back as pleasure coursed through me. With my free hand, I pulled down the shoulder of her dress, freeing her magnificent tits that were covered in royal blue lace. I then dragged the lace down and stooped to take her nipple into my mouth. It was hard and tasted like strawberry.

My heart jumped and I pulled my mouth away to look at Jemma. "You still wear that lotion I bought for you." I was making a statement - I didn't need to ask - I would recognize the taste anywhere. I'd bought it for her when we'd gone to the mall one day. She loved the smell of it, but said it was too expensive, because it was some naturally produced shit or something, so when she went to the bathroom I went back and bought her a tub of it.

Jemma nodded and looked at me with hazel eyes that were full of memories.

"It always reminded me," she replied.

"Jesus Christ." I captured her lips with mine and kissed her. It was hard and passionate and full of everything that I'd felt for her seven years ago; everything that I was feeling for her now. Lust, longing, and desire.

With my lips still covering Jemma's, I shrugged off my jacket and pulled open my shirt, sending buttons cascading around the room. While my hands and lips continued to explore her, I toed off my shoes and socks and kicked out of my pants and boxers. My dick was getting harder as her fingers stayed wrapped around it.

"Damn it, Jemma," I groaned as I backed away.

Her chest was heaving, her lips swollen, and her eyes bright with need. She reached for the hem of her dress and whipped it up over her head and threw it to the floor. I didn't think I could get any harder, but seeing her, in front of me, in royal blue matching underwear and amazing 'fuck me' sandals, my dick grew another inch. It was so hard it was painful.

Jemma looked at me and, with a glint in her eye, she dropped to her knees.

"Jemma…" I started, but as soon as her hot, little mouth wrapped around me, I couldn't speak. I had no words.

As she sucked me, the nails of one of her hands dug into my ass, while her other hand worked my dick. She slowly dragged her mouth along my length and then licked me, lapping at me, running her tongue around in circles. Taking a hard hold of my shaft, she lowered her mouth back on to me and started moving her hand and mouth in a rhythmic motion, slowly taking a little more of me in with each movement.

"Oh my God," I groaned, as I hit the back of her throat.

Jemma looked up at me and smiled around my dick before slowly dragging her mouth up my shaft, adding in a little teeth, with her tongue trailing after. The pleasurable pain of the gentle scratch almost had me exploding, but I held off as best I could, wanting to come inside her. I reached down and pushed my fingers into the curls piled on top of her head, and as I groaned, my hips jutted forward. Jemma gave a low moan and as her hand reached up to play with her nipple, stars flashed before my eyes.

I pulled away and reached down, putting my hands under her arms. "Get on the damn bed, Jemma."

She smiled and locked her lips with mine, allowing me to walk her backwards towards the bed. When we reached it, I pushed her down and then dragged her towards me by her ankles until her butt was on the edge. Hooking my fingers into her panties, I pulled them down and off her legs, and before they'd even hit the floor, I went to thrust into her, but stopped.

"Shit, condoms. I don't have any. Fuck!" I dropped my forehead to her chest, the smell of strawberries driving me wild.

"Garratt, I'm on the pill and I'm clean." I looked up at her, torn over my next decision. "I got checked out."

"I'm clean, too," I breathed out. "Never gone without, but the bank makes us get a health check every year and I've just had my results. I swear…"

Her fingers pressed against my lips. "Stop talking, Garratt, and just fuck me, okay?"

No further encouragement was needed. I pushed inside of Jemma and cried out. It was everything that I'd remembered.

It was perfect.

It was paradise.

We moved together, our mouths joined, our tongues exploring, and we then came together – something that had never happened to me before – I thought I was going to die from the pleasure that swept over me.

"Jemma!" My cry was loud and hoarse as I gave everything to her, and watched in awe as she took it all.

Shuddering beneath me, Jemma clawed at my back and pushed her hips higher. We couldn't get deep enough; we needed more even though we'd already reached our climax.

"Jesus," I groaned as I flopped onto my back, pulling Jemma with me. "Either we've both improved with age, or I'd forgotten exactly how good we were together."

Jemma giggled into my chest as I laced my fingers in her hair that was now more down than up.

"A bit of both, I think," she replied, looking up at me.

"Yeah, you could be right." I smoothed her hair away from her forehead and let my fingers linger. "You're so damn beautiful."

Blushing, she kissed my pec. "You're pretty hot yourself."

We lay there, silently staring at each other, and I knew that we were gearing up for round two. Well, I was, and I was pretty sure that Jemma would be on board. As I reached down to capture her lips with mine, my cell started to ring in the depths of the room somewhere.

"You want to answer that?" Jemma asked, resting her chin on my chest.

"Nope." I pulled her up my body and started to kiss her again. The cell rang again. "Fuck off!" I shouted before going back to kissing Jemma. It stopped and then started again.

"You'd better answer it," she said with a laugh, as she rolled to the other side of the bed.

With a huff, I pushed up off the bed and padded over to where my pants had been discarded. Searching through my pocket, I found my cell and looked down at the screen.

"What do you want, Mikey?" I growled.

"Nice way to speak to your best buddy," he grumbled. "Anyway, what's your room number? I forgot to ask."

I dropped my head back and cursed under my breath. I'd forgotten he was staying with me.

"I'm not there at the moment," I lied. "I'm just taking a walk. I'll be there in ten."

"Oh great, what am I supposed to do until then?"

"I don't know, go to the bar or just stay with Hannah for a little longer." I turned to look at Jemma who was scrambling off the bed. I waved my hand at her and shook my head, trying to get her to stop. "Just give me ten minutes." My comment was aimed at both her and Mikey, but she was already pulling on her panties.

"Okay, I'll go to the bar. Hannah already threw me out of our room. You wanna join me?"

I scratched at my head, wondering how I could get Jemma to stay for a while longer, but she was now pulling on her dress.

"No, I think you need your beauty sleep," I replied to Mikey. "I'll call you when I'm back in my room." Before he could answer, I dropped the call and threw my phone onto the couch.

"You don't have to go," I almost pleaded.

Jemma walked over to me and reached up to kiss the corner of my mouth.

"I'm guessing that Hannah and Mikey have finished whatever "final checks" they were making, so yes I do. She'll be calling me soon, no doubt."

Then, as if by magic, her cell rang in her bag that she'd dropped by the door. Rushing over to it, and giving me a fantastic view of her ass in her tight dress, Jemma pulled the phone out of her bag.

"Hey, Hannah. You ready for me now?...Okay, just give me fifteen or twenty minutes to get myself sorted and I'll be there...room 5193, okay... yep they went to the casino with Deacon...oh, they are, okay, see you in a few."

"You're leaving me," I said with a pout to my lips.

"Sorry, but the bride has requested my presence."

I pulled her against me, and as her body slammed against mine, Garratt junior woke up. Jemma giggled and dropped a hand between us, giving him a little squeeze.

"Don't fucking do that and then go," I cried as she started to walk away. "That's just cruel."

"I have to, and you have to entertain Mikey, and if you leave it too long he'll get drunk in the bar and it'll spoil his day tomorrow."

"Just a quick one?"

"No, Garratt," Jemma replied, with a hint of a smile, her hand on the door handle. "I'll see you tomorrow at the wedding."

"But don't you think we need to talk?" I suddenly felt anxious, worried that would be the last that I'd see of her for another seven fucking years.

Jemma's eyes clouded over, but she gave me a small smile and nodded. "Tomorrow."

She blew me a kiss and then let herself out.

"Shit," I groaned as the door closed, wondering whether I'd have time to whack one off before I called Mikey.

eight

Jemma

As I walked towards Hannah and Mikey's room, I had never felt so conflicted in all my life. I'd just had some of the best sex of my life, with a man who, seven years ago, I'd been days away from falling in love with. I should have been happy at our lust filled reconnection, even if it was only going to be for a short time. And there lay the problem. I wasn't sure I'd be able to walk away and there was a sadness deep inside of me that wouldn't let go of the tight grip it had on my heart.

If I had any sense, I'd forget the wedding and pack my bags now; leave to start my new life. A life without Ollie bringing me down and making me feel worthless.

Garratt was so different to my ex-husband. Garratt made me feel desired and sexy, he made it quite clear that he wanted me, but we couldn't have anything more than today…and maybe tomorrow, because I knew that I didn't have any sense and I wouldn't be packing my bags until it was absolutely necessary. Being with him again, close to him, feeling him inside me – it was everything that I remembered, everything that I'd thought about for years; it was perfection. But weren't all dreams and fantasies perfect, and then you wake up and realize that life is actually pretty shit? Well, maybe I'd keep dreaming for a couple more days and then force myself to wake up.

"Hi, Hannah," I said as she opened the door after a couple of knocks.

"Oh, Jemma," she cried. "Thank God you're here."

She moved into the room ahead of me, clutching at her hair.

"What's wrong?" I asked, laying a comforting hand on her shoulder.

"Shannon, my Maid of Honor, she can't come tomorrow. The girl who was going to help her out at her bed & breakfast has got the measles, and Shannon has tried every agency around to get someone, but there just isn't anyone available. She's got a houseful of guests and can't leave them. What am I going to do?" She turned to me with tears pricking at her lashes. "I have to have a Maid of Honor."

"Come on, sit down." I ushered Hannah towards the sofa and sat her down. "You don't really need one, do you?"

That was totally the wrong thing to say, because the noise that came out of her mouth was a high pitched squeal that almost deafened me.

"Of course I do. Garratt has to have someone in the wedding party to walk back down the aisle with. He has to have someone to do the first dance with. I don't have my mom, so Shannon was going to be it. Everything is going to be ruined. We have to cancel." Hannah dropped her head to her knees and started to bawl like a baby.

"Hannah, stop it, nothing has happened that can't be rectified. What about Eden or Krystal, couldn't one of them step in?" As soon as I said it, I held my breath, hoping she'd pick Krystal. Eden seemed particularly interested in Garratt and I really didn't want him neither walking nor dancing with her.

Hannah shook her head and wailed again. "No! Krystal is far too tiny…" My heart sank. "And Eden's boobs are huge. They're fake, you know."

"No, I didn't know." I mean, I had an inkling; they barely moved after all.

"Yep," Hannah sniffed. "The dress won't fit either of them."

"They could wear something of their own," I ventured.

"No, it has to be that dress." Hannah pointed to a soft grey, embellished gown that hung from the closet door. It was sleeveless, with an art deco beaded design that emphasized the low, v-cut neck and back and it would have looked at home in a 1940's movie.

"Wow, it's beautiful," I whispered.

"I know, right," Hannah sniffed. "It was my grandma's wedding gown, and Mom had it altered for her High School prom. It was her first date with Dad."

Big, fat tears rolled down Hannah's cheeks as she gazed at the dress, and I totally understood why she wanted it to be a part of her big day. I fingered the diamond studs at my ears. They'd been Lauren's twenty-first birthday present from my parents, and I hardly ever took them out.

"I had it fixed so that it fit Shannon. I thought about wearing it for my wedding dress, but…" she pointed down at her own boobs that were bigger than average. "Plus, as much as I love it, I really had my heart set on one I'd seen in a bridal magazine." Her bottom lip trembled as she glanced at the long, black dress bag that was hanging next to the grey dress. "Does that make me a bad person?"

"No, sweetheart, of course it doesn't." I pulled her into my side, and gave her a squeeze. "You're still having it as part of your big day."

"I know, but I just wish my mom was here instead of her dress."

I shuddered in a breath, as I thought about my own mum. I'd thought at one point I was going to lose her, as well as Lauren, so I felt the stab of Hannah's loss.

"Okay," I finally said. "What size is Shannon?"

Hannah looked up at me and wiped a hand under her nose.

"She's a ten on top and an eight at the bottom, why?"

I took a deep breath. "Okay, so in UK sizes that makes her 14 and a 12. The top will be a little big but I can always pin it."

Hannah gasped. "You think it will fit you? You'll be my Maid of Honor?"

Glancing at the gorgeous dress, with Garratt's face flashing through my head, I nodded.

"Before you get too excited, let me try it," I sighed, getting up from the sofa.

Hannah was up and handing me the dress before I had even made it two steps. "Go, try it on. Oh God, I hope it fits," she squealed excitedly.

Ten minutes later, the noise she was emitting was one of the loudest that I'd ever heard.

"Oh shit, Jemma, it looks perfect. It doesn't even need pinning, your boobs must be bigger than you thought."

"Yeah, maybe, but it does depend on the cut. Usually I'm a twelve."

"Who the hell cares?" Hannah cried, clapping her hands together. "It fits and you look amazing. What about your shoes, what size are you?"

"A UK seven, that's a nine I think."

Hannah's face fell. "Oh no, Shannon is a ten, they'll be too big." She put down one of the dove grey shoes with a beaded bow on the front. I slipped my foot inside, and it was indeed too big. It slipped off my foot; I'd end up breaking my neck.

"Hey, I have silver sandals with me!" I cried. "They're a little higher than those shoes, but the dress is a little long without heels." I kicked out my leg to emphasize how the dress was dragging on the floor.

"Shannon is a little taller than you, so your sandals might work. Were they the ones you had on tonight?" I nodded and Hannah sighed with relief. "They'll be perfect."

She pulled me against her chest and gave me a tight squeeze.

"Thank you so much, Jemma. You've saved me from being a complete wreck tomorrow."

"Hey, don't worry about it, but you might want to let me go before you crease the dress and we have another trauma on our hands."

She giggled and let me go, and as I wandered back into the bathroom, I heard a champagne cork pop followed by a knock on the door.

"Hey, Han," Krystal's voice, slightly slurred, cried. "We're here and we come with cookies, popcorn, and candy, so let the sleepover commence."

Smiling to myself, I hung the dress back on its padded hanger, glad that I hadn't got any sense and had not packed my bags to leave. I was going to enjoy the wedding, enjoy Garratt for a couple of days, and worry about the future after that.

nine

Garratt

When Jemma came down the aisle in front of Hannah, I thought my heart was going to blow its way out of my chest, like dynamite blasting a safe. She looked stunning, smiling brightly as she clutched a bouquet, of what I have no idea.

I know that my attention should have been on the bride, but I couldn't take my eyes from Jemma throughout the ceremony. I was so caught up in her that I missed my cue for the rings. Mikey's dad, Ron, had to kick my shin from his seat on the front row of chairs that were set out next to the pool.

"I had no idea that you were being Maid of Honor," I whispered against her ear as we danced to Sam Hunt's, Make You Miss Me.

"Me neither," she giggled. "There was a crisis meeting after I left you. Shannon, Hannah's friend, had a measles situation."

"So you stepped in." I didn't understand or care what the situation was. All I cared about was the beautiful woman in my arms.

As Sam Hunt sang out the words, 'Girl I'm gonna make you miss me', I drew in a breath and moved a curl from Jemma's eyes with my finger. She smiled and rested her cheek against my chest as we continued to dance.

"When do you fly home?" I asked, wanting to know how much time I had left with her.

"Day after tomorrow," she replied without looking up at me. "What about you?"

"Same," I said, mentally making a note to call Jesse and tell him I'd be getting home a day later than I'd planned. "Then I'm driving back home, to my parents' place. Well it's my brother's place now, but Mom and Dad still live there."

I'd taken an extra week's vacation just so I could chill before my three weeks at school. I had already done my lesson plans, so was looking forward to just spending time with my family.

"The ranch?" Jemma asked.

"You remembered." I pulled Jemma closer to me and kissed the top of her hair.

"Yes," she sighed. "I remember everything about our time together. I even remember you scaling the walls of my dorm building because the main door was locked."

I grinned, recalling the night. "I thought the drainpipe was outside your window, but it was actually that real nerdy girl who was studying astrophysics, shit what was her name…"

"Ashleigh Haven, and she screamed the place down when you knocked on the window."

"Yeah and campus police came, and if it hadn't been for her roommate dragging me in, I'd have been in real trouble."

I laughed but Jemma stiffened slightly in my arms. I looked down at her to see that she was pouting.

"That girl really had the hots for you. There was only one reason she dragged you through that window and it was to get you into trouble of a whole different kind."

"Ah, baby," I soothed, kissing her forehead. "Were you a little jealous?"

Jemma giggled and slapped at my chest. "Yes, you know I was. We'd only been seeing each other for a couple of weeks and I was feeling a little insecure."

"You didn't need to." I stopped dancing and lifted her chin with my finger. "I told you, once there was you, no one else existed."

I dropped my head and kissed her. Softly sucking on Jemma's bottom lip, I cupped her face with my hands, my fingers lacing into her hair. My tongue pushed at her lips, making me sigh as she opened up and kissed me back. With her arms twined around my neck, she gave herself up to me, standing on her tiptoes and pushing her warm, sexy body against me. It was a perfect kiss. Soft, yet demanding. We had another day and two more nights together and I was going to make sure that they were more memories that she never forgot.

"Is it too early for us to get out of here?" I asked as I pulled slowly away.

With her eyes still closed, Jemma smiled and nodded. "Yes, it is," she said, pulling me back to her as we danced to Carrie Underwood's, Heartbeat. "We at least should wait for Mikey and Hannah to cut the cake."

"Okay," I sighed. "If you say so."

I stretched lazily in my bed, enjoying the warmth of the Hawaiian sun that was streaming through the window. It warmed my aching body that had been put through its paces the night before.

Jemma and I had some acrobatic sex and made some fucking fantastic memories. The one involving the strawberries and chocolate that we'd ordered from room service being the hottest one.

I grinned to myself as I recalled what Jemma had done with the fruit, and felt my morning wood get to a full blown erection. I could hear the shower running and pushed out of bed to join her, but before I got to the bathroom door, the water stopped. When I reached the doorway, Jemma had already covered her body and was just raking her fingers through her curls.

"Hey," I said, pulling at the towel she had wrapped around her. "I was just going to join you."

She gave me a beautiful smile and kissed the side of my mouth.

"I'm going to say goodbye to Krystal and Eden. They're leaving in about fifteen minutes."

"We said goodbye last night," I groaned, reaching under the short towel for the curve of her ass.

Jemma playfully slapped me away. "I know, but I'd like to grab their numbers and email addresses. Keep in touch, you know."

My spirits rose, wondering whether that meant good things for us, whether we would keep in touch this time.

"Okay," I said. "You go. I'll go to my room, take a shower, and then meet you back there in an hour?"

She nodded and then leaned into me, kissing me deeply, with her hands at the back of my head, her fingers tangling in my hair.

"Hmm," I said, licking my lip when she pulled away. "That was nice. Make that a half hour."

Jemma rubbed a finger down my cheek and shrieked as I slapped her ass as she walked away.

A half hour later I got a text from her.

Jemma: *Got delayed. Will be with you in another half hour x*

"Women," I grumbled to myself with a grin, as I flopped onto my bed and waited.

Almost two hours later, after three texts from me, without response, I finally got a reply from Jemma.

Jemma: *I'm so sorry Garratt but I couldn't say goodbye to you. It would have been too hard. These last couple of days have been perfect and I have loved spending them with you. I'll always remember you and our time together. Be happy, Jemma xxx*

I hit on her thumbnail and paced the room waiting for her to answer; it went straight to voicemail.

"Jemma, what the fuck is this shit? You can't have left, we had damn plans today. I'm not fucking ready to let you go yet." I stilled as I took a breath, running a hand through my hair. "Please, baby, just call me back."

My cell was thrown across the room as I let out an exasperated yell.

"Fuck!"

There was no point chasing after her; she'd left it long enough that she'd probably already taken off. I had no damn idea where she was flying to in the UK, no clue where she lived. I knew that she'd moved from the address that I'd originally had. A Christmas card that I'd stupidly sent almost three years after she'd left had come back, not known at the address. Then I remembered Hannah was in contact with her via Facebook. I snatched up my cell to call Hannah, but then remembered that they took an early flight out this morning to get a connecting flight to Bermuda – fuck again! Instead, I went onto Facebook and put in the name Jemma Stevens but there were hundreds and none of the few I scrolled through looked like *my* Jemma. I entered Hannah's name but her page was locked down, and as I wasn't on Facebook, I wasn't one of her friends. I could make myself a page – that's what I'd do. I could then friend request Hannah, but she was on her honeymoon and probably wouldn't be on Facebook anytime soon, not if Mikey had anything to do with it.

I dialed Jemma's number again, and again it went to Voicemail.

"Shit."

I dropped to the couch and flopped back, rubbing at my sternum. She was gone and there was nothing I could do about it.

ten

Garratt

Over the week following the wedding, I tried everything to get in touch with Jemma, but got nowhere. Her cell had been disconnected, which basically meant she'd changed her number and didn't want to be contacted. I didn't think for one minute she'd dropped it down the john or had it stolen like the characters in those damn romance books that Millie was hooked on. No, she'd definitely changed her number.

"You asked Hannah?" Jesse asked with a stupid smirk on his face.

I looked at him and curled my lip. "What do you think? And what's so fucking funny?"

"You getting so antsy about a woman. Never thought I'd see the day."

"You know how much he liked her at college," Millie said, slapping a hand at Jesse's arm. "So leave him alone."

Jesse laughed and snagged his wife with an arm around her waist, pulling her onto his lap. He nuzzled into her neck and slid a hand up her tee.

"Please," I groaned, pushing up from the Adirondack chair that I'd been planted in for most of the afternoon while Jesse manned the grill. "I don't want to see you two making out like a couple of teenagers."

"I can't help it if my wife is irresistible," Jesse replied with a contented sigh.

"Anyone want another beer?" I pushed open the patio doors, pausing with one foot inside the house.

"Me please, and just get Jesse a Coke, he's had enough for one day."

"I'm not drunk," Jesse cried. "Nowhere near."

Millie leaned into him and whispered something into his ear. Jesse groaned, readjusted his dick, and then turned to me.

"Coke is fine, Garr."

"Fuck," I muttered to myself, wishing I hadn't agreed to spend the day in the yard with my brother and his family. All it had done was show me what I was missing.

Not that I didn't want Jess to be happy, I really did; he deserved it more than most after what he'd gone through with his first wife. I just missed Jemma and the thought of what could have been.

Who the hell was I kidding, though? She lived in the UK and I lived here; it was only ever going to be a 'wedding hook up'. Didn't mean the feeling of emptiness and longing would go away, though. Her disappearing like that had hit me like a brick from a great height. I couldn't explain it – seven years apart but after two days together, I was just as hooked as I had been back then.

Taking two beers and a coke from the refrigerator, I made my way back outside. Thankfully, the lovebirds had stopped making out and were just talking.

"Here you go." I passed them both their drinks, and sat back down in my chair.

"Kids go down okay?" I asked Jesse.

"Yep, Hunter pushed for two stories, but he was fast asleep by the time I'd said no for the fourth time."

"God help you with that one," I laughed, taking a swig of my beer. "He's going to run you ragged when he's a teenager."

Millie groaned. "Oh don't, he's a little monster now."

"No he's not," Jesse protested. "He's got spirit, is all."

Millie and I grinned at each other. Jesse would not have anything said about any of his kids. He was a real papa bear these days. He'd always loved Addy, but hadn't always been the best daddy when she was small. Now, well now he was the best father I knew, only being rivalled by our own dad.

"So," Millie said, nudging my foot with her own. "What information did Hannah give to you?"

I looked up and stared between her and Jesse, who were watching me intently. That's how they'd been for the last week, watching me the whole damn time. For what, I had no idea. It wasn't that I was heartbroken and likely to do something stupid. I was just fucking mad as hell that Jemma had sneaked away from me.

"Her email address," I finally responded.

"And?"

"And I sent an email and put a read receipt on it, and it hasn't been read."

"So what does that mean?" Jesse asked, popping his can of Coke.

I looked at him with cocked brows, wondering whether he was being serious.

"What do you think it means, dufus? She hasn't read it of course."

Jesse pulled a cushion from the empty chair next to him and threw it at me.

"Hey," I cried as it hit my bottle, the beer spilling onto my shirt. "What the fuck was that for?"

"For being a dick. I know it means she hasn't read it, but what does it mean you're going to do about it?"

I threw the cushion back onto the chair and swiped at the droplets of beer on my chest.

"There's nothing I can do. I have no number for her and, other than Facebook, that was the only way Hannah ever contacted her. And," I sighed, "like I said, her cell is no longer in service."

"So you're gonna do nothing," Jesse retorted.

I shrugged, deciding I didn't want to talk about it any longer. It was making my damn head hurt.

"Apathy is alive and well in Bridge Vale," my brother muttered around his can of Coke.

"I'm not apathetic," I argued. "I just have no damn clue how else to find her."

"Jess," Millie said, running her fingers through his hair. "Leave him alone. He's tried his best."

"No, he hasn't, or he wouldn't have let her go in the first place. If you recall, I chased you to the airport, and would have got on a plane to England if I'd had to."

"But he doesn't know where she lives."

"Excuse me," I cried, shifting forward in my seat. "*He* is still here!"

Millie and Jessie looked at me and both grinned.

"Sorry."

"Yeah, sorry Garr, but I do wonder why you let her leave."

"Because, Jessie, I had no damn idea that she was leaving. By the time she sent me the text, she'd have gone. Anyway, let's just change the damn subject, otherwise I'm going to Mom and Dad's."

"But…"

Millie nudged Jessie hard in the ribs, making him groan. Her eyes were wide as she stared at him, silently warning my brother to shut the fuck up. Thankfully, he understood.

"What time you got to be at school on Monday?" Jesse asked as he rubbed at his side.

"I'm meeting the Principal at 7:45, a half hour before class starts. Apparently, there's another guy starting, too. He's teaching English, so Miss Turnbull wants to introduce us both to the rest of the staff."

"You haven't met this guy then?" Jesse asked.

"Nope. Don't think he's local though. Jim Reynolds, ever heard of him?"

Jesse shook his head. "No. Good that you're not the only newbie, though."

"Yeah," I sighed, suddenly feeling a little nervous about the next three weeks. It could mean a massive change to my future, and the excitement I'd been feeling was waning in case this didn't work out. "What if I'm shit at it?" I voiced my concerns.

Jesse laughed and Millie gasped.

"This is math that we're talking about," Jesse said. "You're a fucking nerd, why wouldn't you be any good at it?"

"It's not just being good at math, you idiot. I have to be able to get the kids to understand it."

Millie leaned forward and patted my knee.

"You'll be great. Look how you helped Clemmie with her homework. You made it really simple for her."

"But Clemmie is a bright kid," I protested.

"Garratt, I know it's been a long, long time, but I trained as a teacher, don't forget," Millie said. "And I can see you have a natural ability for it. You'll be great, I know you will."

"Whatever," Jesse said with a grin. "At least the girls will be attentive. We all know teenage girls love a hot, male teacher. And since you're just a darker version of me, you're definitely hot."

Jesse grinned at Millie who sighed and shook her head. Jess might have amused himself, but my stomach lurched as I thought about what he'd said. Benjie had told me how the girls were always trying to flirt with him.

"Oh shit," I moaned. "I've changed my mind. I can't do it."

Millie gave Jesse another hard stare. "Ignore him. You'll be great," she said soothingly. "I just know this is going to change your life."

Taking a huge swig of beer, I could only hope that she was right.

eleven

Garratt

It was the weirdest thing. I felt nervous. Not an emotion I was particularly familiar with. I always felt confident about everything I did. My feeling was, if you can't do something with your balls nailed to the wall, then don't bother. Yet standing in front of Miss Turnbull's door, I could feel my stomach churning. I knocked and then wiped my clammy hands on my jacket.

"Come in." Miss Turnbull's voice was raspy, and I had to smile. Benjie probably got a hard on just listening to her talk.

I pushed open the door and gave the tall redhead that walked towards me, my best smile.

"Garratt, hey. Lovely to see you again." She held out her hand to me and returned the smile.

"Great to see you, too, Miss Turnbull."

"Becky, please. I like to run a relaxed ship here, but believe me, they know if they're in trouble." Her head went back as she laughed loudly. "So, you're still looking forward to this?"

I nodded and sat in the seat that she ushered me to.

"Excellent. The new English teacher will be here soon. Once she's here, I'll take you both down to the staffroom."

I thought she'd said the new teacher was a she, but Benjie had definitely told me it was a guy.

"I'm looking forward to meeting everyone," I replied. "But of course, I know Benjie already."

Becky's cheeks pinked slightly at the mention of Benjie's name. He wasn't bullshitting me then, because I had to admit Benjie had a tendency to over exaggerate from time to time. That blush creeping up the Principal's neck told me this time he was being honest.

"Yes, of course you do," she replied a little breathily.

A knock on the door saved her from any more embarrassment.

"Oh, that'll be our other newbie. Come in," she called.

As the door opened, I swiveled in my chair to greet my colleague.

"Jemma, how great to see you again."

"What the-" My mouth dropped open as wide as my eyes. Standing in the doorway was Jemma.

"Garratt," she gasped, looking as shocked as I'm sure I did.

"You two know each other?" Becky asked, with a little giggle. "How strange is that?"

"I thought it was a Jim Reynolds starting," I said.

"Jim?" Becky asked, ushering Jemma inside. "You're not really a Jim are you Jemma."

"No, no I'm not really Jim," Jemma said, shaking her head, her eyes watching me intently.

"I can vouch for that," I muttered under my breath so no one could hear.

"That's good," Becky sighed. "Because I've put Jemma Reynolds on all your paperwork. Now, you two give me just one minute to speak to Rita, my secretary, and I'll introduce you to everyone else."

Becky went through a door at the rear of her office, and started to talk to someone. The door clicked shut, leaving Jemma and me alone.

"Where the fuck did you go?" I demanded, pushing out of my chair and standing toe to toe with her.

"Garratt, please-," she started.

"No, Jemma, I want to know why you fucking left me like that. And *Reynolds*, not Stevens?"

Her cheeks flushed as she took in a deep breath.

"I had to go. I can't be in a relationship at the moment. I was starting this job and it's just too difficult."

"Did I ask you to have a relationship with me?" I asked, keeping my voice lower than I felt the desire to. "I thought you were going home to England. All I wanted was to spend another day with you. The least you could have done was tell me that you were going. Or even better, just fucking stayed and let us have a good time together."

"I'm sorry, Garratt," she whispered.

"Yeah, whatever Jemma. And again, what's with the Reynolds? Please don't tell me you have a fucking husband in tow." I was practically growling now and my hands were balled up tight.

The way she dropped her gaze to the floor said it all.

"Fuck."

Jemma took a step towards me and placed a hand on my arm. "It's not like that, we're divorced."

I opened my mouth to speak, but closed it again as Becky came back into the room. I felt sick to my stomach. I knew I had no right, but the thought of her saying vows to another man, being married to him, having a life with him, had knocked me right on my ass.

Jemma

Garratt did not look happy when he questioned me about leaving the hotel. Then, when he realized I was married, I thought he was going to actually blow steam from his nostrils.

"Okay," Becky said, grinning widely at us both. "Let's go and introduce you to everyone."

Garratt stood to the side to let us both pass him as we headed towards the door. Once in the hallway, with its shiny tiled floor and rows of pale blue lockers lining the walls, we followed Becky. I could feel Garratt's eyes boring into the back of my head, and could practically hear his brain ticking as we walked in silence. Finally, after two more hallways, we stopped in front of a door with a small rectangular window in it. Inside I could see various people sitting or standing around chatting. We were at the staff room and we were about to meet our colleagues.

I gave Garratt an anxious glance over my shoulder. Whereas I felt nervous, he looked as cool as a damn cucumber. No, cool wasn't the word; pissed off was how he looked. He didn't look at me though, but pointedly stared past me, towards Becky.

"Now," she said. "They're all real good guys and will make you feel welcome. But, I've buddied you up with another teacher, a mentor if you like, so if you need anything at all, and I'm not around, then you go to them. I'll try and sit in on a couple of your classes, Garratt, and Neil, your buddy, will too. Just until you're comfortable with the kids and we're happy you can add and subtract numbers." Becky laughed. "Only kidding, your lesson plan and practical that you did for us a few weeks ago proved you've got this."

She pushed open the door and, as we entered, the chit chat continued until Becky called out.

"Hey everyone, can I have your attention."

Everyone's gaze turned to her, and thus to us, and the chatter dulled. A tall guy, with black hair cut in a short trendy style and wearing a track suit, smiled wider than anyone else and saluted us. I heard Garratt laugh beside me and turned to see him salute the guy back.

"Buddy, you didn't chicken out then." He strode forward to clasp Garratt's hand. "Good to see you, Garr."

"You, too, Benjie."

As the guy, Benjie, thrust his hand towards me, brushing Becky's arm, she coughed and took a half step back.

"Benjie Stewart."

"Oh hi," I said, placing my hand in his. "Jemma Reynolds."

As I said my name, I was sure I heard Garratt groan, but when I looked at him he was smiling at the rest of the group.

Benjie moved back to his place between a woman in a knitted two piece and plaid skirt, and an older guy in a creased brown suit and pale blue shirt.

"So, let me introduce you to Garratt and Jemma. As you know, Jemma is our new permanent English teacher. English teacher in every sense of the word," Becky said, smiling widely. "And this is Garratt who is with us for three weeks for teaching practice. I believe you actually attended this school, isn't that right Garratt?"

I couldn't understand how I'd missed that fact when I'd applied for the job. To be honest, though, when we went out in college, Garratt talked a lot about his family, but rarely about his home town, if at all. Still, the chances of us both coming here to teach absolutely blew my mind. I was sure a mathematics genius like him could work out the probability of it.

Garratt nodded. "I did, in fact..." He leaned forward and peered at the group of teachers. "I do believe I see Miss Winter."

The woman in the plaid skirt shook her head and crossed her arms over her chest.

"Garratt Connor. The pain in my behind," she said playfully, turning to her colleagues. "I taught Garratt along with Benjie, and before that, Garratt's older brother, Jesse, and let's just say the Connor boys could be quite a distraction to the young ladies in this school."

My back stiffened as I thought about Garratt with other girls. Now I was pissed off, even if I was being totally irrational. It was over ten years ago and I didn't even know him in those days.

"How is Jesse?" Miss Winter asked.

"He's great. Married again and has two more fantastic kids."

Miss Winter smiled. "I heard about Melody, I'm sorry for his loss."

Garratt's face darkened momentarily and then he grinned back. "He's good, and Addy is amazing. Millie is the best thing to happen to them both. She's a fantastic wife and mother."

Miss Winter nodded and Becky stepped forward.

"Okay, so, Garratt, I've asked Neil to be your mentor these next few weeks, and Jemma you'll be with Vicky."

A short man in skinny black trousers and a crisp white shirt stepped forward to shake Garratt's hand. From behind the group, a woman around my own age appeared. She was really curvy, and had lustrous burgundy colored hair that fell in waves past her shoulders.

"Hi, Jemma," she said chirpily. "Nice to meet you."

She smiled at me and her pretty face lit up as she reached out her own hand to me. I noticed a huge diamond on her ring finger, and wondered how on earth she could lift her hand; it must have been really heavy it was so big.

"Hi, Vicky, nice to meet you, too."

"You're going to love it here," she said. "The kids are great."

"That's good to know," I breathed out, trying to banish my nerves.

"Yes, we don't have a bad bunch," Becky added, laying a hand on my shoulder. "The seniors can get a little wild from time to time, but hey, that's what senior year is all about, isn't it?"

Instantly, I knew this was going to be okay. I liked Becky a lot, she seemed as though she was a fantastic Principal, and the staff all seemed friendly enough.

I looked around and saw Garratt watching me. His eyes were still dark with temper and his arms were folded across his chest. Whenever anyone spoke to him, his face broke into a smile, but once his gaze was back on me, the glare returned.

Shit.

Maybe this wasn't going to go so well after all.

twelve

Garratt

My first day teaching at Bridge Vale High went well. Becky sat in on it, but pretty much kept in the background taking a couple of notes. There was the usual ribbing of the new teacher, from the senior class, but once I showed them that I wasn't intimidated by their antics, they soon gave up and listened to what I had to say on statistics. Particularly when I used my Star Wars Top Trumps cards to demonstrate what I was trying to teach them. As they left the class, most of them thanked me, and if they didn't at least they were smiling.

Because Bridge Vale and its catchment area wasn't huge, the school was combined with the Junior High. That meant that my afternoon lessons were spent with the 8th graders. The boys in the class listened carefully to what I had to say, while the girls stared dreamily at me. Becky had been called to meet a parent, so I was on my own and it was a little unnerving to say the least. I felt distinctly uncomfortable, particularly when one girl, Brianna, sidled up to me, flicked her long blond hair over her shoulder, and suggested she might need private tutoring. These kids were fourteen years of age, who the fuck taught them to flirt like that? Then I remembered what a horny little shit I'd been at fourteen and quickly sent Brianna back to her seat.

I was making my way back to the staffroom to pick up my things, when someone whistled behind me. I turned to see Benjie jogging towards me, pushing through a group of younger teenage girls who were looking at him with the same hunger that Brianna had afforded me earlier.

"Hey man," he said, as he pulled up in front of me. "How'd it go?"

I smiled and nodded. "Yeah, okay I think. The 8th grade girls are a little scary."

Benjie rolled his eyes. "Fucking tell me about it," he said, lowering his voice, looking around for any lingering kids. "The Senior girls are practically nuns compared to those kids. Who you have trouble with?"

"Brianna Devlin."

"Sheesh," Benjie whistled out. "You know who her mom is don't you?"

"No, who?"

"Clara Devlin."

I gasped. Clara Devlin had been my girlfriend for a while when we were in the 8th grade.

"Oh fuck," Benjie said his eyes getting wide. "She isn't-"

"No, she damn well isn't," I spluttered. "We didn't, but her and Dexter Carmichael did, which was why we broke up."

Benjie considered what I was saying for a moment and then nodded. "Yeah, I remember now. Then her and her folks left town. Now we know why. Brianna only started this semester, when Clara came back to town."

"Knowing she's Clara Devlin's kid answers why she's so damn forward." I thought back to our rolls in my dad's barn when we were fourteen. Clara had taken the lead, and we'd done everything but the dirty deed. In fact, it was Clara who'd schooled me on how to make a girl feel good and bring her to orgasm with everything except my dick - that lesson I'd learned from a senior, Marla Jacobs, when I was sixteen.

"Yeah well, you survived your first day. Quick beer at Rowdy's?"

I thought about it for a couple of seconds and nodded.

"Yeah, why not. Although, it's a little early."

Benjie laughed and slapped a large hand on my back. "It's your first day teaching and it went well. Soon, my friend, you'll realize how welcoming a beer at Rowdy's at five in the evening is. You haven't taught Buddy Dunkley's son yet."

I grimaced. Buddy Dunkley was a couple of years older than Jesse, and was the town bully when we were kids.

"He a bully like his dad?" I asked.

"Yep," Benjie breathed out, guiding me towards the staffroom. "And just as fucking ugly, too."

Once we were settled at a high table at Rowdy's, I tapped the edge of my bottle against Benjie's and grinned at him.

"So, you and the Principal, then."

His cheeks flushed a little as he smiled back. "No one at school knows yet. I suggested we keep it quiet, but after the weekend…well, Becky wants to tell everyone when we break for summer."

I furrowed my brow and took a swig of beer. "What happened last weekend?"

Benjie's cheeks went a deeper shade of red and he coughed nervously.

"We kinda said the "L" word."

I almost spat my beer out across the table. Benjie was the biggest manwhore I knew, apart from Jesse when he'd been going through a bad time, before Millie came along.

"Seriously?"

He nodded. "Yeah. I love her, man."

"She's older than you though, right?" Becky had to be older than us. She was a High School Principal and those jobs usually only went to people with a lot of teaching experience.

"She's thirty-four. I know what you're thinking, she's *too* old for me."

I let out a laugh and slapped Benjie's back. "Fuck no, I'm thinking she's *too* damn good for you."

"Hey, douchebag." He grinned and took a long drink.

"She seems real nice. I like her, and she must have been a damn good teacher to get a Principal's job at thirty-four."

"Actually, it was thirty-two, she was at a school in Oklahoma City before she came here."

"Why would you leave Oklahoma City to come to Bridge Vale?"

Benjie winked at me. "'Cause she knew I was waiting for her."

"That has to be it."

"No, her parents live in Knightingale and her mom has MS, so she wanted to be around more. This job came up and she got it."

"Sorry about her mom."

"Yeah, she's a real nice lady. Doesn't let it get her down, you know."

"But a Knightingale woman, Benjie. Don't tell Jesse, he'll never speak to you again."

"I remember a time when Jesse had plenty of Knightingale women in his bed."

I nodded, he was right, and I was only playing with him. But Knightingale was the enemy when we were in high school.

We sat in silence for a while, before I turned back to Benjie.

"You spend any time with Jemma today?" I didn't look at him, but over towards Janelle who was wiping down the bar. She'd recently bought the place from Rowdy, who'd retired to Miami. According to Jesse, she'd promised everyone at a town council meeting that she wouldn't be changing the name of the place. That was the sort of town Bridge Vale was - the name of the local bar was an agenda item for the town council.

"Nope," Benjie said. "You?"

I let out a long breath before placing my bottle on the table. "You remember that girl at college that I was crazy about?"

"Yeah," he said slowly. "The one who left when you got thrown out?"

"That's the one. Well, that girl is Jemma."

His mouth dropped open as he slowly placed his bottle on the table.

"No fucking way."

"Yes, she sure is. And there's something else."

"Don't tell me she had your kid," he gasped.

I slapped him around the back of the head. "What is it with you thinking I've got fucking kids running around all over the place? As far as I know,

I've never impregnated anyone, you dick."

"Well you sounded kinda dramatic." He gave me a look that, if I didn't know what a softie he was, it might have had me shitting my pants.

"Whatever. The something else, is that she was at Hannah and Mikey's wedding."

"Oh God, yeah. You went to college with Hannah, and she was Hannah's roommate, right?"

"Yep. But let's say at the wedding, she was mine – roommate, I mean."

"So, are you two an item now then, or what?" Benjie leaned closer, evidently eager to hear the juicy gossip.

"Nope, she left me without saying goodbye. Today was the first time I'd seen her since she disappeared on me. Seeing as you said the new English teacher was a guy named Jim, I was a little shocked when she walked through the door."

"Fuck."

"Yeah, buddy, fuck indeed."

thirteen
Jemma

After our meeting in the Principal's office, I didn't see Garratt again. I caught a glimpse of him leaving school, with Benjie, but he didn't see me, or if he had, he didn't acknowledge the fact.

I understood why he was mad at me, I'd have reacted the same way if he'd disappeared on me. Especially after what we'd done the night before. He'd lavished my body with attention, in every way, on every part of it, with some parts getting more attention than others. It had been even better than the night before the wedding. That night had been spectacular, but spending the whole night together had taken things to a different level. A level that, as naïve twenty year olds, we never would have reached.

I couldn't ignore how I felt about him. I was still having vivid daydreams about it for god's sake. I also couldn't ignore the fact that nothing else could happen between us, no matter how much my body yearned for it.

My head was in a mush thinking about things.

How my feelings for Garratt had been reawakened.

How we'd both ended up working in the same place.

How I had to just get through this next three weeks and then he'd be gone.

How that thought filled me with dread.

"Hey, Jemma. How was your first day?"

Vicky was throwing her bags into the back seat of her car that was parked next to mine.

"It was great. I think. I guess you'll have to ask the students that."

She waved a dismissive hand at me. "Ah, I'm sure you did great. I didn't hear you shouting once, so you must have been keeping their attention."

Vicky's history classroom was across the hall from mine, and once or twice I'd see her giving me a thumbs up through the glass in the doors.

"The seniors seem to like the war poets, which is a big surprise."

"Wow, that is a surprise. I know Roger, your predecessor, used to hate teaching it. Always said the kids hated it and were bored stupid."

I shrugged. "Maybe they were being kind, seeing as it was my first day."

Vicky smiled and opened her driver's door. "Well, I'll see you tomorrow. You got plans tonight?"

I shook my head. "No. Bath, dinner, and bed for me. I still have stuff I should be unpacking in my apartment, but it can wait another night. You?"

"Wedding cake tasting." She grimaced and blew out her cheeks. "I really should avoid the calories, I have a real tight wedding dress to get this baby into." She slapped her ample, but pert, bottom and laughed. "But Jonah, my fiancé, insists we try at least four cakes before we decide. Me, I'm just like, honey, lets go chocolate and vanilla, but no, he's too fussy."

She started to giggle and talk of her fiancé turned her from pretty to beautiful. Her dark brown eyes flashing with love as she flicked her hair over her shoulder.

"You'd think being a personal trainer, he'd feel my pain, but no," she sighed. "So cake it is."

"Take tiny bites," I replied, smiling back at her.

"Good idea. Anyways, I'll see you tomorrow."

We waved goodbye and got into our respective cars. Before starting the ignition, I set my phone in its cradle and tapped on to the directional app. Bridge Vale wasn't huge, but I was still a little unsure of where I was going. I'd been here for a couple of weeks, settling in before starting at the school, but I didn't have a good sense of direction at the best of times.

The high school was on the outskirts of town, just off the main road between Bridge Vale and Knightingale, so was easy enough to get to. My problem was how to find my apartment. It was on the new development that the real estate agent had told me was "highly desirable". Personally, I think I'd have preferred something a little more rural, like some of the beautiful farms and ranches that I passed en route. There was little chance of me ending up in one of those though, so my small two-bed apartment would be home for a while.

When I let myself in through the front door, I kicked at a flat package that was lying on the hall floor. It was my redirected post from home. There wasn't much of it, probably only junk and people I wasn't interested in keeping in touch with, but I ripped it open anyway. I was right, in the main, but then the letter with the National Health Service stamp on the front caused me to catch my breath.

My palms got sweaty and my heart jumped up into my throat.

I knew what this was.

I'd hoped that moving here I'd escape it, but things that big just didn't go away. Biting down hard on my lip, I stared at the envelope, holding it with shaking hands.

Should I destroy it - forget all that crap even existed?

I threw it onto the pile of junk mail and walked away. When I got to the doorway, I turned on my heels and went back to it. Snatching the letter up, I tore open the envelope and pulled out the letter. Taking a deep breath I unfolded the stiff white paper.

It was what I'd expected. My family doctor, and family friend, Dr. Monroe, was writing to ask why I hadn't gone for the test that he'd arranged for me. He stated how important it was and that I should call him to arrange an alternative appointment, and that he'd be failing as my doctor and my dad's friend if he didn't insist.

I ripped the letter into quarters and put it back onto the pile of others that needed to be trashed. But, as I threw them away, the words on the letter kept swimming before my eyes.

"Due to your family history, and the results of the tests performed on your mother during her treatment, it is imperative that you have the test for the BRC, TP, PALB and PTEN genes."

When Mum had cancer, she'd been tested for the deadly gene. She'd lost a daughter through cancer, she had cancer, so chances were I would get it, too. Mum wanted to know for my sake and so had the test done. It came back positive - a ridiculous statement if ever there was one.

How could the news that you were dreading be called as a positive result?

Closing my eyes, I gripped the back of the high stool at the kitchen counter. I knew it was imperative that I get tested if I wanted to know whether I was going to get the disease that had killed my sister, and ravaged my mum's body. But I didn't want to know.

I didn't want to know whether my future was going to be blighted with pain and sickness inducing treatment.

I didn't want to know whether I might have to have parts of my body removed, just in case.

I didn't want to know that my dreams for the future would be shattered into a million pieces.

I simply didn't want to know.

That's why I'd left Garratt in the hotel. It was why I couldn't possibly start anything with him. That one night had to be enough, because I knew anything more and I'd be addicted. I was half way there now. So any more time spent with Garratt and there'd be no way I'd want to give him up.

Everything was better this way. I could live in ignorance, and no one would but I would be shattered when the inevitable happened. Not even my parents. They knew I was here, living and working - we'd argued for weeks about it - but now that I was here, I was avoiding their calls. I didn't want them pressurizing me.

It was better for everyone if I just go on with my life. Alone.

fourteen

Garratt

"Hey, Caleb," I said to the kid who was still seated at his desk. "You do know it was time to go home about ten minutes ago, right?"

Caleb was a senior, and I noticed over the last few days that he always hung around after class. Either he'd engage me in conversation or mess around with whatever was in his bag. Today was the first time he'd stayed in his seat, just reading.

He looked up at me through dark blonde hair that fell in front of his eyes.

"Sorry, Mr. Connor, I guess you need to lock up the classroom." He started to pack away his books, shoving his chair back with a scrape.

"No, I'm good," I replied, moving towards him. "I just don't want your parents worrying about where you are."

He shrugged his shoulders. "It's fine, no one will be home for a couple of hours."

"Well, you can stay if you want to. I'll be here for a little while yet."

Something told me that the kid was stalling for time if no one was home. He had friends, I knew that because I'd seen him at lunch throwing hoops with a couple of other guys. I'd even seen a few girls milling around him. I wasn't so sure Caleb had seen them though. While he was a good looking boy, he was quiet and extremely studious - he'd gained nothing less than 90% on any of the quizzes that I'd given the class over the last four days.

He gave me a small smile and nodded. "Thanks, Mr. Connor. I guess I'd better go. I got English and Spanish homework."

"You can start it here. Like I said, I'm going to be here marking papers for another hour at least."

"You sure?" He appeared to sag with relief. "That would be cool."

I nodded and went back to my desk, leaving Caleb to pull his books back out of his bag and settle at his desk.

I wasn't sure about the rules around being alone in a classroom with a kid, after hours, so sent Neil, my mentor, a quick text.

Garratt: *Marking papers and one of my students is staying behind to do homework. Is that OK?*

His response came back quickly.

Neil: *Sure. Keep door open. Vicky is running detention down the hall if you need anything.*

As I put my phone back into my pocket, Caleb let out a frustrated groan.

"Something wrong?" I asked.

His head shot up and he looked at me with startled eyes.

"Oh, sorry. I didn't mean to disturb you."

"You haven't. Just sounds like you're having a few problems. What is it, English or Spanish? Although, I have to be honest, I'm not sure I can help you with either. I'm a total math nerd."

He laughed and his whole face lit up. It struck me then that in the few days I'd been teaching him, that was the first time he'd shown me any emotion. Even when the rest of the kids in the class had been laughing at the expense of Brian Maynard, the captain of the wrestling team, for losing a tooth in a fight with his twelve year old brother, Caleb had stayed quiet - just taking it all in without even a hint of a smile.

"Hey," I said, grinning widely. "Being a nerd is not something to be laughed at."

Caleb dropped his head, but I could still see the tip of his lips.

"You are so not a nerd, Mr. Connor."

"Well, thank you, Caleb, but I think my brother would disagree with that."

At the mention of Jesse, Caleb sat up straight in his chair.

"Is he really that good with horses?" he asked, leaning forwards. "I read he was, it was in a magazine. When the other kids said you came from around here, I just put two and two together."

"Wow, you're a math nerd too," I quipped, bringing another smile to Caleb's face. "But yeah, he really is that good. You interested in horses, too?"

"Oh God, yes sir," he breathed out, his face becoming animated. "I think they're the most beautiful creatures on this planet. My dad used to have a couple, when I was a little kid."

"He doesn't have them anymore?"

Caleb shook his head and sighed. "No, sir. We live in apartment above the food mart in town now."

"Oh, okay."

I guessed the family had hit hard times if they lived above Rick Hannigan's food market. That place was tiny. I knew, because during my senior year at this very school, I'd dated Rick Hannigan's niece. The apartment was empty at the time, and Uncle Rick never knew what sweet little Polly did during her lunch break, on the days that she helped out in the shop.

"He works in Knightingale now, as a mechanic." Caleb's shoulders slumped.

"You lived on a farm? I know most people around here, but don't recall any Tremaine's."

"Nope, you won't. We came from out of state a couple of years ago." He gave me a quick glance and then went back to his books.

"You still need help with that homework?"

Caleb shook his head. "No thank you, sir. I'll be fine."

That was the last thing he said to me until he left an hour later and said goodbye.

As I made my way across the parking lot, I noticed Jemma pacing up and down next to her car. My stomach lurched as I watched her long, tanned legs in a pair of fuck me heels. There should be some damn rule about her wearing them while teaching horny teenage boys. Especially with that damn tight skirt that stopped just above her knee and hugged her beautiful ass.

I'd successfully managed to dodge her over the last four days. Preferring instead to take my lunch to one of the picnic tables outside, and spend the time catching up with Benjie, or chatting with a couple of the other teachers. Becky had called one staff meeting the night before, but I'd watched and waited for Jemma to go in before I did. That way I could sit as far away from her as possible.

The problem I had, was that I had no fucking idea why I was avoiding her. I was mad at her because she'd run out on me in Hawaii, but I was desperate for us to take up where we left off. Only that morning I'd whacked off in the shower, with images of Jemma in my head.

"Hey, you okay?" I asked as I approached her.

She stopped pacing and swung around to look at me.

"Oh hi, Garratt. I-I erm, I seem to have lost my car key."

"Right, so that's why you're patrolling the car." I moved my index finger backwards and forwards in the direction she'd been pacing.

"Yes," she said on a long sigh. "I was trying to think where I last had them. Obviously I locked my car with them this morning, and I've only been in the staff room and my classroom today. I even ate lunch at my desk, so I have no idea where they can be."

"You checked the staff room and your classroom?"

Jemma's nostrils flared as her hands went to her hips.

"No, Garratt. I just assumed the key fairy took them. Of course I did."

I held my hands up in surrender. "Okay, just asking. So, do you have a spare?"

"Yes," she snapped petulantly. "It's at home."

"Okay, you'd better get in then." I aimed my key and beeped my own car unlocked.

"I can get a cab." Jemma backed up against her car, holding up her cell.

"I doubt it very much. We don't have many cabs around here. We have one Uber, and he's probably on his second beer by now."

I was lying of course, Bobby never started drinking until at least seven on a week day.

"It's only just gone five-thirty," Jemma exclaimed, calling me out on my lie.

"And? This is the country, Jemma. There isn't much excitement going on except a night at Rowdy's and Wednesday night is quiz night. Things start a little earlier on a Wednesday night."

She watched me warily for a few seconds and then huffed out a breath.

"Okay, as long as you don't mind."

Mind? Fuck, I was desperate to have her in a confined space where she couldn't run away from my questions. I was done with fucking sulking over her.

"I'll take you home and then bring you back if you want to pick it up tonight…" Jemma opened her mouth to say something, but I ignored her and carried on. "…failing that, I'll pick you up in the morning and bring you in. No arguments."

She heaved a defeated sigh, picked her huge bag up from the hood of her car and followed me to mine.

Yep, I was done sulking, it was now time for action.

fifteen

Jemma

As Garratt drove us back to town, the atmosphere in the car was decidedly icy. So much so, I was convinced if I touched the window, my fingertips would sting against their icy coldness.

The only sound was the low hum of the radio; that and Garratt drumming his hand against the steering wheel.

"Why don't you just say what you have to say, Garratt?" I turned to look at his profile and his jaw was tensed so tightly it was pulsing.

"I don't think it's me that has anything to say," he replied without looking at me. "You're the one that left."

I let out a sigh and turned back to watch the landscape. Everywhere was a lush green, from the fields to the mountains in the distance. It was beautiful, and although my parents weren't there, I couldn't wish to be anywhere else.

"Well?" Garratt asked.

I could feel his eyes on me, but didn't turn back. I couldn't, he was just too beautiful. I'd succumb and we'd end up in a relationship only to be separated in the end. And whether that separation was in a little over two weeks when he went back to his job, or in the future, it didn't matter. It was inevitable and it would bloody well hurt.

"I'm talking to you, Jemma with a J."

My lips twitched at that comment, and I couldn't help but look at him now.

"I only ever said that once, but you keep making fun of me about it."

Garratt shrugged. "It made me smile when you said it. One of the many things that you said or did that made me smile, if I'm being totally honest."

"*Garratt.*"

I didn't want him talking about those days. It made my heart hurt.

It ached for the days when I still had my sister. When cancer wasn't a part of our lives. When Garratt and I were just starting out on something good and we both knew it was going to be special. When the only thing we had to worry about was avoiding Tyler, his roommate, who seemed to think Garratt had stolen me from him; which was absolute rubbish, I'd only ever said hello to him before I started seeing Garratt.

"Okay," he breathed out, shaking his head. "Safer subject. How is Caleb Tremaine doing in your class?"

"Caleb? Dark blonde hair, handsome, quiet boy who has no idea he's the latest heartthrob?"

"Yep. If the girls who hang around, watching him at lunch mean he's a heartthrob, then that's the one."

"He's doing okay. He needs to go deeper with some of his analysis of the topic at times, but okay. Why?" I half turned in my seat, intrigued. "Is he having problems?"

Garratt glanced at me and shrugged. "Not as such. I just get the feeling that he's struggling at home."

My heart started to pound. "He's being abused in some way."

"God no," Garratt exclaimed. "No, he just seems to hate going home. He stayed behind to do his homework when school finished today. And a couple of nights he's been dragging his feet to leave."

I then remembered something.

"A couple of nights ago I had dinner at the diner, and I saw him in town."

"Yeah, he lives above the food market," Garratt said, turning onto the road towards my apartment.

"No, he was sitting on a bench outside the diner, reading. I didn't know whether to speak to him. I thought he might be embarrassed of his teacher saying hi. But by the time I left, he'd gone anyway."

Garratt chewed on his bottom lip. "Why sit on a bench reading, when you only live across the road?"

"It was a nice night," I offered. "Maybe he just wanted some fresh air."

"Yeah, maybe. He did say they used to live on a farm, and his dad had horses. He could be just struggling with living in a tiny little apartment."

I hoped that was all it was. "You think?"

Garratt looked at me and smiled. "Yeah, maybe. Even so, I think I'll mention it to Becky tomorrow. I was going to ask Jesse if Caleb could help with the horses, but I'd better check its okay first."

"I'm sure she'll agree, especially if it helps Caleb." I smiled and instinctively reached a hand out to cover Garratt's that was resting on his knee. "That's really thoughtful of you."

He didn't say anything, but pulled into one of the designated parking bays outside my apartment block.

"Nice," he said, stooping to look through the windscreen.

It was okay, not the rural location I'd have liked, but there was a communal garden on the side of the block. The apartments were in a quiet, dead end, at the back of a road of large detached houses. According to my real estate agent, the original development was nine years old, and the detached houses and apartments had been added because more of the locals were leaving the land but wanted to stay in the area.

"You want to get your car tonight, or am I picking you up in the morning?" Garratt asked, unclipping his seatbelt.

"I don't want to put you to any more trouble. I'll book an Uber for the morning."

Garratt sighed and shook his head. "Oh Jemma, when will you learn about living in the country? Bobby doesn't get out of bed before nine."

"He really doesn't do much *"ubering"* at all, according to you." I frowned at him, beginning to think he was telling me lies about Bobby, just to get his own way.

"No," Garratt replied, with a wry grin. "He doesn't. Now, let's get inside and you can make me a cup of coffee as thanks for bringing you home. Unless of course, you want to make some of that damn tea you Brits love."

"I don't think-"

"It's best you don't think where I'm concerned," Garratt butted in and leaned forward to kiss me quickly. "Because it'll make your fucking toes curl."

And I couldn't disagree.

sixteen

Garratt

"**O**kay," I said, as soon as we got inside Jemma's apartment. "Talk."

Her head snapped around as she moved to put her purse down on a side table.

"About what?" she asked.

She couldn't keep her eyes on me. They were looking everywhere around the room, and she was twisting her fingers together in front of her. Jemma definitely had secrets, and the biggest one was why the fuck she ran away from me in Hawaii.

I walked over and stood inches from her. She stiffened and took a deep breath. Yep, I affected her. Her nipples poking through her sexy-as-all-get-out blouse told me that if nothing else did.

"Don't bullshit me, Jemma."

"I-I'm not," she stammered.

I let out a sigh, grabbed her hand, and pulled her down onto the couch with me.

"Okay, you obviously don't want to offer any information, so I'll ask questions, and you'll damn well answer them."

"You can't tell me what to do."

She tried to push up from the couch, but I caught hold of her forearm.

"Sit, otherwise I'll damn well spank that ass of yours."

There was the hitch of her breath again, and a sexy little moan that she didn't think I'd hear. Yeah, well I had the hearing of a bat.

I looked at her with wide eyes, silently bidding her to do as I said. With a sigh, she flopped back against the cushions.

"You can ask," she said. "But there's no saying that I'll answer."

"We'll see."

Cocky shit that I was, I winked at her.

"Why didn't you tell me in Hawaii that you were living over here?"

"You didn't ask."

"You could have told me anyway. Seeing as I damn well fucked you any which way I could for two nights, I'd have thought you might have mentioned it."

"Garratt," she gasped. "Do you have to be so coarse about it?"

"Sorry," I replied. "But that's me, you know that. So?"

Jemma chewed on her thumbnail and stared at me. Gorgeous eyes, the color of whisky, flashed with a hint of fear as she watched me carefully.

"I knew that if I told you I was moving to the states you'd want to see me again."

That sentence caused a pain in my chest.

"I'm not some fucking stalker, Jemma." My aching heart was pounding. "Yeah, I admit I would have wanted to see you, but all you had to do was be honest and tell me no. Is that why you damn well left without saying goodbye? In case I hassled you about seeing each other again?"

My jaw clenched. The thought of her running because she didn't want to be with me, caused the anger to continue its swell inside of me.

"I knew you wouldn't take no for an answer. I don't want a relationship."

"A relationship in general, or just one with me?"

I waited anxiously. If it was just me and she was going to be available to someone else, I think I'd lose my shit.

She looked at me and then her shoulders dropped.

"In general," she whispered.

I sagged in relief. I had a chance if at least she liked me. "And you didn't think you could tell me that?"

"Oh, like you'd accept that," she snapped back, her voice louder and more confident than before.

"Like I said, I'm no fucking stalker. You know that, but yeah, you're right. I'd have tried to persuade you otherwise. Because, correct me if I'm wrong," I said, turning my body towards her. "It was my fucking name you were screaming most of the night. Which leads me to think, why the hell wouldn't you want more of that?"

"God, you are so conceited," she gasped. "Sex isn't everything, you know."

I thought about it for a few seconds. She was right, it wasn't, but sex with her was pretty close.

"I know, but you and I both know that not only are we amazing in the sack together, but we have fun and we were damn good friends once upon time."

"Yes, seven years ago when we were just kids. Things change, Garratt."

I watched her carefully as she picked at one of the buttons that were down the front of her tight black skirt. She was pushed up against the arm of the couch, as far away from me as she could get. She was damn well scared of me, but I sensed it wasn't in a bad way.

"Okay, we'll park the subject of you living here. Tell me about the husband."

Her head shot up, and her fingers stilled on the button she had been playing with.

"We're not together any more. We're divorced."

"Yeah, you said as much in Becky's office. Again, why didn't you tell me in Hawaii?"

"For goodness' sake, Garratt," she said, pinching the bridge of her nose. "I hadn't seen you for seven years, we were having a wedding fling. Why would I tell you?"

I took a deep breath and edged closer to her. Jemma tried to move back, but she had nowhere to go. Taking advantage of that fact, my arm moved in front of her, putting my hand on the arm of the couch that she was pushed up against. My other arm rested on the back. Not only could she not move away from me, but she couldn't get up. I had her caged in.

"If we were just a wedding fling, as you call it, then fine. I'd understand. Two people, mind blowing sex, no questions asked and no answers given. You and I, though, we are far from a wedding fling, and you know that."

"No I don't," she protested.

I glanced down at her chest that was stretching the silky material of her blouse. Two perfect little peaks were formed.

"Those," I said, circling my finger in the area of her nipples, "beg to fucking differ. As do those." I pointed at her eyes that were full of fear.

Jemma glanced down at her rack, and crossed her arms over it with a muttered curse.

I caught hold of her chin with my thumb and forefinger and looked directly into her eyes.

"We both know but for circumstances, you and I would have stayed together through college. We'd have been fucking amazing together. Just one month with you showed me that. I've never forgotten you these last seven years, and if the way we were together in Hawaii is any indication, you never forgot me either. Straight from the off, in that bar, the chemistry was there. Eden and Krystal knew it, too." I let go of Jemma's chin and combed my fingers through her hair, my eyes taking in every inch of her face. "So don't you dare tell me we were just some fucking wedding hook up, or fling, or whatever you want to call it. We weren't. We were two people who had something amazing once, and were remembering how good it had been, and realizing it could be even better."

Jemma whimpered and closed her eyes as her tongue darted out to wet her lips. That one little action made my dick hard. Fighting back the urge to just push up that tight skirt and rip off her panties, I leaned forward and kissed her forehead.

"Now," I said, as her breath stalled. "Tell me why you're so damn scared to be with me, when everything inside you is screaming for it to happen."

"I-I-"

"No, Jemma. No bullshit, baby. Your heart is beating so fast and loud, I can almost hear it. Tell me the truth. I'll listen, give you my viewpoint, and then if after that you still feel the same, I'll walk away."

And I would…well I thought I would. As much as I wanted more with this beautiful woman, if she seriously didn't want to be with me I wouldn't push it. Trouble was, I knew she wanted me, every instinct I had told me that. I just needed to find out what the hell had her so spooked.

seventeen

Jemma

I looked at Garratt, his face just inches from mine, and I knew I'd have to tell him the truth - well, a version of the truth anyway. There was no way I was going to tell him that we were never going to be an "us" because I was petrified that I'd fall in love with him and then find out I was dying.

"Ollie, my ex-husband, cheated on me, almost from the minute we got home from our honeymoon," I blurted out.

Garratt's eyes darkened as he sat back, giving me room to breathe; room to breathe without having to inhale his cologne, inhale him.

"You're kidding, right?"

I gave him a small smile. "Yes...well kind of. He did cheat on me and we had only been married for about six months, so it's close."

"The fucking douchebag," Garratt said taking my hand in his. "How did you find out?"

My mind went back to that night.

"I'd been away on school trip, as one of the chaperone's to the kids I was teaching. When one of the girls broke her arm during a pillow fight, someone needed to take her home, so I volunteered. I'd jumped at the chance to be honest."

"Not enjoying the trip, hey?" Garratt's voice was soft and tender as he stroked his thumb down the back of my hand.

"No, it wasn't that. Since I'd left home two days before, I'd felt uneasy. Had a strange feeling in the pit of my stomach and I wasn't sure why. Things had been good before I left and Ollie had sounded normal during a call that morning, telling me he missed and loved me, but something just wasn't right."

"You had no idea before then? That he was playing around?"

"Ollie was never one to keep his eyes to himself," I replied with an empty laugh. "But there'd been no unexplained absences, dropped calls, or late nights at work, so I wasn't suspicious. But, when we talked on the phone that morning, I was sure that I heard heels clicking on the tiled floor in the background. I didn't question him, though maybe I knew deep down and didn't want to hear his pathetic lies. It was seven-thirty in the morning and he was at home, what logical explanation could he give me to put my mind at rest?"

"So what, you pushed it to the back of your mind?"

"Yep. Until I dropped Mia, the student, off at home, and tried to call him." My whole body sagged at the memory. "I'd already tried about three times on the two hour train journey, but just kept getting his voicemail, which was unusual. It was a Thursday evening, he never had plans on a Thursday evening. I figured he must have had a last minute call to play pool with his friends, or was maybe at the pub and couldn't hear his phone. But, when I pulled up on the drive, there was a mini parked behind his Audi and I knew exactly why I couldn't get hold of him."

"Oh fuck, Jemma."

Garratt moved closer and pulled me onto his lap. My head was telling me to protest, and not get too close, but my heart was longing to be in his arms and feel the comfort of them as I recalled the night my marriage ended.

I rested my cheek against his chest, took a deep breath and carried on, feeling remarkably calm, despite my pain at what had happened. "I let myself in and as soon as I set foot through the door, I heard her, Natalie, moaning like she was auditioning for a porn movie. I'd had sex with Ollie," I scoffed. "And no way was he that good, but you had to give the girl a gold star for her acting skills."

"Knew I'd fucking ruin you for anyone else," he muttered, his chest shaking with his quiet laughter.

I slapped playfully at his arm and was rewarded with a kiss to my forehead.

"What'd you do?" he asked.

"I burst into laughter." I looked up at him and grinned. "Her noise was so ridiculous I couldn't help it. I think losing Lauren had been the absolute worst thing that could happen to me, so Ollie getting his rocks off with someone other than me didn't really register on my trauma scale."

"But to find them like that. Shit, you must have been devastated."

I shrugged. "Not that night, no. It's been painful since, but that night I marched up the stairs and, while he was pumping into her from behind, I stormed into the bedroom, opened my wardrobe, sorry, my closet, and started to pull out my clothes."

Garratt groaned. "Shit, *really*? What the fuck did the douchebag do?"

"He left Natalie with her damn arse in the air and tried to stop me. Told me it wasn't what it looked like."

"Fuck off, you're joking?"

I shook my head. "Nope, I'm not. He actually said those exact words. When I dragged a suitcase from under the bed, he even told her to go and to stop pestering him."

"You still left that night though, right?"

"Of course I did. He begged me to stay, said the usual; it wouldn't happen again, it was just the once, she'd been stalking him. I think he even accused her of giving him date rape drugs."

"What a fucking dick. Why the hell did you marry him in the first place? In fact, scrap that, why the hell did you even date him?"

My heart juddered as I thought about the answer to that question.

Because he reminded me of you, was not an answer I wanted to give.

"He was charming," I replied.

"Sounds it. So what happened?"

"I left, oh after finding her toothbrush and face cream in my bathroom." I paused, letting Garratt take that little nugget in. "Because of course, all stalkers and date rapists take their toiletries with them."

"Prick," Garratt growled.

"I went back to live at mum and dad's house and filed for divorce. Ollie bought me out of our house, and he and Natalie now live there with her fat, slobbery pug, Desmond. Ollie is miserable because Natalie keeps him on a tighter leash than Desmond, and I'm glad that I'm out of it and away from him."

We were silent for a few seconds. The only sound was our breathing, as Garratt brushed his hand down my hair.

"So," he finally said on a sigh, pulling me closer to his chest. "I have that dicktwat to thank for you not wanting a relationship."

I wanted to say 'no, I could give two fucks about him, I'm just scared of dying on you,' but I didn't. I nodded.

"We're not all like him, you know."

"I know," I whispered.

Garratt grabbed hold of my chin, and pulled it up to look at him. I resisted at first, not wanting him to see the truth in my eyes. The truth being that I wanted him, and this wasn't about me being scared of getting hurt again.

"Jemma," he demanded. "Look at me, baby."

Swallowing, I did as he asked.

"I swear I won't hurt you."

"I know that, Garratt, but-"

"No, I want you to listen," he said, stopping my denial of him. "I have no idea what's going to happen after my teaching practice, and I know I'm six hours away, but in the short term, if things work out how I'd like, we can do the long distance thing."

His Adam's apple bobbed as he paused to look at me - his beautiful blues full of hope. He took my breath away, and I so wanted to tell him we could try, but it wouldn't be fair to him. I knew we would be great together, my gut instinct told me that. Our past, however brief it had been, told me that. But could I risk the heartache that would be coming my way, coming his way?

"I work in a bank, Jemma," Garratt continued. "I can get a transfer easily, and then when I start looking for teaching jobs, I'll look around here. Fuck, Becky even said herself that if Jim Taylor doesn't come back from teaching in Africa, which he's hinted at, then there's a job for me. As long as the school board agree, and seeing as how most of that school board know my family, I'd say I have a damn good chance."

"The distance doesn't worry me," I said, honestly. "I'm just not sure I want to be in a relationship again." I chewed on my lip, hoping that he didn't see through my lie.

"Not like the one with your prick of a husband, no, but one with me would be different and you fucking know it."

He was right, it would be different. In the month that we'd dated all those years ago - been boyfriend and girlfriend, gone out, whatever you wanted to call it - I'd had the best time ever. It had been fun and exciting and Garratt had been the perfect mix of sexy, sweet, charming, and downright dirty.

"I'm not going to beg you, Jemma," Garratt said, giving me a tight squeeze. "Take some time to think about it, and if by the end of Friday you're still not feeling it, I won't mention it again. That gives you two days, sweetheart."

My heart stopped momentarily. I didn't want him to give up on me, but I wasn't ready to say yes, either. So, what was I waiting for? We could do this for a while, then when I became ill I'd end it, maybe blame the distance. But how long was 'a while' likely to be? A month, a year, ten years?

"I'll think about it," I replied, snuggling against Garratt's chest.

I felt safe there; so damn quickly, he'd given that to me. It felt like we'd never been apart, and the last seven years had simply brought us closer together. How could that be? I looked up at cornflower blue eyes. Garratt, that's how.

"Okay, if that's what you want," he whispered and then pushed forward.

Garratt's mouth took mine and he kissed me hard. His fingers threaded deep into my hair as he held me captive against him. My fingertips dug into his back as heat flooded through my veins and I could feel myself getting wet with desire for him. Pushing myself closer to Garratt, I let out a moan before whispering his name. Garratt's hands came around to cup my face as he pulled away and very slowly released my bottom lip. I was panting, desperate for more.

"Just remember that kiss when you're thinking things over."

Garratt pulled me off his knee and pushed up from the sofa. Before I could catch my breath, he'd gone.

"Oh shit," I whispered, touching my swollen lips. "I am in so much trouble."

Garratt

Yeah, like fuck I wouldn't be mentioning it again. After hearing why she didn't want a relationship and that damn kiss, even if she said no, I would do whatever possible to persuade her otherwise. That woman needed to realize that we were meant to be together.

eighteen

Garratt

When I got to Jemma's apartment the next morning, part of me expected her to have already left. She hadn't, and thrust the door open as soon as I pressed the buzzer.

"I'm running late," she said breathlessly, turning and walking back up the hallway, wearing a rock band tee over the top of a pair of black pants. "My stupid alarm didn't go off."

"You don't use the one on your cell like most people?" I asked, picking up a photograph from the side table. "Nice tee by the way. Not a fan myself."

Jemma's head poked around a doorway. "Are you deaf? How can you not like Oasis?"

I shrugged. "Trying too hard to be like The Beatles, I guess."

Jemma huffed and disappeared back into her room. My eyes went back to the photograph. It was Jemma in a cap and gown, and she was flanked by, whom I assumed, were her parents. She looked just like her dad but had the same curls and coloring as her mom, although her mom's hair was cut short, close to her head. Jemma had told me her mom had also had breast cancer, so wondered if this was her hair growing back after treatment.

"I'll be five minutes," Jemma called from her room, breaking my thought pattern. "Coffee is made if you want to grab a cup."

I carefully put the photograph back and walked up the hallway, past the lounge room that I'd sat in the night before. It was a small kitchen, but tidy, and on the counter a coffee pot bubbled away.

"You got into the habit of coffee already, I see," I called over my shoulder.

"Yeah." Jemma appeared in the doorway, fastening up the blouse that had now replaced the tee that she'd answered the door in. "I still love my tea, though."

She smiled and it was so fucking beautiful I had to force myself not to drag her into my arms. I'd said I'd give her time - she had today and tomorrow to decide. I was such a cocky bastard, though, I'd already emailed my boss about getting a transfer to the Knightingale branch. He hadn't responded yet, but I didn't think it would be an issue, particularly as I knew the loans manager at Knightingale was leaving. Everything was falling into place, I just needed Jemma on board now. Maybe I was being stupid pinning my future on a girl who I'd had two nights with after seven years apart, but I'd never been one to be cautious. That's where I was different to my brother. Jesse thought everything through, about ten times, before he did anything. Shit, he almost lost Millie because he was too busy thinking. Me, well I was a no holds barred kind of guy, something that had given my folks many a sleepless night. I knew that Jemma and I could have something good. I'd been falling hard for her all those years ago, and I had no doubts that if she'd stayed around we'd still be together now. Okay, who the fuck knew, but I did know we'd have been awesome together and I wanted that again. Plus, I damn well hated being six hours away from my family, especially the kids. I was missing out on seeing them grow up, so why not come home?

I poured some coffee into a mug that was standing on the counter. "You want one?"

"No thanks," Jemma said, reaching around me to pick an apple from a huge glass bowl full of fresh fruit. "I've had one."

I lightly grabbed her wrist and nodded down at the apple. "That your breakfast?"

"Yep. I don't really do breakfast."

I shook my head and took the apple from her hand, putting it back in the bowl. "That's a snack, not damn breakfast. I'll take you to the diner."

"We don't have time for the diner." She reached for the apple again.

I took her arm and swiveled her around, away from the counter. "We have time to call and get takeaway French toast. Now finish getting ready." I slapped her ass and gave her a gentle push.

"Garratt." Her hand went to her tight, little ass cheek and rubbed it.

"That didn't hurt. Now go."

She threw me a glare and left, muttering something under her breath about sexual harassment - yeah, whatever, sweetheart.

"Oh. My. God. Garratt, that's amazing."

I readjusted my trousers as Jemma's sexy moans filled my car, and wrapped around my dick. She had a mouthful of French toast and was savoring every little bit of it.

"Told you. Isn't that better than an apple?"

She nodded vigorously, putting a hand over her mouth. "Yes, but I can't eat this every morning," she said around the toast. "I'll be fatter than a pregnant elephant within a month."

I laughed and thrust the car into park. "I'm not suggesting you eat the diner's French toast every morning, just something a little better than an apple."

My dick got a little harder as Jemma put a long finger into her mouth and licked off the sugar, before pulling it out with a pop.

"I think we'd better get inside," I said on a cough.

Jemma looked at me and whatever was written all over my face said it all and made her blush.

"Oh, God, yes. Erm, so thanks for the lift."

"No problem. It's still here anyway." I nodded towards her sedan that was still parked where it had been the night before. "Let's hope your other key turns up."

"Yes," she sighed. "I have no idea where it could have got to."

I put my hand to my pocket. "Oh shit, this wouldn't be it would it?"

I pulled out a car key on a Union Jack, heart shaped fob. Jemma's mouth opened wide as she snatched at the key.

"Where did you find it?" She looked up at me with blazing eyes and I couldn't hide my smile. "You had it all this time, didn't you?"

I bit down on my top lip, trying desperately not to laugh, but she looked so damn pissed I couldn't help it.

"I'm sorry," I uttered around a laugh. "I found it on the floor in the staff room at lunchtime, and knew it must have been yours. Who else would have a UK flag on their keyring?"

Jemma slapped at my arm. "You let me worry myself sick, when all this time you had it. You-"

"Let me stop you there," I laughed, grabbing hold of Jemma's hand. "Me keeping your key meant we got to spend some time together. It also meant you got one of the best kisses of your life - if I remember correctly."

I closed my eyes, flicked my tongue out, and licked at my lips.

"Yep," I groaned. "I do remember correctly."

"This is not funny Garratt. Not funny at all."

Jemma unclipped her belt and went to open the door, but I was not finished with her yet. Putting a hand around the back of her head, I pulled her to me.

"Not so fast."

As her mouth fell into an O, my tongue pushed its way in and I began kissing her. Slowly at first, with my hands cupping her face, but when I felt her beautiful rack press against my chest, I notched it up a level. Jemma's hands moved to my biceps and I coaxed a quiet moan from her as one of my hands moved to thread into her hair. She was so damn addictive that I knew I needed to stop. I'd be happy to take her there and then, in my car, oblivious to the kids and other teachers that could see us.

I pulled away before my sensibility was totally hijacked and Jemma let out a gasp. Her eyes were still shut, long lashes brushing her pinked cheeks.

"I'm still mad at you," she whispered, desperately trying to get her breath.

"Yeah, baby, I know." I dropped a quick kiss to her forehead and then unclipped my seat belt. "Come on, let's get to work."

As we walked across the parking lot towards the main school building, Jemma kept throwing scowls at me.

"You're not helping your cause you know?" she finally said as we reached the front door. "Pulling sneaky tricks like that."

I shrugged. "Just fighting dirty. That way if you do decide we can't be together, at least I got some more action from those hot lips of yours."

"Whatever." She was just about to turn towards the door when she started blowing and flapping a hand at her nose.

"Wait a minute," I said and reached for the tiny white feather that had landed on her. I plucked it off and held it up to her. "An Angel's kiss."

"What?" she asked, and held out her palm.

I placed it on her outstretched arm. "My mom says that when a small white feather lands on you, it's a kiss from an angel. Someone up there is thinking of you."

Jemma looked up at me and gasped. Her eyes were shining brightly with unshed tears and I wanted to kick myself. I put a hand out, but she shook her head, swallowed hard and turned away, closing her hand around the feather.

"I'll see you later, Garratt."

She pushed through the door, letting it slam behind her. I watched through the glass as she rushed down the corridor towards her classroom, passing the door to the staff room on her way.

"Fuck," I muttered. "You dick, Garratt."

Kicking at a loose stone, I made my way inside, wondering when I would stop stuffing things up.

nineteen

Jemma

itting down at my desk, I gently curled open my hand and looked down at the feather Garratt had just given to me. Gazing down at it, I thought of Lauren.

Was this a message from my sister?

Was she up there thinking of me?

I wasn't a great believer in God; After all, who would allow someone as beautiful and kind like my sister to be given cancer? Yet, the thought that she was sending me a message gave me comfort. This proved that I was one of those cynical people who only believed when it suited them to do so. And at this moment in time, it suited me to believe in heaven; to believe in a greater being.

With tears in my eyes, I reached inside my desk drawer for a tissue, and wrapped the feather up in it before placing it in my bag.

"Oh, Lauren," I whispered. "I wish you were here." She'd have known what I should do, and she'd damn well keep on at me until I did it. Truth be told, *I* knew what I should do, but was too much of a coward to do it.

With a sick feeling in the pit of my stomach, I was wiping my eyes, when my classroom door was slowly opened and Garratt walked in.

"Jemma, I'm so sorry for being an insensitive dick." His blue eyes were pleading with me to accept his apology. An apology that wasn't really necessary.

"Garratt, don't be silly," I protested. "You did nothing wrong. I'm just still a little emotional about it. It still hurts."

He perched on the edge of one of the desks on the front row and sighed. "I should have realized and kept my stupid thoughts to myself."

I shook my head. "No. It's actually quite comforting to think that she might be up there thinking about me."

"You sure?" He leaned forward and peered at my face. "You can call me a prick if it helps."

I laughed and wiped my eyes again. "No, I'm fine, and you're not a prick."

As we watched each other carefully, the door opened again, this time it was Becky.

"Fantastic," she said breathlessly. "You're both here."

She flopped down onto one of the chairs and fanned herself. "Sorry, I've been running around the track trying to catch up with Benjie."

"You're not exactly dressed for track," Garratt said, one side of his mouth turning up into a half smile.

Becky's face was red from exertion and I had to wonder what was so urgent she needed to chase our gym teacher around the track. .

"Oh no," she gasped. "I needed to talk to him, but he was running. It was…erm…I had to ask him…a school thing."

I looked over at Garratt as he coughed around a laugh. I also had to wonder what he found so funny.

"Okay. Anyway," he said. "You wanted to see us about something?"

She drew herself up straight and pulled her shoulders back.

"Oh yes. Garratt, I saw your email about Caleb Tremaine and I'm in total agreement. Spending time on your brother's ranch would be extremely beneficial to him, especially as he wants to work with horses in the future.

So, from an educational view point I'd be happy to sanction it."

"But," Garratt said, sensing, as I had, that there was one.

"But, we need his father's permission too and I'm afraid Mr. Tremaine has been pretty difficult to get hold of."

"What about his mother?" I asked. "It's doesn't have to be his dad does it?"

Becky shook her head. "No it doesn't, but according to Caleb, his mother left the family home some months ago."

"When he said no one was home, I just assumed he meant both his folks were working." Garratt sighed heavily. "He's been staying behind to study."

Becky nodded. "I know. Neil told me that you'd asked if it was okay." She paused and tapped her nail against her tooth as she thought. "Okay, I'll try and get in touch with his father again and see if we can't get this agreed on sooner rather than later."

She got up to leave and then hit her forehead with the heel of her hand.

"God, I'd forget my damn head. The other reason I wanted to see you."

I glanced anxiously at Garratt, wondering why on earth she wanted to speak to us both. Were we in trouble for having had a relationship in the past? Had she found out somehow and was going to warn us off rekindling it?

"The senior geography class is going on a field trip to Wilmington Park. I thought you two could go with. Vicky was supposed to go with Gladys Winter and Frank Desouza, but she's had a wedding venue trauma, so needs to be home to get it sorted. That means I need someone else."

"So which of us do you want to go?" Garratt asked.

"Oh, both of you," Becky replied nonchalantly. "It'll be good experience for you Garratt, and I need a male teacher there, too."

She smiled widely, as did Garratt.

"Great, no problem," he replied, giving me a sly wink.

"What about Frank?" I asked, thinking about the large, sweaty music teacher.

"Oh yes," Becky said on a sigh. "He's got a note from his doctor to say he's not fit to hike or sleep outside."

"We're camping?" I tried not to groan, but camping was just not my thing.

"Yes. You go on Monday, two nights. Is that okay?"

"Yep, sure is." Garratt was looking far too happy and pleased with himself.

"Jemma?"

"Yes, sure, Becky," I answered, trying to sound bright. "No problem at all."

I groaned inwardly. Firstly, I would be sleeping outside on the hard ground, and secondly, I would be spending forty-eight hours with Garratt. Whatever decision I came to about our 'relationship', the trip was going to be difficult to say the least. Either I'd be trying to keep my hands off him, or keep him at arm's length. I didn't fancy my chances at either.

twenty

Garratt

At the end of the day, a day where I'd upset Jemma over a damn feather, I parked up outside Mom and Dad's house. Opening the car door, I could hear a ruckus from over at the main house. Looking over, I could see Hunter running around, as naked as the day he was born, with Millie, Addy, and Clemmie chasing after him. I couldn't help the huge smile that came to my face. That kid was crazy and I think both Millie and Jesse were glad he'd been the youngest of their kids. If he'd come after Addy there would have been no way Millie would have had Clemmie. Hunter was enough to put doubt in anyone's mind about having a kid.

Slamming my car door, I threw my jacket and keys onto the swing on the porch, and started towards the main house. As I reached the edge of the pasture where Jesse sometimes kept his horses, I heard Hunter's high pitched squeal followed by Millie and the girl's laughter.

"Hunter John Connor!" Millie cried. "You'd better stop now before I call Daddy."

Hunter stopped, turned and looked at his momma, and then carried on running towards the back of the house.

"Geez, Millie," I called. "You can't catch a two year old? You're slipping, girl."

Millie pulled to a stop and stared at me, her hands on her hips. "He's quick for his age."

"Momma, quick, grab him," Addy called as Hunter double backed to run past them.

Millie made a grab for Hunter, but missed him.

"Uncle Garratt," Clemmie cried. "Get him."

Hunter was now on his way towards me. I waited, and as he drew level with me, I flung out an arm and snagged him around the waist.

"Gotcha."

Hunter wriggled in my arms, giggling, and it was one of the best sounds I'd ever heard. How on earth had I survived living away from them all this time?

"Down," Hunter demanded.

"No way, buddy." I dropped a kiss to his soft blonde hair and strode over to Millie, depositing him in her arms. "Here you go, Momma."

As Millie took hold of him, Hunter realized his game was over and instantly laid his head on Millie's shoulder and started to suck his thumb.

"Looks like he's tired himself out," I said, running a hand over his head.

"Yeah. He didn't nap this afternoon, so I'm sure he's pooped after that burst of energy." Millie kissed his cheek. "Okay girls, you go inside and start your homework, and I'll get this little monster his dinner, before he falls asleep."

"Are you coming for dinner, Uncle Garratt?" Clemmie asked, pulling on my hand.

"Yes, stay," Millie said, turning to the house. "We're having your mum's chicken pot pie. She made a batch before they went away. I think she still worries about my cooking."

It was common knowledge that when Millie first came here, she could only cook the basics, but Mom taught her a few recipes as well as Millie taking some cooking classes in the evening. She was determined to take on the role of rancher's wife, and wanted to take the strain from Mom, who usually did all the cooking for the ranch hands as well as the family. Nowadays, Millie and Mom shared the work.

"I'm sure she doesn't think that," I replied, following Millie and the girls into the house.

"She loves your chilli, Momma," Addy said, giving Millie a beaming smile. "She told me it's better than Janelle's."

Janelle had made Rowdy's chilli famous, it was so good, so for Mom to say Millie's was better really was high praise.

"Well, that's good to know." Millie beamed with pride - she sure loved my mom. "Okay, let's get inside and get dinner started. Daddy will be home soon."

Just a half hour later, Hunter had been fed and was fast asleep in his crib, the girls were doing homework at the kitchen table, and Millie and I were enjoying a glass of lemonade while Mom's pie was warming in the oven.

"So," Millie said with a grin. "What is it that you have to tell me?"

"What makes you think I have something to tell you?" I asked.

"We've hardly seen you all week, and it's your first week at the school, so you must have something to tell me. Something must have happened."

I shrugged and took a sip of my lemonade.

"Garratt?"

"What?"

"What's happened? Something has, so tell me." Millie's eyes were wide and questioning. She never fucking missed anything.

"Jemma is actually the new English teacher."

"Sorry?"

"Jim Reynolds, the new English teacher, was actually *Jemma* Reynolds, my old college girlfriend and recent wedding hook up."

Millie watched me open mouthed.

"Nothing to say, Armalita?" I laughed at her astonishment as she shook her head. "Okay, well, I've spent some time with her, trying to get her to see we'd be good together. She's a little reluctant, but I've given her two days to think about it. What she doesn't know is, even if she says no on Friday,

I'm still going to work on her. I'll just have to be subtle about it. Oh, and we're both taking the senior geography class camping in Wilmington Park next week, so if she does say no, I'll use that time wisely."

"You're joking, right?" Millie asked.

"Which bit? The fact that she's here or that I'm hoping to share my sleeping bag with her?"

"That's she's here," she replied, pulling her feet up onto the couch. "I have no doubt that you'll persuade her what a catch you are. You're nothing if not persistent."

I let out a laugh. "Yeah well, you know me when I want something."

"And why doesn't she want you to be a couple, has she said? Is there someone else?"

"No, there isn't anyone else," I growled. "She just doesn't want a relationship. She's been married, not long divorced, and he was a cheating bastard. She's hurting and it's up to me to show her that not all men are douche nozzles."

Millie watched me for a few seconds and then reached for my hand. "You really like her don't you?" she asked softly.

I took in a deep breath and nodded.

"I just remember how good we were, Millie. I could easily have fallen in love with her all those years ago. Think I'd already started, to be honest."

"And now?"

"And now," I sighed. "Nothing's changed. She's as amazing now as she was then, if not more."

"Well, I hope it works out for you, Garratt."

"Yeah, me too, Millie. Me too."

And I really did, because I didn't think getting over Jemma would be as easy the second time around.

twenty-one
Jemma

It was Friday evening, and a few of the teaching staff had decided drinks at Rowdy's were in order. A few lived in Knightingale, but as most were in or around Bridge Vale, the turnout was good. Even Gladys Winter had turned up in her best dress and some seriously hot, red, ankle strapped shoes. Becky was there, too, but was acting a little weird. Every time Benjie went near her, she moved away to talk to someone else. After a few minutes, Benjie would join that conversation, only for Becky to move on to the next person.

"What's going on there?" I asked Garratt as he passed me a bottle of beer.

"Don't know what you mean." He smiled around the lip of his own bottle.

He was definitely lying.

"Yes you do. Spill. Now."

I glared at him, trying to look menacing. Garratt almost spat out his drink.

"Seriously, Jemma? You trying to scare me?"

His wide, perfect smile showing off those straight white teeth, was infectious, and I, too, broke out with a grin.

"I know you know something. Benjie is one of your best friends."

"Doesn't mean he tells me everything about his love life."

I gasped. "Hah, you just let the cat out of the bag. You said his love life. I never mentioned his love life."

Garratt groaned and shook his head. "Okay, but keep it quiet."

I mimed zipping my lips.

"They're seeing each other. It's pretty serious and words of love have been spoken."

My head whipped around towards Becky who was talking to Vicky and Marcus, the drama teacher.

"Don't be so obvious," Garratt hissed.

"Sorry. But I have to say, you were so easy to crack. In fact, you were pathetic."

"I was not," Garratt protested. "I knew you'd keep at me until I told you, and in any case, they're telling everyone at the end of the semester."

"Like I said, easy." I laughed as Garratt cursed. "It's nice though. They make a good couple."

"Talking of couples, have you made a decision about us yet?"

Garratt grinned and took a swig of his beer. There was a twinkle in his eye and my heart thumped rapidly at the sight of him. God, he was sexy, and there was no way I was going to be able to keep my hands off him for much longer.

"You said I had until the end of today," I replied. "That means I have about another three hours."

"Yep, you do, but I'm proposing we have a quiet chat. Then, maybe," he said, pointing his bottle at me. "*I* can persuade *you* to make your mind up in the next half hour."

"You can't change the rules. We had a deal."

Garratt took a step closer to me, moving his mouth inches from my ear.

"We did, but I think you'll be happy with the rule change when I explain it fully."

I felt his breath against my skin, and his seductive voice and close proximity made my clit start a gentle throb. He was making me wet simply by speaking softly in my ear; no wonder the orgasms he gave me were epic.

"Go on then," I replied. "Tell me what the rule change is."

He moved his bottle into his left hand, placing his right on the small of my back, and edged himself closer to me, until his chest was brushing the side of my breast. As he spoke, his lips whispered against my ear. A shiver ran through me and my nipples hardened.

"My new rule is this. You go to the bathroom, and when you get there you lock the door. Then," he said with a quick nip at my ear, "I will follow you. I'll knock on the door, twice, and you'll let me in."

God I was so wet, and so turned on, I could already feel my orgasm building. If he touched me I felt sure I'd scream his name. No man had ever had this effect on me before. Only ever Garratt. Even when we were young, naïve twenty year olds, he'd talk dirty to me and have me begging him to touch me. Inside or outside my knickers, it didn't matter, one touch and I went off with shards of joy piercing every one of my nerve endings.

"And then what?" I asked breathily.

"Then I come inside the bathroom, I lock the door, and I tell you to drop those tight, sexy as fuck jeans." His hand with the bottle came up, and he pointed his finger, slowly ghosting it over my nipple.

"Then?" I asked, licking my lips.

"Then," he continued. "Well then, I'd take that tiny scrap of lace that I know you're wearing, and rip it off. Once it's gone, I'll push my hard as rock dick inside you and fuck you. I'll fuck you so good and so hard, that once you come, you'll have no damn idea what your name is, where the hell you are, or even how to speak."

I sucked on my bottom lip and fought against my inner desire to open my jeans and touch myself. At that moment, I couldn't care that I was in a crowded bar with my new work colleagues. I just wanted to soothe the ache. I wanted *Garratt* to soothe the ache.

"What then?" I asked. "What would you do once I came?"

Garratt's breathe against my ear faltered, as his hand at my back dropped to my backside.

"And then I'd drop to my knees and eat that magnificent pussy of yours until you screamed my name again. After that, you'd be so fucking addicted to me you'd wonder whatever made you doubt we could have a relationship."

My chest was heaving, I was wet, and I wanted him.

"How does that rule change sound, Jemma?" He asked quietly, his eyes on the group of teachers standing away from us.

It sounded pretty good to me.

"I suggest you go and talk to Gladys for a few minutes, so as not to draw attention to the fact that I've gone."

Garratt's eyes darkened with lust as he pushed up against my side, allowing me to feel his hardness that was forcing itself against his jeans.

"If I talk to Gladys and she sees this boner, she may well get the wrong idea," he groaned. "Anyways, I've changed my mind-"

"No," I cried, loudly, not caring that I might be coming across as desperate.

Garratt gave a soft laugh. "Let me finish. I've changed my mind, we're both going together."

"We can't, people will see us. They'll guess-"

"Jemma," he interrupted. "Move that sexy ass of yours *now*, because I'm telling you if I don't get inside you soon, I'm gonna come in my pants like a virgin at a strip joint."

I turned towards the bathroom, only to be pulled back by Garratt.

"No." He shook his head. "I'm not fucking you in a bathroom, baby."

"But you said-"

"I know what I said, but you're a high school teacher, and you're too damn classy to be treated like a quick fuck. Bobby is waiting outside with his car for us."

I drew in a sharp breath. "Bobby the *Uber* driver? I thought he hardly worked, and never after seven thirty."

"He does if you book him." Garratt drank back the rest of his beer, placing the empty bottle on one of the high top tables. "Come on, let's go."

"How could you book him? Were you always planning on leaving this early?"

Garratt grinned and my belly flipped. "No, baby. He's been waiting out there since we came in and he'd be waiting until whatever time we decided to leave. I paid him for the whole night."

My eyes widened. "You're not serious?"

"As a fucking heart attack, Jemma. Now move unless you want me to embarrass myself and have to pretend I spilled beer on my crotch."

"But-"

"No buts, Jemma. I said move, or I'll throw you over my damn shoulder and spank your ass in front of everyone."

With his words making my knickers wetter and my clitoris even more sensitive, I picked up my bag and left Rowdy's. I didn't say goodbye and didn't even check that Garratt was following me. Once the cool night air hit me, I turned to see him just appearing through the door.

He pointed to a large, black car parked across the street from the bar. "There's Bobby. Let's hope we get you home before that bad chicken rears its head again."

Looking at him questioningly, Garratt grabbed my hand and dragged me to the car.

"Told them you've got a bad case of food poisoning."

"Garratt," I cried indignantly.

Garratt grinned.

"Keep that name on your lips, baby, because you're going to be shouting it a lot before the sun comes up."

And there was the end of my knickers.

twenty-two

Garratt

The drive home was fucking torture. All I wanted to do was strip off her clothes and lay her down on the back seat of Bobby's *Chevrolet* and fuck her brains out. Obviously, I didn't. For one, she deserved better than that, and two, Bobby never shut the fuck up the whole way back to Jemma's apartment.

By the time I handed over the three hundred bucks I owed him, I was just about ready to deliver it with an accompanying punch to the nuts; let's see if he liked aching balls as much as I did. It wasn't Bobby's fault, he was doing his job being a jovial *Uber* driver, but when you're desperately trying hard not to jump the woman next to you, or blow your load in your pants, it's kind of difficult to concentrate on the whys and wherefores of the damn town's Founder's Day festivities.

"Hurry," I whispered into Jemma's ear as she fumbled with the key in the lock. "I can't wait much longer."

My chest was to her back, and my arms were wrapped around her waist with my hands fumbling at the button of her jeans.

Suddenly, the lock clicked and we fell forward as Jemma stepped into the hallway. Throwing her keys down onto the side table, and her purse on the floor, she turned in my arms and our mouths were instantly welded together.

"Oh fuck," I groaned. "Bedroom?"

Without stopping from kissing me, Jemma pointed behind her and started walking backwards. Stumbling and ripping at each other's clothes, we made our way past the lounge, the kitchen, and another door that I guessed must be the bathroom. Finally, after seconds that felt like damn hours, she maneuvered us into her room. By now, both our shirts were gone, Jemma's bra had also been discarded, and both sets of jeans were undone. I pulled myself away from her, toeing off my shoes and socks.

"Strip," I commanded as I pushed down my jeans and boxer briefs, before kicking them away.

Jemma did as she was told and pulled off the rest of her clothes, until she was standing in front of me in nothing but, as I'd thought, a tiny piece of lace that doubled up as panties.

"You're incredible," I whispered as my eyes roamed over her glorious body.

"So are you." She stepped forward and took hold of my hand, pulling me towards the bed. "I need you, Garratt," she whispered. "Now."

I didn't need asking twice. I pushed her down onto the mattress and watched as she bounced and opened her legs for me. Crawling up between them, my eyes watched Jemma as she reached behind her for the brass headboard.

"Hold on," I said, as my head dropped and I sucked on the inside of her thigh. She was mine and I was going to mark her as such.

"Oh God," she cried, as I pushed two fingers inside her while still biting at her smooth skin. "Garratt, please."

"What?" I asked. "What is it that you want? More fingers or my dick? Tell me."

"You, I need you, Garratt."

"Which part of me, Jemma? Tell me, baby. Fingers or dick?"

I curled my fingers, hitting the spot that made her back arch off the bed.

"I need to hear you say it, Jemma."

"Your dick, Garratt," she gasped. "Oh shit, your dick."

Christ she was amazing. I would never get enough of her.

"I've got to get a condom," I said, removing my fingers from her hot wetness.

"No, don't go. We did it before, without one."

Her belligerent moan made me smile.

"Stop acting like a princess." I laughed and leaned down to kiss her. "Are you sure? You still okay going bare? Because I've got to say, I'm more than okay with that."

"Yes, I'm sure," she hissed before putting a hand around my neck and dragging me back down for another kiss.

"Thank fuck," I said breathlessly. "But you may want to stock up on cranberry juice."

"What?" Jemma asked, craning her neck to try and kiss me again.

"Cranberry juice. It's good for bladder infections, and a lot of sex can bring those on."

"How do you even know that?" Jemma looked at me with a frown, her impatience growing.

"I heard Mom and Millie talking about it once, when Millie and Jess were trying for Clemmie. Not a conversation I ever want to hear again, but I heard it. That shit is now seared into my brain. I now know the consequences of having a lot of sex, and I intend on fucking you a helluva lot for the next two weeks. So, stock up on the cranberry juice."

"Don't." Jemma shook her head. "Don't talk about how long we've got."

I smiled and bent down to kiss her softly. "Hey, that doesn't mean it'll be the end of us, it just means that after two weeks we might have to do the long distance thing for a while. I'll only see you on weekends, so I'm going to get as much of you as I can, while I can."

A shadow passed over her features and I saw her chest expand as she took a deep breath.

"Jemma, baby."

I smoothed a hand down her leg, wanting her to feel exactly what I was feeling, know exactly what I knew; it was going to be alright, we were going to be fine. Jemma broke out a smile and reached to pinch my nipple.

"Just fuck me already," she giggled.

I pushed inside her and let out a cry. She was tight, warm, and fucking perfect.

Lying in the bed, with my arms wrapped around Jemma, I didn't think I'd ever felt more content. We'd had two rounds of amazing sex, and were taking a breather. At least in my head we were - I wasn't sure Jemma was up for another go at it, she was real sleepy.

"You okay?" I asked as I rubbed small circles on her back.

"Hmm." She snuggled into me, tightening her arm around my waist. "This is nice."

"Yeah, it is," I agreed.

Dropping a kiss to her nose, I knew that I wouldn't be able to cope with the long distance thing for long. I didn't give a shit whether my boss had been successful in arranging my transfer or not; I was damn well coming home.

"I'm going to come home." My inner thoughts blurted right out.

Looking down at Jemma, I expected to see her smiling. My heart faltered as she bit on her lip and took a deep breath.

"You don't look too happy about it," I laughed, trying to make light of it. Jemma didn't join in my laughter, but remained silent. "Jemma, sweetheart, don't you want me to come home?"

Her head slowly turned up to me, but her eyes remained closed.

"Jemma?"

"I don't want you to change your life just for me," she whispered, finally letting me see the whisky colored windows to her soul. "You don't know whether we'll even want to see each other again after this next two weeks."

As I lifted onto my elbow, Jemma fell away from my chest, onto her back.

"What the hell?"

"I'm just saying," she replied. "At the end of two weeks you might have had enough of me."

"Not going to happen." I shook my head. "Now tell me why the hell you'd think that."

Pulling the comforter up to her chin, she didn't reply.

"Jemma, why would you think that? Do you think *you'll* be glad to see the back of *me* in two weeks'?"

"No," she said quickly, her eyes widening. "I just think that we need to consider it. Don't rush into anything."

I reached down, brushing blonde waves from her face. "I've waited seven years, I hardly think that's rushing into anything."

"I doubt you've been waiting for me, do you?"

Jemma snuggled further down under the covers and turned on her side. Away from me.

"Hey," I said, pulling on her shoulder so that she was on her back again. "What's going on in your head? First you say we'll be done after two weeks, and then you get all jealous because I've obviously had a sex life since college. This from you who has been married. To a douche admittedly, but you made vows to spend the rest of your life with him. So, if anyone should be feeling a little insecure, it should be me."

Jemma looked at me. Her brow furrowing as she studied me.

"You shouldn't feel insecure about Ollie," she said quietly.

"Why not? He was your husband. You only left him because he cheated. If he hadn't been such a prick, you'd probably still be married to him."

I knew I sounded like a sulking kid, but I couldn't help it. I was pissed that she'd been married to someone else. I didn't love her, or anything like that, but I still thought of her as mine. She had been seven years ago and she damn well was now. And if truth be told, I knew it wouldn't take much longer to fall in love with her. Fuck, I'd been halfway there when we were just twenty years old.

"Still find it hard to understand why you dated the fucker in the first place. He sounds like a real tool."

Jemma let out a blast of laughter.

"You are such a baby." She reached up and flicked at my pouting lips with her finger. "Ah, does baby feel jealous," she said in mocking tone.

I grunted and moved my head to the side. Yep, I was being a jealous prick and I couldn't help it.

"Wait there a minute." Jemma sighed and, throwing back the comforter, she dropped her feet to the floor.

"Where you going?"

"Just a minute," she said with an impatient sigh.

She padded out of the bedroom, only to return minutes later with her cell in her hand. Getting back into the bed, she messed with the phone and then passed it to me.

"What?" I asked.

"Look at it." She nodded at the cell in my hand. "That's why I '*dated* the fucker in the first place',￼" she said, doing a decent impersonation of me.

I looked down and saw she'd gone onto a company website – the 'Meet our Team' page. A bunch of suits all looked up at me. All of them sitting sideways, with smarmy grins and matching preppy boy haircuts.

"It's a bunch of people who work for a company. I don't understand."

Jemma sighed and leaned over and poked at the screen.

"There, that's Ollie."

I looked down at the guy smiling back at me from next to her finger. "Oliver Reynolds, Finance Executive." I read aloud. "That's him, the douche?"

"Yes," she said. "That's my ex-husband. Who does he remind you of?"

I looked closely and then started grinning.

"Me, but not half as good looking."

Jemma sighed. "Exactly."

"Let me get this right," I said, glancing down at the screen again. "You dated a guy because he looked like me, yet apparently *I* can't possibly have been waiting for *you* for seven years? Plus, I'm probably going to want to be rid of you at the end of the next two weeks. Is that right?"

Jemma didn't answer, but jutted out her chin with determination, daring me to argue.

"Listen to me," I said, putting an arm around her neck and bringing her face closer to mine. "I was as into you as much as you seem to have been into me. I was miserable when you left, and you know how hard I tried to get in touch. Fuck, you saw all the emails and text messages to prove it. So, don't ever doubt how much I cared about you, or how much I'm starting to care about you again. Two weeks with you would never be enough."

I took Jemma's mouth and kissed her, desperately trying to get her to understand from the feel of my lips and tongue, just how honest I was being. As she let out a little moan of pleasure, her cell trilled out in my hand, startling us both.

"Fuck," I cursed and looked at the screen. "Shit, it's your mom."

The screen said 'Mum', and a picture of the woman in the photo in the hallway flashed up. Her hair was a little longer in this one, and the tight curls had loosened to waves.

Jemma snatched the cell from me, and quickly silenced the call.

"You could have taken it," I said.

Jemma shook her head and threw the phone onto her night stand. "No-no, it's fine."

"You sure?" I looked at her quizzically as she started to chew on her thumb nail.

"It's fine, don't worry about it." Jemma looked at me and plastered on a fake smile, before pushing down under the covers again.

Something was wrong, she seemed agitated by the call from home.

"What's wrong?" I asked, pulling Jemma against my chest.

"Nothing," she answered, too quickly. "I don't want to talk to my mum while we're in bed after having had sex."

Her smile was watery and a little too wide to be real, but I'd let it go. For now.

twenty-three

Jemma

I woke with beautifully aching muscles, and a huge smile on my face. Garratt was in my bed, a strong arm wrapped around my waist and a long tanned leg intertwined with mine. I turned my head to look at him and my heart did a little flip in time with my stomach. He looked beautiful.

His face was turned towards me, and his soft breathing was causing the disheveled hair that was falling over his face to blow in the breeze he was creating.

I softly traced a finger down his cheek and his hand that was resting on the pillow dropped to scratch at his hair. My finger now went to his nose, tracing his profile. Garratt huffed and wiggled his nose, making me giggle quietly. I leaned forward and blew softly onto his face. Garratt's hand that was wrapped around me came up and swatted at his face. Holding back a snorting laugh, I leaned forward and nibbled at his chin, with its sexy stubble. Before I even had chance to pull away, I was on my back and

Garratt was on top of me. His mouth was at my neck, blowing raspberries on it, while his hands were at my waist, tickling it.

"Garratt, no," I cried, amidst my giggles. "Stop it, please."

"No," he said, lifting his mouth from my neck momentarily.

He continued his torture of me, his fingers on one hand travelling up to under my arm.

"Oh my God. No. Garratt, I'm going to pee myself."

With lightning speed, he stopped and pushed back to the other side of the bed, leaning up on his forearm.

"Ugh, dirty girl." Garratt grinned at me and it was sleepy and sexy, doing all sorts of things to my insides.

"I was kidding," I said, reaching a hand up to smooth down his bed hair. "I hate being tickled."

"Well in that case, morning gorgeous," he said, dropping a kiss to the end of my nose.

"Hardly," I replied, stifling a yawn.

"Yes, you are." Garratt's voice was soft and low, almost whispered. "So damn gorgeous."

The smile left my lips as his words pounded my emotions. I wanted to fall in love with this man so much. He was everything that I wanted. Everything that Ollie had never been, and could never be. I stared up at him, tears stinging at the corners of my eyes. He could be my life, if I let him.

"Hey," Garratt cooed, brushing his thumb against my eye. "Baby, what's wrong?"

What did I say? If I told him, would he run back to the city and never come back? After last night, I didn't want him to leave; I wanted what he was offering, no matter how long it lasted. Now, I wanted to be selfish, but could I really do that to him?

"You just make me happy," I said through a sniffle.

"Really, because it doesn't look like it." Garratt smiled and brushed hair from my face. "But I can't say that those words don't make me feel happy, too, because they do. Does this mean you've changed your mind about having a relationship?"

He gave me a cocky grin, knowing full well what that answer was.

"You and your sexy moves," I replied with a shake of my head. "They've managed to blur the edges of all my decisions."

I took a deep breath, thinking about the one decision that I wasn't sure I would change.

"That's good." Garratt's mouth was on mine instantly, devouring me and flooding my senses with his magnificent taste. "Now, I suggest we have us some morning sex before breakfast. What do you say?"

"I say, that sounds like a brilliant…Oh God, Garratt."

I was then given the best morning orgasm of my life.

"What's your plan for today?" I asked Garratt, as he helped himself to more coffee.

He looked up at me and smiled. "You fancy coming home to the ranch with me?"

"Your family ranch?" I asked, shocked.

"Yeah, my family ranch." Garratt laughed and shook his head. "My folks are away, so it'd just be Jesse, Millie, and the kids. Oh, and any ranch hands that are around."

I hugged my coffee mug against my chest and watched Garratt as he sat at one of the tall kitchen stools. He was wearing only his jeans, seeing as I had on his shirt from last night, and his feet were bare. His hair was damp from the shower he'd taken and it was all mussed up from rubbing a towel over it. He'd wanted me to get into the shower with him, but I'd been adamant I was going to cook him breakfast. It had only been fried egg sandwiches, but he wolfed down every bit, with noises of satisfaction. The pleasure he evidently got from my cooking had almost managed to dull the ache between my legs that I'd had since declining to shower with him.

"Well?"

I startled. "Oh, well I don't know. Won't they all be busy?"

"Not so much on a Saturday. Jesse tries to work a little less on the weekends these days. He wants to spend as much time with Millie and the kids as he can, so they'll probably just be kicking back in the house or the yard."

"They won't want me hanging around then," I replied, not sure whether

I was ready to meet Garratt's family just yet. "Messing up their Saturday."

"You're not nervous at meeting them are you?" he asked, laughing softly.

"No." I answered quickly and a little strongly.

"Jemma," Garratt said in a warning tone.

"Alright, maybe just a little bit. We've only been back together a night. Don't you think it's a little soon?"

"Nope." Garratt shook his head and took a swig of his coffee. "Told you, I'm moving back to be with you, so makes sense you'll get to know my family."

Garratt's back was ramrod straight as he watched me carefully. He'd already made his mind up and no matter what I said, today would be spent on the Connor ranch.

As we pulled up outside the most beautiful house I think I'd ever seen, the nerves in my stomach started a riot. I was going to be meeting Garratt's family. Surely it was too soon; didn't you only do this once you knew you were in a serious relationship? But, how on earth could we even contemplate *that* after one night together? Okay, so it wasn't exactly our first night together, but we hadn't actually had the conversation about whether we were in a relationship or not. Garratt did his magical hip gyration, gave me multiple orgasms, and I gave in and more or less agreed that we were together.

"Hey," Garratt said, grabbing hold of my hand and squeezing it. "Stop worrying about something that isn't even a problem. Yeah, it may seem a little soon to most people, but we're not most people and we have history."

"How did you know that's what I was worrying about?" I asked, frowning.

He shot me one of his cheeky grins and shrugged. "I just know you. It might have been a long time ago, but that month we were together we were barely apart. Besides which, I'd been studying you in class way before we started dating."

"Oh, did you now?" I giggled and leaned forward for a quick kiss.

"Yep," Garratt said as we parted. "I studied that fine ass of yours mostly, but I also spent a great deal of time watching your face and wondering how I could get you to just smile at me. You always seemed so worried."

I thought back to college and Garratt was right. "I think I was a little scared that I'd fail all my classes and get sent home, meaning all the arguments I'd had with my parents about studying overseas would have been pointless."

"Yeah, and I see that same look on your face now." Garratt lifted an index finger and gently stroked between my eyes. "You have that little V shaped, frown thing going on."

I batted his hand away. "I do not." I pouted and lifted my own finger to feel. I started to laugh. "Oh God, I do. I'm going to need *Botox.*"

Garratt took my finger and pulled it away, kissing the tip of it. "Nope. No way. I'd like to be able to see your expression when I'm making you come. I don't want you looking surprised every time I stick it in you."

"Garratt," I cried. "Oh my God, you are so disgusting."

I tried to hold back my smile, but I couldn't help it. He was so crude at times, but he made me laugh like no one ever had before.

"Disgustingly handsome." Garratt started to laugh and, before long, I was joining in with him. "Okay," he said finally. "That's stopped your nerves, so let's go and meet my family."

When we got out of the car, I leaned back against it to look up at the house. It really was gorgeous. For starters it was big, but not ostentatious in any way. The grey slate roof sloped down to lighter grey walls that had windows that were so clean and white they appeared to pop out. My favorite part, though, was the porch that you walked up to via wooden steps. It reminded me of the house in *The Walton's*, one of my mum's favorite shows that she used to get us to watch repeats of on a Sunday morning when Lauren and I were children.

"Wow, this place is gorgeous," I said in awe.

Garratt came to stand next to me and dropped his head back to look at the house. "Yeah, Jesse did it all," he said proudly. "Mom and Dad never had the time or the inclination, so when they signed the house over to Jesse, he did a whole lot of work on it. Mainly for his wife Melody, but it still wasn't good enough for *her*."

I turned to look at Garratt. His tone had hardened and I felt him tense beside me.

"That was his first wife? The one that died?"

I remembered at college, Garratt telling me that his brother was struggling to come to terms with the loss of his wife. He'd been really worried about him, and often called his parents to see how Jesse and his niece, Jesse's daughter, were doing.

"Yep, that's the one," Garratt sighed. "But he's happy now. I can't imagine him with anyone else but Millie. She's his life."

A ball formed in my throat that I was struggling to swallow around. Stupidly, I could only think of Garratt finding someone else if I died. I was being ridiculous, but I couldn't help it. I couldn't ignore the pain in my chest.

Garratt moved from beside me and, taking hold of my hand, pulled me towards the house, dragging me from my inner thoughts.

"Come on, let's go and see what they're all doing. If we're lucky, Millie might have made her famous sausage and chips for lunch."

"Oh my God," I said, forcing a smile. "Really? I forgot she was from the UK."

"Yeah," Garratt said, leading me up the steps. "And she trained as a teacher. How weird is that? My big brother and me have more than good looks and a huge penis in common."

With a sigh, I shook my head and followed Garratt into the house, holding a hand against the turmoil in my stomach.

I don't think I had ever met such cute, adorable children as Addy, Clemmie, and Hunter in all my life. Addy, the eldest, and Hunter, the youngest - and loudest, were most definitely Connor children. They were the image of their daddy, with lighter blonde hair than Jesse but the same striking blue eyes. Clemmie, on the other hand, was the image of Millie, with olive skin, brown eyes, and long black hair to her waist, she was a real mini-me of her mum. The three of them had greeted me with hugs and kisses and after only half an hour, Hunter was already climbing onto my knee so I could read him a story. They were so loving and it made my heart ache.

"You okay?" Garratt asked, handing me a bottle of beer.

"Yes, I'm having a lovely time." I smiled up at him before glancing over at the children, who were now splashing around in a blow up paddling pool. "They love the water."

Garratt's gaze followed mine. "Yeah, they sure do. Jesse is thinking about building a swimming pool, but Millie likes her garden as it is."

From my spot on the deck, I had a good view of the garden and it really was beautiful. The grass was lush and green and had a border of beautiful wild flowers, with a path curving through it to a pasture at the back.

"I feel bad sitting here while Jesse and Millie do all the work," I said, looking back up at Garratt.

Jesse was cooking meat on the grill in the far corner of the deck, while Millie was inside making salad and cutting bread. The meat smelled delicious, and while good old British sausage and chips would have been nice, I was looking forward to the steak.

"Don't worry about it," Garratt replied, plonking himself down in the chair next to mine. "They love days like this - the kids having fun, and family being around. There were too many dark days in this house before Millie came along."

Garratt's eyes drifted over to his brother and a small smile lifted his lips. It was evident how much he loved his brother, and Millie, too. They were obviously close, the huge hug he'd given her when we arrived showed that, but they enjoyed great banter with each other; making fun of each other and cracking jokes. They also had their love for Jesse in common. I noticed that Millie's eyes shone brighter when her husband was close by, but it seemed pretty mutual to be honest. He couldn't keep his hands off her, whether it be one at her waist, touching her hair, or landing a playful smack on her bum, or ass, as Garratt kept telling me to call it. They were a beautiful family and pangs of envy were tugging at my chest. I wanted this, but it was all just a pipe dream.

"Okay," Millie said, appearing through the sliding doors holding two dishes. "We've got a green salad and a shrimp salad. Garr', can you go inside and bring out the bread and baked potatoes for me, please?"

Garratt saluted her and stood up, placed his bottle on the table, and disappeared inside.

"Are you sure there's nothing I can do?" I asked, taking one of the dishes from Millie and placing it on the table.

"God, no," Millie protested. "You're a guest. When you're family, then you can help out."

She grinned at me and I smiled back, but my stomach dropped.

"Oh, I'm not sure about that." My face was heated. Yes, maybe one day it would be nice to be a part of this lovely family, but despite it being too soon to think about that, it was never going to happen. Once I told Garratt about my situation - and I knew that I had to - he wouldn't want to continue to be with me. Why would he want to invest time in a relationship with someone who might have a death sentence hanging over them?

"Believe me," Millie said. "If I know anything about Garratt, it's when he's serious about something, and he's really serious about you."

She squeezed my shoulder and looked over at Jesse.

"Those Connor boys are really hard to forget once they're in your system, I can promise you."

As I watched Millie stare at her husband, Garratt appeared back at the table.

"Where do you want these, Millie?" he asked.

Roused from her daydream, Millie turned and made a space on the table. "Just here. Jesse, are the steaks ready yet?"

Jesse didn't turn from the grill, but held up two fingers. "Two minutes, baby."

Millie walked to the edge of the deck and, leaning against the post of the steps, called down to the children.

"Time to dry off and wash up, kids."

"Momma, do I have time for a shower?" Addy asked, running across the lawn towards the steps.

"No, baby. Get dried and wash your hands."

"But-"

"Addy, you heard your momma," Jesse called, still not turning around. "Do as she asks."

I laughed quietly as Addy rolled her eyes and clomped up the steps, snagging a towel from a chair.

"Adeline Marie Connor, you better stop stomping girl." Jesse's voice was stern as he continued to concentrate on the steaks. "Take your brother and sister with you."

Addy stopped at the top step and turned to yell for her siblings.

"*Clemmie, Hunter,* come on we have to dry off *and* wash up!"

The smaller two children instantly stopped what they were doing and chased after Addy, before all three of them disappeared inside. As soon as they were out of sight, Garratt started to laugh.

"Sheesh, that girl has suddenly got attitude," he said to Jesse who was bringing a plate full of meat to the table.

"That girl has always had attitude," Jesse replied. "It's just gotten worse over the last few months."

"She's not my baby anymore," Millie lamented. "As soon as she hit eleven, she became so grown up. Now she wants to shower all the time. Not a *bath*, but a *shower*."

"She's hit that age when hygiene suddenly becomes important," I said.

"Yes, I know, but bath time was always her favorite thing. I miss that."

I watched Millie, who sighed heavily. I knew Addy wasn't her daughter by blood, but she evidently saw her no differently to the two she'd actually given birth to. I'd always thought it wouldn't be possible to love a child that wasn't yours with the same intensity as your own children, but Millie had proved me wrong. She'd made me rethink my opinion.

"Maybe that's a good thing," Garratt said. "With her going away to school, maybe she needs to be more grown up to deal with it."

Jesse made a growling noise as he sat down in the chair next to Garratt. "Less said about that the better."

"You don't want her to go?" I asked.

"Nope. She's too young."

Millie sighed. "Babe, we've talked about this. She needs to go to that school to fulfil her potential. No disrespect, Jemma, but Bridge Vale High just isn't good enough for her."

"She's going to a school that has a gifted kids program," Garratt explained.

"Oh, okay," I said, nodding my head. "Well, in that case, I agree, Bridge Vale isn't the right fit for her."

"Not you too," Jesse groaned, picking up a beer from the iced bucket on the floor next to him. "It's bad enough I have these two going on about it."

Garratt and Millie shared a conspiratorial smile.

"Jesse doesn't like that she's going to be boarding at the school, do you, babe?" Millie leaned across and kissed her husband on the cheek.

"Nope. Don't see why she needs to – she could come home every day, it's only two fucking hours away. Anyway, I don't want to talk about it. I've got a little under four months left with her at home and so I'm gonna try and forget about it until then."

With that, it was evident the subject was closed. Garratt went on to ask Jesse about the possibility of Caleb Tremaine coming to help him out with the horses, as long as his father gave permission. Jesse was more than happy to have Caleb, and the conversation then moved on to horses, so Addy's school was definitely forgotten.

The rest of the afternoon went blissfully by with the two younger children playing in the water again, Addy sitting reading, and us four adults chatting and joking. I couldn't remember a time when I'd felt so content and happy and I really didn't want the day to end. Finally, at six-thirty, when Millie called the kids in for their bath, or shower in Addy's case, Garratt announced that he'd better get me home.

"Why are you going back to town?" Jesse asked. "'Cause I'm assuming you'll be staying over, so why not just stay at Mom and Dad's?"

"I never said we were going back to town," Garratt replied. "Besides, have you not noticed that I've been drinking beer all afternoon?"

Jesse looked down at the empty beer bottles next to Garratt's chair. "So if you're staying at the house, why are you going now? Millie has got some bottles of that sparkling white wine shit that she likes. I bet Jemma would like some, wouldn't you, Jemma?"

"I would, but also I don't have any spare clothes with me," I said to Garratt.

"You don't need spare clothes, in fact, any clothes," he said quietly around the mouth of his bottle as he swigged the last dregs of his beer. "And," now much louder, "as much as I love you big brother, I've had enough of you for one day."

Jesse looked between me and Garratt, grinned widely, and nodded. "Okay. Well, have a good night, both of you."

With that, he stood up, collected some of the dishes, and disappeared inside the house.

"Garratt," I protested. "That was rude."

Garratt laughed loudly as he stood and offered me his hand. "No, baby, it wasn't. Jesse understands."

"Understands what, that he's given us his hospitality all afternoon and you've just told him that you don't want to spend any more time with him?"

Garratt pulled me to my feet and close to his chest. His head dipped and his mouth whispered against my ear.

"No, he understands that I'm ready to get you naked and make you scream."

He slapped my *ass* and then dragged me away, through the house and across the pasture to his parents' house. There wasn't a thing I could do about it, but to be honest, I went more than willingly.

twenty-four

Garratt

When Jemma walked out of her apartment building on Monday morning, my heart thudded hard, and a growling groan escaped my lips. She looked un-fucking-believably sexy in her skin tight yoga pants, tight black, tee and her hair in a high pony tail, swishing around behind her as she jogged towards my car. I met her halfway, taking her backpack from her and leaning in for a kiss.

"Well, good morning Ms. Reynolds. And how are you today?"

Jemma smiled against my mouth and let out a little sigh.

"That good, huh?"

She grinned at me, a little blush touching her cheeks. "Happy to see you."

"Good. That's what I like to hear. My girl is happy to see me."

I turned towards my car, popping the trunk to throw her backpack inside. Jemma came beside me and put a coat and a hoodie on top of our bags.

"Can't say I'm happy to be going camping, though," she said, moving towards the passenger door. "I've only been a couple of times, and both times I got soaking wet due to the weather."

"Well, it won't be the weather getting you soaking wet on this trip, gorgeous." It was corny, I knew, but I liked my cheesy lines and I think deep down, Jemma did, too.

"You can't say things like that," she scolded. "If any of the kids find out we're together, and it gets back to Becky, we could be in trouble."

"Becky can't say anything," I replied, climbing into the driver's seat. "She and Ben are together."

"I know, but I'd still rather we tell her before any of the kids do."

I took Jemma's hand in mine and gave it a squeeze. "Okay, if you insist. I'll be a good boy for the next two days."

"Promise?" she asked, holding out her pinky finger.

"Seriously? You want me to pinky promise?" I looked down at her finger, and then back up into her eyes with my brow furrowed. "I'm not doing that."

Jemma's eyes widened as she tilted her head, daring me to disobey. When I stared back at her, she jutted out her chin with her eyes getting even bigger.

"Fucking hell," I groaned, and linked my little finger with hers and gave it a little shake. "Happy now?"

I was rewarded with a beautiful smile and a quick kiss to the lips.

"Shit, Jem', if I'd known I was going to have to deny myself of you for two days, I'd have never let you sleep here alone last night. I'd have been here making sure we had enough orgasms to get us through."

Jemma started to giggle. "I had to have *some* sleep. You've kept me awake until all hours, all weekend. And worked every damn muscle in my body, I should add."

I had to admit, my heart and dick kind of swelled at that statement.

"I needed to have some sleep before tackling two days in the woods with a bunch of hormonal teenagers."

"Yeah, well, I think a half dozen orgasms would have worked just as well," I pouted.

I really was wondering how I was going to keep my hands off her for the next couple of days. It was going to be a struggle. But, I had to agree, she was right. We couldn't get caught by the kids – it wouldn't be professional for a start.

"Just think of how exciting the wait will be," Jemma said. "The anticipation of it all."

I gave her a small smile and shook my head.

"If you say so." With that, I maneuvered the car out of the space I was in and on to the road to school where the bus was picking us up.

An hour later and most of the kids had arrived and were milling around, talking in their groups, while Jemma and Gladys ticked off their names on the attendance register. I, in the meantime, helped Dan, our driver, load all the gear and backpacks.

"They all here?" Dan asked, as we loaded up the last of the tents.

"We good to go, ladies?" I shouted over to Gladys and Jemma.

Jemma shook her head. "We're just waiting for Caleb Tremaine."

I walked over to Jemma and looked down at her list, wondering how late Caleb was going to be. One of the boys left the group he was in and sidled up to us.

"He's not coming, Ms. Reynolds," Matthew Cutter, a kid who I'd seen hanging around with Caleb, said quietly.

"How do you know?" I asked.

"He said on Friday." Matthew looked over his shoulder, checking no one was close by and then leaned in closer. "Said he didn't have the stuff, so wasn't going to come."

"He didn't tell me," Gladys chimed in. "And he knows he needs to complete this project to pass Geography. If he doesn't, then it won't go towards his GPA."

"Could it affect it badly?" I asked.

For some reason, Caleb Tremaine had got to me, and I hated the idea that he might be jeopardizing his choice of college, for the sake of a weather-proof coat and some walking boots. Ever since he'd told me he loved horses, and was evidently in awe of my big brother, I'd felt as though I needed to look out for him.

"He wants to go to Colorado State on a scholarship for their Equine program – so, yes I'd say he needs to complete this project." Gladys gave me a thin lipped smile, and I could sense that she was concerned about Caleb, too.

I turned to Matthew. "What stuff is he missing, did he say?"

Matthew shrugged. "Not sure, I think he said he doesn't have any walking boots or a sleeping bag. His pop is always working, so he said he hasn't had chance to get them for him. To be honest though, Mr. Connor, I'm not sure he could afford them anyways."

I looked at Gladys and Jemma and knew we were all thinking that Matthew was probably correct.

"Okay, Matthew," I said, laying a hand on his shoulder. "Thanks for letting us know. And I think you were right to keep it on the down low from the other kids. You're a good friend to Caleb."

Matthew smiled, brushed his shaggy brown hair from his forehead and jogged back to the group of boys he'd been with.

"What do we do?" I asked.

"Nothing we can do," Gladys replied. "He'll lose points for not completing the project, which goes a big way to passing his geography class. But he's a bright kid and hopefully he'll make them up with his grades in other subjects, or maybe CSU will see the potential and take him with a lower GPA. I just know how strict they are. There are hundreds of kids who want to go there and get onto that program, especially farming and ranch kids. It's not only their future they're working for, but that of their families."

I knew what Gladys was saying to be true. My mom and dad's ranch had survived because Jesse was forward thinking and read up on everything, studying the best practices for his cattle and horses. He never rested on his laurels, knowing he had to continually move forward. Ranching was a hard life, and gone were the days when having a few hundred pairs was enough to survive – so no wonder families were sending their kids to college to learn more.

"He told me he wants to work with horses," I said.

"The boy is obsessed with them." Gladys sighed. "But, what else can we do? If he isn't coming, he isn't coming."

I made my mind up. Caleb was damn well coming on this trip, and he was damn well getting the GPA he needed to go and study everything horses.

"You take the kids ahead, on the bus," I said to Jemma and Gladys. "I'll meet you at the lunch stop."

"*What*?" Jemma asked, astonished. "What are you going to do?"

"Garratt Connor," Gladys growled. "Don't you dare make me pull rank here."

She gave me the look that I remembered from when I was a kid – the one she gave me when I'd forgotten to do my homework.

"He's a good kid, Gladys. He deserves a chance."

"There's nothing to say he won't get the required GPA without the project," Jemma said, looking between me and Gladys.

"But why take the risk?" I'd thrown my education away, not that I regretted it – what was the point, it was over and done a long time ago - but I was damned if Caleb was going to throw his education away through no fault of his own.

"This is most inappropriate, Garratt." Gladys shook her head, but I could sense she was in agreement with whatever I planned to do.

"Jemma, you understand, don't you?" I asked, hoping getting Jemma onside would sway Gladys.

Jemma was silent for a moment and then turned to our colleague. "Garratt's right, Caleb is a good kid and shouldn't lose out because he can't afford a pair of boots."

Gladys let out a long sigh. "Okay, but you'd better be at the lunch stop because if you're not, we don't go. Which means you have the GPA for all those kids on your head." She nodded towards the group of kids still waiting for us.

"Shit, way to make a guy feel guilty, Gladys."

"You're the one that's flouting all the rules, Garratt. Not me, honey pie."

I looked up at the sky and sighed, putting my hands to my hips. "Okay. Whatever happens, with or without Caleb, I'll be at the lunch stop at one."

Gladys eyed me warily. "Okay, we'd best go. Come on Jemma, say goodbye to lover boy."

My mouth dropped open and Jemma gasped.

"H-how, did you…"

"Shit, Gladys," I groaned. "You related to NCIS' Agent Gibbs, or something?"

Gladys waved a dismissive hand at us. "Food poisoning my ass. Anybody with eyes could see you two being all kissy over each other. You were desperate to be alone."

"Oh God," Jemma gasped. "Does everyone know?"

"No, don't be silly. They were all too busy watching Ben and Becky and wondering who was going to win the wager on what time he sneakily felt her ass."

I burst out laughing, mainly at the look of horror on Jemma's face. Gladys gave us a little shrug and walked off towards the kids.

"Oh shit," Jemma whispered. "Thank goodness we didn't go to the bathroom and…you know."

"Baby, stop worrying. There was no way we were going into that bathroom for sex. Told you, you're too classy for that. Now stop worrying." Giving a quick glance over to the kids, making sure no one was looking, I planted a quick kiss to her pouty lips. "Go. Go and get on the bus and I'll see you at the lunch stop. I promise."

Jemma sighed heavily. "Okay, and please be careful. Don't speed, and if Caleb really doesn't want to come, don't push him."

"He'll come."

"I'm guessing you're going to buy him the stuff he needs."

I nodded. "Yeah, I am."

"Well don't force it, he's probably got his pride. Remember that."

"I will, baby. I swear. Go on, and I'll see you later."

She gave me a beautiful smile. "You're a good man, Garratt Connor."

"Ah well, you know some are born great, other have to strive for it. I think I was just born that way."

Jemma started to laugh and, with a shake of her head, joined Gladys in herding the kids onto the bus. I started to walk to my car, and took out my phone, dialing a number.

"Hey Garr'," my brother answered. "What's up?"

"I need a favor, bro. You got time to take me to the roadside café at

Bennington in an hour or two?"

"Aren't you supposed to be on that school trip to Wilmington Park? What happened, you miss the bus?"

"Yes and no. I let it go. I need to help that kid out, the one that you said can help you with the horses."

Without question Jesse said yes. My brother was amazing. I knew he'd be busy, but I had no one else to ask.

"Thanks, Jesse. I'll see you outside Sloane's in an hour. Oh and you'll need to follow me to school, to leave my car there."

"Anything else?" Jesse asked with a hint of laughter.

"Not for now."

I ended the call and got into my car, hoping that Caleb was home.

twenty-five
Garratt

A s I pulled up outside Hannigan's food market, it crossed my mind that I was doing the wrong thing. I should just let Caleb have his pride and figure another way for him to get to CSU. That thought was brief, because I knew that while the kid was bright, he didn't need the pressure.

Getting out of my car, I saw the door next to the main shop door open. Caleb appeared, pulling a backpack over his shoulder while studying a piece of paper in his hand.

"Hey, Caleb," I called, averting his attention.

Caleb looked up and when he saw it was me, stopped dead in his tracks.

"Mr. Connor. What are you doing here?" His cheeks blushed and his eyes widened.

"You missed the bus. I'm here to pick you up and we're going to meet up with everyone at lunch."

"I'm not going. I-I can't go," he stammered. "I don't want to go."

Taking a step closer to him, I shook my head. "Not an option, Caleb. You need to finish the project to get the grade in Geography, to get you the GPA you need for CSU. For your scholarship."

Caleb's gaze dropped down to the floor, watching his feet as he kicked at the sidewalk. "It'll be fine," he said, without looking up.

"Caleb, it won't be fine. You have to do this project. So, like I said, I'm here to make sure you do."

"You don't understand," he replied, lifting his head back up.

"I understand perfectly. Now, what say you go back inside and pack your backpack with everything you need?"

"But-."

"Everything you need that you have. The rest, we'll go over to Sloane's for."

His shoulders stiffened and his nostrils flared.

"Who told you? I bet it was Matty, wasn't it?"

"Don't be mad at him. He was just being a good friend." I took a step closer and laid a hand on his shoulder.

"The whole damn senior class will know. How do you think that'll make me feel?" Caleb's voice cracked as he stared at me with eyes full of emotion. "I'll be humiliated."

I shook my head. "He only told me," I replied with a half-truth. The kid was embarrassed enough that I knew of his situation, he didn't need to know that Gladys and Jemma knew, too. "He told me in confidence away from Ms. Winter and Ms. Reynolds."

"It's still embarrassing that *you* know."

Caleb ran a hand through his hair and groaned.

"Hey," I said to get him to look at me. "It's not embarrassing. I want to help you out because you're a bright kid who wants to do well for himself. Times are hard, Caleb, for everyone, so you've nothing to be afraid of. Plus, if you learn anything on that course, you might just be able to pass it on to my brother when you're working on the ranch during your college breaks."

Caleb's eyes went as round as saucers. "What?"

Yep, I'd have to owe Jesse for that one when I told him, but I'd pay the kids wages myself if Jesse had a problem with it.

"You heard me. Jesse said you can work on the ranch during your breaks while you're at college. That way you're both a winner. You're learning from him and he might learn something from you."

"Seriously?"

I nodded. "Yeah. Now, go back upstairs and let your dad know you've decided to go on the trip. Get your stuff and meet me at the outdoor section of the department store in ten minutes. And, if you don't turn up, I will chase you down and drag you there. Oh, and if it makes you feel better, you can pay me back when you start earning from my brother."

Caleb managed a small smile and gave me a short nod of his head before disappearing back through the door. As I walked over to Sloane's department store, I shot Jesse a text.

Garratt: *I've told Caleb he can work with you on the ranch when he's on break from college. I'll explain more when I can.*

Jesse: *Caleb? The kid who is going to work for me on weekends?*

Garratt: *Yep*

Jesse: *WTF?*

Garratt: *I know and I'm sorry. Promise I'll explain. Just go along with it when you take us to Bennington.*

Jesse: *OK but you owe me!*

Garratt: *I know and thank you.*

A half hour later, after a quick dash through the outdoor department, Caleb and I piled into Jesse's truck – Caleb in the back changing into his walking boots and pushing the rest of the gear we'd bought into his backpack.

"You left the message for your dad?" I asked. "Telling him you'd decided to go on the trip after all?"

"Yes, sir. I called him at work."

"Good. You're going to have a great time, as well as get that GPA you need," I said, looking over my shoulder at him.

"Thank you, Mr. Connor. And I'll pay you back every penny."

"Well, you need to start earning first."

"Yeah, about that. Thanks to you, too, Mr. Connor. You don't know what it means to me. I mean, the weekend job offer was awesome, but to have me working for you while I'm at college, well that's just…it's just *even more* awesome."

"Yeah, no problem," Jesse said, giving me the side-eye. "But let's see how the weekends go first. If you're not cut out for it, or I don't feel comfortable with you around my horses, then there'll be no job."

"*Jesse*," I snapped.

"No, it's fine, Mr. Connor," Caleb said, shaking his head. "Mr. Connor is right. He has to trust me with the horses. They're too valuable and too precious to have someone working with them that doesn't know what they're doing. Really, it's okay, I understand."

Jesse turned to me. "Maybe this kid will work out after all. He has a good attitude about the most magnificent beast on this earth."

I glanced at Caleb to see a huge ass grin on his face and I knew that he would do whatever it took to work with my brother.

"Oh, and Caleb, call me Jesse, hey."

"Yes, sir, Mr. Connor, I mean J-Jesse," he stammered, nervously.

"Good. Now tell me all about this course you're wanting to get on."

And so, for the next two hours, they talked, and I listened, to everything horses.

twenty-six

Jemma

Looking out of the window, I almost squealed when a huge, black truck pulled up and Garratt and Caleb got out, waving to, who I recognized was Jesse, in the driving seat. Caleb was carrying a backpack and had a huge smile on his face. I glanced at Gladys, who closed her eyes in relief and let her shoulders sag.

When they came inside, Garratt said something to Caleb, and pointed towards the counter. Caleb nodded and jogged away, I guessed to order his lunch that the school had pre-paid for.

"Hey, you did it," I said to Garratt as he joined us, standing at the end of our table.

"Yeah," he said on a sigh. "But do me a favor, ladies, don't let on that you know he couldn't afford the gear. *He* thinks that *you* think he slept in by mistake."

Gladys nodded and gave Garratt's forearm a squeeze. "Well done." She smiled and then turned back to her lunch.

"I'm so proud of you," I whispered as Garratt pushed into the booth beside me. "You did a good thing there, Garratt."

"I've put myself in Jesse's debt for the next fifty years, but shit, who cares if the kid gets to go to the college he wants to go to."

My heart swelled and was flooded with warmth for the gorgeous man sitting next to me. I knew that I was starting to fall in love with him – probably hadn't stopped from seven years ago – but this time my feelings were more intense. Those of a woman falling in love with a man she wanted to build a life with, not a young girl excited about the possibilities that a new romance was bringing. Every day, Garratt showed me a little bit more what a good man he was. For me, he'd been near on perfect when we were at college, but now, along with the handsome looks and cheeky smile, were kindness, strength and determination.

"He wasn't happy about the two hour drive out here?" I asked, getting my mind back on track.

"No, that he was fine with. It was my offer to Caleb of a job on the ranch during his college breaks." He laughed and reached for my cup of coffee. "I had to think of something to get the stubborn, little fool to agree to me buying him the gear."

I giggled and shook my head. "You're incorrigible."

"Yeah, maybe, but I'm fucking good at it."

Gladys looked up and raised her brow.

"Sorry, Gladys. Totally forgot where I was."

Garratt squeezed my knee under the table, making me bust out a laugh.

"Mind you start remembering," she said. "I'd hate to have to put you in detention."

Garratt saluted her. "Yes, Ms. Winter, consider it done."

"And also remember kids have eyes." Gladys' eyebrows arched. "Don't let them catch you feeling Jemma up under the table."

I gasped as Garratt's hands both shot in the air, palms facing Gladys.

"Nothing going on here, Ms. Winter," he replied, with a wink.

"Just be careful, that's all I'm saying."

I shuffled further down the booth, away from Garratt, who turned to frown at me.

"Where you going? To sit in the parking lot?"

"No, but Gladys is right," I hissed. "We need to be careful, in front of the kids *and* until we've told Becky."

Garratt let out a sigh. "Fine, I'll try and keep my distance."

"You don't need to do that," Gladys said, adding salt to her sandwich. "Just don't be kissing and cuddling where you might get caught. Now, tell me about Caleb. What's the situation?"

With that, Garratt purposefully moved closer to me and told us everything that had happened with Caleb.

When we got to the campsite, after checking in with the park ranger, almost two hours later, the kids were just about ready to burst with all the pent-up energy. Things had got a little raucous on the bus, and Garratt had needed to go to the back and calm things down. It was just kids being kids, but Dan had threatened to pull over and throw them all off the bus if they didn't quiet down. So, Garratt got the job of sitting with them.

"Okay, guys," Gladys shouted above the chatter. "I need you to get the tents from the bus, and split into groups of four to put them up – each group of four will then share that tent."

"Hey, Cindy," a tall, gangly boy named Derek called. "You wanna share with me?"

As everyone laughed, Gladys clapped her hands for some quiet. "Hey, settle down, and no, Derek, Cindy will not be sharing with you. There will be no mixed sexes in the tents," she replied with a warning tone.

"As if I'd want to share with you anyway, Derek Pederson," Cindy grumbled. "Your feet likely smell like cheese and I know for a fact you fart like twenty times an hour."

More laughter broke out as Derek's friends all started to rib him, jumping on his back and messing up his hair.

"Hey, come on guys, let's all listen to Ms. Winter, because the quicker you do, the quicker you can have some free time," Garratt shouted above the noise.

For someone who was just getting his first experience at teaching, he was doing a great job. He'd fitted into the role perfectly, and the kids seemed to have a lot of respect for him - I hadn't seen anyone mess with him like they did most trainee teachers.

Everyone stopped talking and let Gladys continue to tell them that once the tents were up, they could have some free time. There wasn't an awful lot around for them to do, and practically zero phone signal, so I hoped that boredom wouldn't lead some of them into doing something they shouldn't – we were in the middle of a woodland park, with a group of twenty hormonal teenagers, it could be asking for trouble.

"Are we allowed to leave the camp?" One of the girls asked.

"No, Darla," I replied. "You need to stay where we can see you."

Darla pouted and gave a side-long glance at Matty, Caleb's friend. Okay, so there was a couple I'd be keeping an eye on.

"It's going to be a little boring, don't you think?" another girl complained.

"Let's get the tents up first, and then think about how we fill our time, hey, Bethany?"

Bethany gave Garratt a small smile and nodded, fluttering her eyelashes at him. "Okay, Mr. Connor."

And that was something else I'd be keeping an eye on. Bethany most definitely had a crush on Garratt.

As the kids all scattered to get their tents set up, Garratt sidled up to me.

"Can't believe you're sharing with Gladys and I've got to share with Dan," he said in a quiet voice. "It's going to be torture. Lying next to big, hairy Dan all night. And, I'm guessing Derek isn't the only one that farts a lot."

"Stop it," I giggled. "I'm sure you'll be fine."

"I was talking about Gladys, not Dan. It's you that's going to need some sort of mask. That woman eats more than I do. There's only one result for that amount of consumption, and that's bad ass gas."

I looked over at Gladys who was indeed snacking on some sort of chocolate bar as she supervised the selection of the tents from the bus.

"That's her second in the last hour, and don't forget the family size bag of potato chips she scarfed after a bag of peanut M&Ms. I'm telling you, gorgeous, you're going to be gagging for air later. You should just cut to the chase and insist on sharing with me."

Rolling my eyes, I slapped at Garratt's arm. "Not happening, so don't ask."

"Can't blame a man for trying," he whispered, leaning into me. "Just have to wait until we get back I suppose - to make you scream my name while your pussy tightens around my cock."

His words created an immediate throb between my legs, and I could feel myself getting wet.

"Garratt," I breathed out.

"Just let me know when you need *that* little problem taking care of," he said, nodding towards my crotch. "I can always suggest we go and get some wood for the fire. Then while we're out there, I'll make sure you feel real good, fingers or tongue, it's up to you."

He winked and walked away, leaving me with a throbbing clit and hard nipples.

For the rest of the afternoon, the kids all hung around either chatting, reading, or desperately trying to get a phone signal. Garratt had taken three of the boys with him to look for some fire wood, and an hour later they'd returned with enough wood to last a week, not just a couple of nights.

"Just put it down there boys," he said, nodding towards a circular area created with boulders. "We'll be building the fire inside the circle."

"Are we cooking on the fire?" Drew, one of the boys asked.

"We sure are." He looked to me. "I believe it's stew for dinner, isn't that right, Ms. Reynolds?"

I nodded, my stomach lurching at the thought of the huge tubs of stew that the school cook had made for us, and were now sitting in a cool box.

"Yes, that's right," I said, feigning a smile. "Mrs. Walsh made it for us. It's going to be delicious."

The three boys all stared at me wide-eyed.

"Miss, have you ever *had* Ms. Walsh's stew?"

"Yes, Christopher, I have. It's lovely," I lied.

"Ugh, gross," he spluttered. "Mr. Connor, sir, can't we cook something else?"

"Sorry boys, but that's what's for dinner. It'll be great, warmed up over the fire. You'll feel just like cowboys out on the range."

"If you say so, sir. If cowboys eat shi-."

"I suggest you stop it right there," Garratt said, stopping Christopher in his tracks.

"Sorry, but it is."

"It's either that or nothing, boys," I replied with a small smile.

They all groaned and, shoving their hands into jeans pockets, shuffled away to their tents.

"He's right," Garratt whispered, as we watched the boys. "It is shit."

I nudged him with my elbow and leaned a little closer. "You know that, and I know that, but we have no choice."

"I can always get Dan to drive the bus into town and we could bring back pizza. It'd only take an hour there and back."

"No way," I replied, arching an eyebrow at him. "Gladys would never allow it, and Dan wouldn't want to drive into town. He's already asleep in your tent, and said not to be disturbed."

"He's really not going to help out at all over the next two days, is he?" Garratt asked, rubbing a hand over his head.

"Nope. Gladys asked him to help with our tent while you were collecting wood. The poles wouldn't go in the ground because it was so hard."

"He said no?" Garratt frowned and cast a glance towards his tent, where Dan was sleeping.

"Said his purpose on this trip was to drive the bus, nothing more."

Dan was the school janitor, and regular bus driver, and according to Gladys had worked there for years, getting more cantankerous with each year.

"Serious? He refused to help you?" Garratt asked, leaning in with his hands to his hips.

"We got one of the boys to do it. It's fine."

"No, it's not. You needed his help. It's not acceptable," he snapped and turned on his heel and strode away.

"Garratt, what are you going to do?" I called after him.

"You'll see."

I watched as he disappeared inside his tent, and waited for a noise, a shout of anger - anything at all to indicate that Garratt had done something to Dan, but there was nothing. I didn't see Garratt again until it was time for dinner and he refused to tell me what he'd been doing for the last hour.

twenty-seven

Garratt

As we watched the kids collect all the specimens of plants and bugs they needed, I could feel Jemma's eyes on me. I didn't look at her, I couldn't. I knew if I did I'd give the game away. She'd know that I was responsible for Dan stumbling out of our tent at breakfast, clutching his gut as he ran toward the toilet block, with Jemma immediately asking me what I'd done.

Of course I denied it. Why would I admit to getting laxative from the medicine case and putting it into Dan's bowl of stew? That would just be a fucking stupid thing to admit.

"I know what you did."

I turned to see Jemma was now at my side, glaring at me.

"What's that, gorgeous?" I gave her one of my most winning smiles, hoping to disarm her.

"You did something to make Dan ill, didn't you?"

I frowned and shook my head. "No idea what you're talking about."

"Don't act stupid, you know exactly what I mean."

"Seriously," I cried, holding my hands up. "I have no damn idea. All I know is, his guts were gurgling like a hot mud pool all night, and then this morning he ran out of the tent saying something about needing to shit." I shrugged and turned back to watching the kids.

"I know you, Garratt," she whispered. "You were really angry with him, you disappeared, and then he got diarrhea. I know you were responsible."

"Not sure how you work that out, but hey, if that's what you want to think. Personally, I think it was more likely to be Mrs. Walsh's stew.

"No one else is ill, only Dan."

"Hmm, unlucky I guess."

Jemma took hold of my chin and turned my head to face her.

"I'm not stupid. It was you and I have one thing to say."

"Oh yeah, what's that?" I asked cocking a brow.

"Thank you. You're amazing."

Fuck if my dick didn't just spring to life as her beautiful eyes sparkled and she gave me a cute smile. Shit, I was totally hooked on this woman, and never wanted to be let loose.

"My pleasure, baby," I whispered. "You can show me your appreciation when we get home tomorrow. That okay?"

She nodded her head and flicked her tongue across her bottom lip. "Oh yeah. More than okay."

After a long day trekking through the woods and collecting specimens, the kids were all in bed and asleep by eleven-thirty, as was Gladys, leaving just me and Jemma by the fire. Dan was also tucked up snug in his sleeping bag. Poor guy had had one hell of a day, shitting every five minutes. He'd been sweating so much, I reckon he'd lost at least six of his two-hundred and fifty pounds - which I was sure he'd thank me for, if he wasn't so worn out from sitting on the john all day.

"How've you enjoyed your first field trip?" Jemma asked, pulling the shawl thing she was wearing tighter around her body.

We were sitting on the ground, leaning against a long trunk seat, and I so wanted to wrap my arms around her, be the one that warmed her up, but we couldn't risk one of the kids waking up and seeing us.

"It's been good," I replied with a grin. "Made it even clearer that this is what I want to do."

"I have to say, you're pretty great with them. And, they respect you."

That in itself made me more than happy. I remembered all too well how assistant or trainee teachers were treated when I was at school - like crap.

"They're good kids," I said, edging closer to Jemma.

As my leg touched hers, I felt Jemma shiver beside me. Her breathing got a little heavier and she caught her bottom lip between her teeth. We'd had almost forty-eight hours of not being able to touch each other and it was getting too much for both of us. Not able to hold out much longer, I looked around to make sure that all the tents were firmly zippered up, and kissed her neck.

"I miss you."

Jemma turned into the kiss, rubbing her soft cheek against mine. "I miss you, too," she sighed. "But we have to be careful."

"I know, gorgeous. I just needed to feel you."

Moving my lips along her jaw line, I took her earlobe into my mouth and gave it a gentle suck. My dick twitched and I knew I had to stop before I did something I shouldn't. Slowly, I pulled away, eliciting a quiet groan from Jemma.

"I need to stop now, otherwise I can't promise I won't have you naked and up against a tree in record time."

Jemma giggled. "Well, if that's the case, you're right, we should stop."

I didn't move away from her, but figured a little hand holding was okay, and linked my fingers with hers.

"If we weren't surrounded by twenty kids, Gladys, and Dan, this would be *the* best date ever," I said, looking into the flickering flames of the camp fire. "Just you and me and the silence."

"Yeah, it's lovely. So peaceful." Jemma squeezed my fingers and sighed. "I wish it could be like this all the time."

I turned to look at her. "I thought you were happy. Working at the school, living in Bridge Vale."

"I am," she protested. "But sometimes life gets in the way. Things happen that you have no control over, and before you know it, your happiness is gone."

I knew she was talking about her sister. It still cut her deep; the loss and grief still lay heavy on her heart.

"Tell me about Lauren."

Jemma took an intake of breath. It was small, but I heard it and felt her stiffen beside me.

"Only if you want to," I said, softly.

"I do. It just hurts thinking about what she went through."

"So tell me about her before then. What was she like before she became ill?"

I turned to see a tear rolling down her cheek and, lifting my hand, I wiped it away with my thumb.

"Was she a good big sister?" I asked, fucking the consequences and letting go of her hand to put my arm around her, pulling her close.

"Yes, she was. We argued like any siblings, but on the whole we were great. We weren't best friends, or anything like that. She was just over three years older and had a big group of friends, but she always looked out for me. It was Lauren that persuaded my mum and dad to let me come here to study."

I smiled. "Yeah, I remember you telling me that when I was pestering you for a date. You said you hadn't argued with your folks just to come here and waste your time with some - and I quote - 'cocky little shit who thought he was the dog's bollocks'."

Jemma let her head drop back and laughed. "Oh my God, I did didn't I?"

"Yeah, but I soon persuaded you otherwise."

"Hmm, I think it took you all of twenty minutes to change my mind." She shook her head. "God, I'm a disgrace to the sisterhood."

"Nah, I'm just a cocky shit who actually *is* the dog's bollocks."

Jemma giggled and leaned her head against my shoulder.

"You know I had to Google that. You English and your sayings, I had no fucking clue."

"I just didn't want to be distracted from my studies, but," she sighed. "I guess I couldn't resist you. Plus, you were a pretty good study buddy, so it worked out okay in the end."

"Told you then and I'll tell you now, going out with me is the best fucking thing you'll ever do in your whole life. You'll be thanking me in twenty years when you're still as happy as a hog in shit."

Jemma lifted her head and pulled her knees up. The air around us seemed to thicken and I felt her move away from me, creating a gap between our bodies. I turned to look at her.

"Hey, what's wrong?"

She shook her head, looking down at her knees. "Nothing."

"Jemma, there's something, so tell me."

When she didn't answer or look up at me, I took hold of her chin and turned her head to face me.

"Jemma."

She rubbed her forehead with her fingertips as her gaze finally landed on me.

"I'm just so happy when I'm with you, and I'm scared it's all going to go wrong."

"When I go back to the City, you mean?" I knew she was worried about the distance, but I'd already told her that we'd make it work. Plus, I still hadn't heard about my transfer.

Jemma didn't answer, but just looked at me with tear filled eyes.

"Listen, I wasn't going to say anything," I started, "but, I've requested a transfer. That way we don't have to do the long distance thing, so you have nothing to worry about."

Jemma's breath hitched as she reared back slightly. "You've asked to come back here?"

"Yeah, I have. I need to be near you."

"B-but, you can't just change your life because of me," she hissed. "What if, what if things don't work out between us, or I go back to the UK, or-"

"Hey," I said, breaking her flow. "Things are going to be great between us, and are you considering going back to the UK?"

"No, but-."

"So, why worry about that now? If you do decide you want to go back, then we'll talk about it, see where we are in our relationship and we'll work something out. If I need to come with you, then I will."

Jemma gasped and shook her head. "But you can't do that, this is your home. Your parents, Jesse, Millie, and the kids are here. You miss them *now*, living in the city, how would you feel all those thousands of miles away?"

I moved closer until our lips were almost touching and ran my fingers through her hair.

"I'd be with you," I whispered. "That's all I want."

Without a thought of being caught, I kissed Jemma's beautiful, trembling lips. Holding her face in my hands, I told her everything through that kiss. I held on as I sucked her bottom lip, pushed my tongue into her mouth, and gently caressed her cheeks with my thumbs. I wanted the kiss to tell her she was everything to me already, and I was only going to fall deeper and deeper. No damn doubt about it.

With both of us breathing heavily, Jemma was the first to pull away. With her hand resting on my bicep, she stared into my eyes and took a deep breath.

"I'm so damn scared, Garratt," she whispered. "You have no idea."

"I'll be here, and nothing is going to go wrong. I swear."

Jemma shook her head. "You can't say that, you don't know."

"Okay, but I do know that whatever happens, we'll get through it. I know we can be strong and get over any hurdle that's put in front of us."

"We're so new, though. What if this is as good as it gets? What if we-?"

"What if we're happier than anyone could ever imagine? What if we spend the rest of our lives loving each other and building a life together?"

Suddenly, without any warning, Jemma pushed away from me and scrambled to her feet.

"I need to go to bed. I'm tired and we have another long day tomorrow, travelling back."

"Jemma?" I pushed to my feet and put a hand out to her, but she took a step back.

"Night, Garratt. I'll see you in the morning."

"Jemma," I hissed into the darkness, but she was gone. "What the hell…"

As I heard Jemma's tent zipper, I shook my head and wondered the fuck was going on in her head.

twenty-eight

Jemma

When we got onto the bus, I had barely spoken to Garratt. Not that I was ignoring or avoiding him, but after breakfast he'd taken charge of taking the tents down with a couple of the boys, while Gladys and I organized the rest of the kids to pack everything else into the bus, and to tidy up the camp. I did catch him studying me a couple of times, probably wondering what the hell had been wrong with me the night before.

I'd had a restless night, worrying about what Garratt had said. The thought of us loving each other for the rest of our lives filled me with warmth and excitement, but what if the rest of our lives wasn't that long? I knew that I needed to talk to him about things, but I was absolutely petrified; scared of losing what we had because he couldn't cope with the idea that I was quite possibly on borrowed time, or at the very least he might have to nurse me through treatment. And, could I actually put him through that? I knew how hard that had been for my family, caring for Lauren when she was constantly sick or tired from her chemo and radiotherapy. There were days when Mum and Dad could barely hold it together, or even think straight, they were so tired - and I didn't want that for Garratt.

"You okay?"

Garratt's voice dragged me away from my thoughts and I looked over to see him stood in the aisle of the bus, looking down at me.

"Oh hey," I smiled up at him, not able to stop myself. He looked tired and disheveled, but was still breathtakingly handsome. "I'm fine, what about you?"

He quickly looked around the bus, and bent down. "Desperate to get home with you. Two reasons; I need to be with you in a bed, even if it's just to hold you. Secondly, we need to talk about last night and what got you so spooked."

I opened my mouth to protest that nothing had spooked me, but I knew I couldn't. He was right, we did need to talk.

"Okay, we can do that. As soon as we get back?"

Garratt nodded. "Talk first, then I'll get you naked."

Not giving me the chance to respond, he moved away, down to the back of the bus.

"Okay," Gladys shouted. "Let's get this bus on the road."

When we got back to school, some of the kid's parents were there to meet them, but there were a few who had left their own cars at school, and were giving rides to others. I was pleased to see Caleb happily get into a car with Matty and their other friend Jasper. He seemed to have enjoyed the trip, and had come up to Garratt when we'd been unpacking the bus to thank him, and as he got into Matty's car, he gave us a wave and had a huge smile on his face.

"You ready?" Garratt asked, as we watched the last of the cars disappear.

I turned to him and took a deep breath. "Yes, let's go."

Picking up my backpack, Garratt walked over to his car and, opening it up, threw all our gear inside. He then moved around to the passenger door and held it open for me. I looked at him, feeling an ice-cold trepidation run around my body, wondering whether this would be the last time I'd ride in his car, or that'd we'd be this normal.

"Okay," Garratt said, putting his beer bottle onto the coffee table. "Go ahead, tell me what's going on in your head."

I hadn't expected him to go straight for it. I'd thought he might at least lead me into it gently. I should have realized that wasn't Garratt. As he often said, he did everything with his balls nailed to the wall. So, I took a deep breath, trying to gain the courage and strength to tell him.

Garratt took my hand in his and squeezed it tight before leaning closer and kissing my forehead, waiting patiently. My pulse slowed a little at his kiss, but with fear still gripping my stomach, I started to speak.

"It was you talking about us loving each other for the rest of our lives," I finally said. "It scared me."

"Too much? Okay, you're not there yet," he replied, slowly nodding his head. "I get that it might scare you after your divorce, but you have to know, to feel, that me and you are in this for the long haul."

"I do," I whispered. "And it's what I want, too, but that isn't what scared me."

I looked at him, expecting him to ask a question, but he was silent, waiting for me to continue. So, I did.

"I told you Lauren died of breast cancer and then my mum had it."

Garratt nodded and his grip on my hand tightened.

"Well, when Mum had it, she had some tests done. The tests were checking for two genes. They've probably got long, complicated names, but the doctors called them BRCA 1 and 2."

"They're the breast cancer gene, right? I've read a little about them."

"Yes," I said on a shaky breath. "The fact that both Lauren and Mum had breast cancer, couldn't possibly be a horrible coincidence, which was why she went for the test. They don't always find something, the consultant told us it's kind of like knowing that there's one tiny spelling mistake in the whole of the Bible and having to find it. So, even if they don't find anything, it doesn't mean it isn't there."

"Shit," Garratt groaned. "It must have been torture waiting for the results. I don't know how you managed to get through that."

"It was hard. The wait seemed to be interminable. My dad pretty much lost it on a daily basis when there was no news. And then the day we finally got the results, I think we all wished we hadn't had them."

"She had the genes?"

I nodded and bit on my lip.

"Yes, she does."

Garratt took a deep breath, and I saw the realization on his face and it was heart breaking. I knew that everything he'd thought about his future, and a future with me, was suddenly drifting away. He wanted us to be together, be a couple for, as he said it, 'the rest of our lives'. That hope was now floating around in the wind, maybe never to be caught.

"Fuck. So what you're saying is…shit, this is just-."

He pulled me closer, burying his face into my hair and wrapping his arms tightly around me. After a few seconds, I gently pushed away.

"No, I'm not saying that."

His eyes widened and a smile broke onto his beautiful face. Hope was there again, at his fingertips but, once again, I was going to force him to let it go, back into the wind.

"No, Garratt, I'm not saying that, either. What I am saying is that I have no idea."

"What do you mean? You have no idea. Why?"

His tone was louder and the way his back had stiffened and his brow furrowed, I knew that he already knew the answer to that question.

"I haven't had the test and I'm not going to."

There, that was it, I'd finally said it out loud - to Garratt.

People say that once you've let go of a secret, you feel so much better, but I felt anything but. His face showed confusion, understanding, hurt, and then anger, all in a matter of seconds, and I hated that I'd been the one to have done that to him. I'd gone through all those emotions when Lauren refused any more treatment – she'd wanted some peace before she died. I couldn't understand why she couldn't simply suffer the constant lethargy, pain, and nausea, if it meant that she was alive, for *us*. Then, one day, I'd watched her trying to do the simplest thing of putting on some clothes and it was pitiful to see. She could barely lift her arms, and once she had managed to put a sweater on, she immediately had to lean over and vomit into a bucket. The way Lauren saw it, dying was a better option than the life she had. She'd been a vibrant, funny, energetic woman and it wasn't only the cancer that was killing her - life was, too.

"You can't be serious?" he asked. "You are fucking kidding me?"

"No, I'm totally serious. I'm not having the test. I'm going to get regular checkups and take my chances."

"You can't fucking take a chance on your life," Garratt stormed, pushing up from the couch to pace up and down. "This isn't you putting all your chips on a fucking number in a game of roulette, Jemma. This is your life. It's about you taking the opportunity to avoid fucking dying before you should. You need to get this test done." He stopped dead in his tracks and turned to me. "You need to get it done today, okay maybe not today, but soon. This week, tomorrow. Becky will give you time off. We need to be prepared."

The words spewed from his mouth in a rush, without stopping for breath, and as I watched the pain on his face, my heart thudded to a rapid beat as if it were providing the tempo for a quick step. This was exactly why I hadn't wanted to tell him, or even to get back together with him. It was too much having to consider someone else. It was hard enough getting through the day as it was, now I'd have to watch Garratt's pain.

"Garratt," I cried, standing up to face him. "There is no 'we' in this. This is my decision and I'd rather not know."

"No we. No fucking *we*, are you kidding me?" He grabbed hold of my upper arms, and bent slightly to look me directly in the eye. "We have something good, we *had* something good seven years ago. You belong to me and I belong to you. Seven years apart couldn't stop that, so don't you dare tell me that there's no fucking *we*."

His voice wavered as he said the words and I saw the pleading in his eyes. He let go of my arms and turned on his heel, striding to the other side of the room, hands gripping at his hair.

"You can't say all of that. We had one month together and this time around we've had days. You can't say I'm yours and you're mine. We're just starting out." Even I knew how stupid that sounded. He'd always been in my heart. Even when I'd been married to someone else, I'd never forgotten the beautiful, dark-haired boy with the vibrant blue eyes and sexy smile.

"Cut the bullshit, Jemma. You feel it just as much as I do. You know it as well as I do. Time is immaterial when you feel it in here," he slammed an open palm against his chest, "when it's so damn deep you know it's rooted in there for life."

"You can't want that with me, Garratt. You can't."

Tears were starting to fall down my cheeks as the pain engulfed me. I wanted this man, so badly, but we couldn't do this. We couldn't start something good and special, knowing it might be ripped away from us.

"Yes, I damn well can," he spat back.

"I won't let you. I won't put you through all the worry and heartache," I sobbed, brushing the wetness from my face.

"You have no fucking choice." His tone was hard, but there was a softness in his eyes, as he looked at me. "I'm in, Jemma, and I'm not getting out. Now, you are damn well taking that test."

He rushed towards me and dragged me against his chest, as I continued to cry, soaking his shirt in the process.

"Any chance I have of keeping you until I'm old and grey, I'm damn well taking it. Whether that's me moving back here, moving to the UK, or you taking a damn test, it's done, period."

"But, I'm so scared." I said, breathing in his scent and pressing my body to his, wanting to memorize every part of him; to always feel the imprint of him.

"I know, baby," he soothed. "But I'll be with you every step of the way. Is the test why you dropped your mom's call that day? Does she want you to take it?"

I nodded and sniffed. "She won't let up, every conversation we have these days is about it."

As more tears came, Garratt rocked us gently as I stayed in my favorite place in the world; pressed against him.

"We're going to go to bed," he murmured. "You need some sleep and I need to feel you, have you in my arms."

I nodded. "Okay."

"Afterwards, we'll eat some dinner, and then you can tell me what your options are. Okay?"

"But-"

"No, Jemma. That conversation is going to happen. Whether you like it or not, we are sorting this out, even if we have to talk until dawn. Is that clear?"

I looked up and saw the determination in his eyes, and somehow, from somewhere, I gained a little courage.

twenty-nine

Garratt

I let Jemma sleep for a couple of hours before waking her and insisting on making us some dinner. She didn't have much in the way of food, so we managed to throw together some chicken and pasta. A little basic, but it stopped the grumbling sound in both our stomachs.

We ate sitting on the couch, while a guy that Jemma liked, Sam Smith, played softly in the background through her docking station. She'd also lit some candles around the room, so that, along with the couple of glasses of wine we'd both had, meant we were relaxed. I kind of think Jemma was trying to distract me from talking about the gene test, but even if she'd done a naked, feathered fan dance in front of me, it still wouldn't have worked.

"Okay," I said, pulling her legs across my thighs. "Tell me what happens if you have the test and it turns out you have the genes."

"Do we really need to do this tonight?" she asked.

"Yep. So start talking."

"Okay," she sighed. "But I'd rather not."

"*Jemma.*"

"Alright, I'm going to," she huffed out. "The short story is, if they find either of the genes, or both of them, then I'll be offered a mastectomy."

Her voice cracked on the word, and I wondered whether I'd pushed her too hard. But, I knew deep down I'd done the right thing. We had to decide what the next steps were, and the sooner the better. If I didn't force Jemma to talk about it now, I knew she'd keep putting it off until it might be too late - and that thought fucking terrified me.

"Go on," I whispered, rubbing a hand along her calf. "Tell me the longer version. What happens then?"

"So, I'll be offered a mastectomy. I could have everything removed and have implants at the same time."

"That's both breasts, when you say everything?"

Jemma nodded and took a sip of her wine.

"Nipples too, to be on the safe side."

"Okay, and those would be silicone implants?"

"They could be, yes."

"I've heard they can be dangerous," I said with a frown.

Jemma tinkled a laugh. "I don't know, but I think it may be a myth about them exploding at high altitude."

"I'm not sure, gorgeous. I know plenty of women have them, but I'd be unhappy at you having something that might have a hint of risk to it. Not that it's my decision of course," I added, aware that while I knew Jemma was it for me, she was right We had only been a couple for a few days, discounting our hook up at the wedding.

"No, you're right and I must admit, I'm not sure how I'd feel about carrying two airbags around with me. I've never really liked how they look, but then I've never been faced with having a mastectomy before," she said as her face paled.

"So, the alternative is no implants and no reconstruction?"

I could see her mulling it over, and then she looked at me with concern.

"How would you feel if I didn't have it done?" she asked hesitantly.

I knew what she was thinking. I loved her body, and often told her what amazing tits she had, so she had to wonder how I'd feel.

"You know how I feel about your rack, but I'll be honest, baby, I'd rather have you here, with scars, than just have to live with memories of you and your body. Plus, I'd rather you didn't have something put in your body that could be dangerous. What about you, how do you feel about it?"

"Being totally vane about it, how I'd look afterwards was a tiny part of why I had been avoiding the issue." Her head dropped as she sighed. "I feel so superficial saying this, but I'm twenty-seven years of age and still want to be able to wear low cut tops and bikinis, but moreover, I still wanted to be attractive and sexy. For myself and for you."

My heart felt constricted as a deep sadness for my beautiful girl washed over me. This was going to be the most difficult decision of her life. It was *for* her life, yet I fully understood her concerns about how she was going to look.

"You'll always look beautiful to me," I replied with honesty, taking her hand and dropping a soft kiss to her wrist.

"There are alternatives," she said with a sigh. "I could have reconstruction using muscles from my back, or even my stomach fat. Although, using my stomach fat comes with the risk of infection."

"Well, that's out then," I stated. "I mean, I know it's up to you, but why take the risk?"

Shit, I had to make sure I reeled myself in a little. While I was definitely in for life, we were still new and Jemma had been living with this for years, so I shouldn't pressure her into choices that I preferred.

"No, I agree. I think I'd go for the back muscles, which means there'll be some scarring. Whatever happens, I'll need seven or eight weeks to recuperate."

I gave her what I hoped was a dazzling smile. "I'll be here to take care of you, so no worries about that."

Then a thought struck me. "Will you have the surgery here, or back in the UK?"

Jemma shrugged. "I haven't thought that far ahead. My mind was made up I wasn't getting the test done. I mean," she paused and looked at me warily before continuing, "I'm still not totally sure."

"No way, gorgeous. We discussed this." I shook my head and gently pulled at her hand. "We talked about this, Jemma."

With wary eyes she watched me, but I looked back at her, unblinking, daring her to argue. Finally, her shoulders dropped in defeat.

"Okay, I know you're right."

I breathed a sigh of relief. "So here or the UK?"

"I have medical insurance, through the education department, so I could have it here."

"I'd rather you did. I want to be able to look after you. But if you go home, I'll come with you. I'm going to quit my job anyway, so may as well do it then."

"Garratt, no. I can't ask that of you," she cried.

"You haven't, I offered." There was no question I'd be going with her, if that was her choice. I had money saved so could easily take some time off.

Jemma leaned forward and placed her soft hand on my cheek. "What did I do to deserve you?"

"You deserve the best in everything, baby, and if I can give that to you, I will. You have no idea how deep my feelings run for you, and if I didn't think you'd jump off this couch and run all the way back to the UK, I'd tell you. Just know this, you have my heart and I never want you to let go of it."

Jemma whimpered and then flung herself at me, smothering me with kisses. She straddled me and began to grind against my hardening dick, and with her fingers lacing through my hair she pushed her body against my chest. Her nipples were hard and the friction caused us both to gasp.

"Garratt, I-"

She didn't finish her sentence but moaned breathily against my neck.

"What is it?" I asked, gripping hold of her ass. "What do you want to say to me?"

"I need you to…oh my God, Garratt."

I smiled lazily as I thrust my hips upwards, knowing that my dick was hitting her in just the right spot, sending her into a state of ecstasy, which made me feel amazing. Taking the hem of Jemma's tee, I pulled it up and over her head, throwing it over the side of the couch onto the floor. When I looked down to see her beautiful breasts, I swallowed hard and leaned forward to take her white lace covered nipple into my mouth. Jemma gasped and threw her head back, pushing herself closer to me. Still sucking, I palmed her tit with my hand, while the other reached behind to unfasten her bra. As the straps fell down her arms, I stopped laving at the hard, pebbled nipple and pulled back to look at the pure look of desire on my beautiful girl's face. Her lips were parted and her eyelids fluttered as she continued to move her hips to gain the friction that we both needed. Desperate to feel my skin against hers, I reached behind to pull my own tee up and discarded it alongside Jemma's. Watching me carefully, Jemma moved her arms to rid herself of her bra, before adding it to the growing pile of clothes on the floor. Placing a flat palm in the middle of her back, I pushed her closer to me. The feeling of skin on skin, more importantly her skin against mine, made my body heat and caused my heart to increase its pace, going so fast it felt as though it was about to burst through my chest. Reaching between us, I pushed my hand inside Jemma's tight, black yoga pants, pushing aside the strip of lace that covered her wet pussy. As soon as my fingers touched her clit, I knew she was already close. The nub was swollen and hard and I could almost feel it pulsing.

"Garratt," she cried as I pushed two fingers inside her and grazed my thumb over her heated bundle of nerves.

"I'm going to get you off and then while you're still trying to get your breath, I'm going to fuck you hard."

My words were coarse and dirty, and I knew Jemma liked them, especially since I felt her getting wetter as she squeezed her thighs against my hand. My two fingers stroked her inner walls and my thumb spread her wetness around and over her clit, and before I could even take another breath, Jemma came apart.

"Oh my God!" she screamed, thrusting her hips and grinding harder against my hand. "Yes, oh shit, yes."

Jemma's hands grabbed at my hair and tugged hard on it, as she pushed closer to me with her breasts flattening against my chest. The pain she inflicted with my hair only added to the pleasure, and I felt my balls contract; I was going to fucking come like a teenager in my pants.

"Fuck," I growled, and with my spare hand, reached for the button of my jeans.

Quickly, I freed my dick and grabbed the shaft and started to pump. Jemma looked down at us and watched as I pleasured us both; my fingers continued to push in and out of her, while my hand tugged my thick, granite hard cock. When I felt the orgasm start in the pit of my stomach, I groaned, and as I spurted the hot liquid onto my abs, Jemma gasped and her second orgasm was released as her muscles clamped down on my fingers.

"Fuuucck," I cried.

As I continued to milk myself, my legs stretched out and stiffened and Jemma's back straightened as she pushed herself up, using her hands on my shoulders for leverage. She thrust her hips in a quick rhythm as she rode out her orgasm, and as the last wave of it ebbed away, she buried her face into my neck and sucked and bit at my skin.

Panting heavily, Jemma lifted her head and I grinned when I saw her face was covered by her hair. She looked as though she'd been thoroughly fucked, and all I'd used had been my fingers. To say I felt ten-fucking-feet tall was an understatement.

Reaching up, I pushed her hair away from her face and kissed her gently on her pouting, gasping mouth.

"Give me a few minutes and then I'll fulfil the second part of my promise," I whispered against her lips.

"Hmm, okay," she murmured, letting her head flop against my shoulder. "Whatever you say."

"You done for, gorgeous?" I asked with a laugh as I wrapped my arms around her.

"Hmm. Be okay. Five minutes." She could barely utter the words.

As Jemma dropped a soft kiss onto my bare shoulder, I inhaled deeply and held my breath. I wanted to remember this moment always. Remember how it felt to have her in my arms. Remember her scent. Remember this moment in time. This was the moment that I knew that I loved her, and this was the moment that I became petrified that I would lose her.

thirty

Jemma

The thought of telling Garratt my secret had filled me with fear because I wasn't sure what his response would be. He was either going to run a mile, or force me to face my fears. Thank goodness it was the latter, and the relief I felt through telling him was immense. My brain felt free of the cloud of thoughts running around in it, and everything about life seemed much clearer, more precise, and brighter. The worry about the results was still there, but selfishly, I was glad to finally have someone to share it with. I knew I'd been stupid and should have told Garratt sooner, but the main thing was he now knew and was being supportive. Okay, so he'd pretty much forced me to take the test, but whenever I looked at him and felt my heart fall in love with him a little bit more, I was glad he had. I wanted a life with him.

As I watched him flick through a magazine in the doctor's office waiting room, I couldn't help but smile at the way he pouted and frowned over various articles.

"Fuck." Garratt leaned towards me without taking his eyes from the magazine. "It says here that at least one in three women struggle to have an orgasm."

He turned to look at me and arched his eyebrows, shock etched on his beautiful face.

"They're fucking the wrong men," he whispered.

"Oh, and you've never had a woman fail to orgasm when you've had sex with her?" I asked.

It was a totally rhetorical question, because I was damn sure he never had. Garratt had skills of the like I'd never experienced before. I'd thought he was pretty talented when we were just a couple of kids, but boy had he improved with practice.

"Yeah right," he scoffed, turning back to the magazine. "If the dick doesn't do it, which to be honest is rare, then I have a perfectly good tongue and fingers that I can seal the deal with. Any man that can't pleasure his woman properly doesn't deserve her."

I couldn't help but laugh at the seriousness of his tone. He was genuinely affronted for the sisterhood.

"Maybe you should do some YouTube videos," I said, trying to hide my smile. "You know, giving hints and tips."

Garratt's head shot up and he grinned at me.

"No, Garratt," I hissed, shaking my head. "I was joking."

"No, I really like that idea, gorgeous. I could run masterclasses, you could be my on-screen assistant."

"No way," I cried. "It was a joke, so don't you dare even think about it."

As my hand fluttered at my neck, Garratt burst out laughing.

"Hah, you're face," he said as he grabbed my hand. "You thought I was being serious, didn't you?"

"You idiot." I slapped at his arm. "I actually think you were, and if I'd have said yes, you'd have definitely been up for it."

He shook his head and frowned. "The hints and tips maybe, but no way would you be seen on screen. No chance any hormonal, teenage boy, whose nuts have barely dropped, is going to get a view of what's mine."

"I teach hormonal teenage boys every day," I replied. "So you can't say that."

"Yeah, but you're wearing clothes at school, not nipple pasties and a nude colored thong."

I shrank back and stared at him wide-eyed. "What the hell sort of assistant did you want me to be?"

"Well, how the hell would I teach my skills otherwise? "Cause I have to be honest babe, my drawing skills are shit, so diagrams of stick men just wouldn't cut it."

"You'd have had sex with me on screen?"

As my voice became high-pitched, I looked around the waiting room, checking whether anyone had heard our conversation. Luckily, it appeared the woman with the grumbling child and the guy with his arm in a sling weren't listening.

"As a teacher, you should know, show is better than tell," Garratt said, his lips twitching into a half-smile.

"Garratt!" I scolded, realising he was indeed joking. "I believed you."

"Honestly, you are so easy to wind up," he laughed, pulling me into a side hug.

Our laughter was interrupted by a nurse appearing and calling out my name.

"Jemma Reynolds."

I took a sharp intake of breath and looked at Garratt. He smiled and kissed my forehead.

"You want me to come in?" he asked.

I stood up and gripped hold of his hand. "Hmm, please."

He gave me the brightest smile and got up from his chair. "Let's go then."

Nodding, I turned, and with Garratt's hand still firmly in mine, followed the nurse.

"I can't believe you still have to wait," Garratt grumbled as we walked back to his car. "Why the fuck couldn't he do the test today?"

"Because Dr. Crowther isn't qualified to do it," I said, trying not to sigh on the fourth time of explaining it to him. "Dr. Kruger at the cancer center is.

It's a genetic test, not just a simple blood test."

"Well, it's a damn good thing she had a free appointment for tomorrow, because I'll be honest with you, gorgeous, I was ready to kick up some shit in there."

"I know," I said, rolling my eyes. "I saw the perspiration on your top lip and that muscle tensing in your jaw."

"I'm that obvious?" he asked, as he clicked open the locks.

I nodded. "Yes, baby, you really are."

We got into the car and immediately, Garratt turned on the engine and cranked up the AC. The heat inside was oppressive, stifling. Add to that Garratt's simmering anger and the atmosphere was thick.

As cool air blew onto our faces, we both let out a sigh. The whole visit to the doctor's office had been tense, apart from Garratt's attempt at taking my mind off things with his live sex videos idea.

"I'm sorry," Garratt finally said. "I just want to get this done as soon as possible. I want to know what we're facing so that we can put things into place quickly, if need be."

I turned to look at his profile and lifted a hand to run my fingers through his hair. His jaw was tensing again, and his hands were gripping the steering wheel, even though we were still parked up and not moving. As I saw how tense his whole body was, I wished I hadn't told him. I wished I still had my secret.

"This was why I didn't want to tell you," I said, dropping my hand from his hair.

Garratt slowly turned to me, shifting in his seat. "What is?"

"You, your fear, your anger. I didn't want you to feel any of that. But you are."

Garratt reached for me and pulled me across the console and onto his lap. His arms wrapped around me as he buried his face into my hair. We sat in silence for a few minutes, while his hands gently rubbed up and down my arms.

"I would gladly feel this a million times over, if it meant you were safe," he eventually said. "I admit I'm scared of what is going to happen, but I'm glad I know. If you hadn't told me, you might never have made the decision to get the test done. So, yeah, I'm fucking shit scared and damn angry, but I'm kind of happy, too, because it means that I've more chance of keeping you and you being healthy and safe, now that I know. I know I can be like a charging bull, going at things full speed, and I know I'm kind of bossy, but I don't give a fuck. I need you with me, always, and if me acting like a prick gets me that then so be it."

He lifted my chin with his finger and kissed me softly and slowly. It was warm and deep and full of love.

"Garratt," I whispered.

"Yeah."

"I need to tell you something."

I felt him stiffen beneath me. "What?" he asked, his voice full of trepidation.

"I love you."

And, oh my God, I really did. We'd only officially been a couple for a matter of days, but I knew that with every breath that left my body, every beat of my heart, and every piece of my soul, that I adored him to the point that my heart physically hurt when I wasn't with him. My feelings for him were more powerful than any I'd ever felt before, even those for Ollie, the man I'd married.

Garratt's gaze was intense as he drew in a ragged breath and brushed my hair away from my face.

"I love you, too," he replied. "So fucking much. I started falling the day I met you and haven't stopped since. Okay, my plummet kind of paused for seven years, but it started again the minute I saw you in that hotel bar looking sexy as shit."

I giggled and wrapped my arms around his neck, touching my nose to his. "You're so romantic, Mr. Connor."

"Yeah, I know. My brother taught me everything I know."

We both laughed and the gap between our lips lessened, until we were mere inches apart. Garratt's arms tightened around me.

"We'll get through this, baby, I know we will."

"I know," I said, with an air of determination. "I have a reason to fight."

"Yeah, you do," he agreed.

I kissed him softly and sighed.

"You and your sexy moves have done it again, haven't they?"

Garratt nodded.

"First you entice me to be your girlfriend and now you've enticed me to love you."

"Yeah, well, it was inevitable," he said with a shrug. "The sexy moves, the cute smile, the huge penis; there could be no other outcome."

While I laughed, Garratt kissed me and, at that moment, I was the happiest I'd ever been. There was no threat of cancer, Lauren hadn't died, and we hadn't wasted seven years by being apart. We were just us, in love and happy.

"Okay, let's get home and get some dinner."

Reluctantly, I shifted from my spot on Garratt's lap and moved back to my seat and buckled myself in. Garratt put the car into drive and as he pulled out into the road, I turned to look out of the window and floating slowly down, gently drifting in the breeze, was a small white feather. Silent tears crept down my cheeks as I smiled and felt the warmth of my sister's kiss.

thirty-one

Garratt

I could barely concentrate during classes on the day of Jemma's genetic test. Her appointment had been made for after school, just like her doctor's appointment, so for a second day I taught math with an air of anxious anticipation, keeping it together just enough that the kids didn't notice I was off.

When we'd got back from the Cancer Center, I'd taken Jemma to the ranch to see Jesse, Millie, and the kids. I'd hoped that three raucous rug rats would take her mind off things, which it seemed to do. We stayed and ate dinner with them, and then I took her back to her apartment, demanding that I stayed the night. I had a feeling she'd need me to distract her some more before she fell asleep. I was pretty successful in loving her into a sleepy stupor, but in the early hours I woke to find Jemma's side of the bed cold. Reaching for my boxers, I pulled them on and padded out of the bedroom in search of her.

When I got to the lounge room, I stood in the doorway and watched her, not wanting to move and break the spell that her beauty cast over me. Jemma was standing in front of the window, looking out into the darkness, wearing her favorite Oasis tee that just covered her ass, and she was hugging a mug of something to her chest. Her wild, blonde curls cascaded down her back and she was sucking on her bottom lip as her slim shoulders rose up and down with her steady breathing. Her face was lit by the silver of the moon and I don't think I'd ever seen her look more beautiful. I took a deep breath and closed my eyes, memorizing the picture, imprinting it into my brain, so I'd never forget it. When I opened my eyes, she was taking a sip of her drink.

"Hey, gorgeous," I whispered, not wanting to startle her.

Jemma turned to face me and gave me a soft, tired, smile. "Hey, did I wake you?" she asked, holding out a hand for me.

"No, I woke and you were gone."

Taking her fingers into mine, I pulled her into my arms and sighed when she wrapped herself into me, snaking her arms around my waist. I kissed the top of her head and tightened my hold.

"You should have woken me if you couldn't sleep," I said.

"I thought some hot milk would help."

"Has it, do you feel sleepy now?"

Jemma sighed. "No, not really. Lots of things are still going round in my head."

"Maybe I can help you with them," I suggested, hating that she was so scared.

"It's the same things we've already talked about," she sighed, lifting her head from my chest and looking up at me. "Nothing else can be said that will change anything."

"You still should have woken me. We can talk about it as often as you need. All night, if it helps."

She lifted to her toes and gave me a soft kiss on the lips. "I know we can, and I love you for wanting to do that for me, but it's fine. I'll be fine."

"Fine isn't good enough, gorgeous. I need my girl to be better than fine. Amazing is what I'm aiming for."

Jemma grinned and kissed me again.

"That is another reason I love you."

My heart thudded as I looked down at her. Admitting that she loved me appeared to have opened the flood gates on the declaration of emotion for her. She'd whispered it to me, over and over, when I was making love to her earlier and now she'd said it, twice, in the last few minutes, and I was on a high from it. Not even the nagging insecurity about her health could mar the feeling. Yes, I was scared what the test results would bring, things could end up being real hard, but at least we would know. At least I'd have Jemma with me and I would move mountains to help her get through anything that the results brought to our door. Without the test we could be facing much worse in the future, when it might be too late.

"Okay," I said, kissing the end of her nose. "Let's get you back to bed. We don't want you falling asleep half-way through your classes tomorrow."

"Yeah, okay," she said, and as if on cue, yawned. "We're doing Shakespeare tomorrow, so I need to be alert."

"Shit, yeah," I groaned. "That's enough to send anyone to sleep."

"Oh, and equations are *sooo* exciting," she replied with a heavy hint of sarcasm.

"Duh, yeah." I frowned and looked at her as though she'd just told me the moon was really made of cheese. "Equations are sexy as all fuck."

"If you say so, you nerd."

Jemma giggled and moved away from me, making her way to the kitchen, giving me a view of her beautiful, rounded ass cheeks that peeked out from beneath her tee, and I decided that I'd rethink that sleeping thing, once we got back into bed.

My first class of the day was with the seniors, and when I perched on the edge of my desk to discuss the lesson, I noticed that Caleb's seat was empty.

"Hey, Matty," I said, giving him a chin lift. "Where's Caleb today?"

Matty shrugged. "No idea, Mr. Conner. I went to pick him up this morning, but he didn't answer the door. Then, when I got to school he sent me a message to say he wasn't feeling too good."

"Okay," I replied, nodding my head, but feeling something was off.

I had no idea what, but Caleb was a hard-working kid, who knew how important these last couple of months of high school were. I knew I hadn't taught him for long, but I also knew him well enough to know he wasn't the sort of kid to take time off because he 'didn't feel too good'. I made a mental note to speak to Becky about it and carried on with my class.

At lunch I was making my way to Becky's office, when I bumped into Vicky, the pretty history teacher, coming the other way.

"Hey, Garratt," she greeted me with a huge smile. "How are you? Still enjoying things?"

"Yeah, I am, thanks, Vicky. Really enjoying it."

"That's good." She grinned and brushed a strand of hair from her face. "I hear good things about you."

I ducked my head, and shrugged my shoulders. Not usually one to be embarrassed about being given praise, this seemed different. It was important to me to do well, so to hear that I was doing okay knocked me a little off kilter.

"Well, I hope so," I replied, feeling a little heat to my cheeks.

"So, where are you off to, not to see Becky?" Vicky asked, looking over her shoulder at the door to the Principal's office. "Because she's out for the rest of the day. She went to a meeting with the education board about a half hour ago. I was just in the office with Rita organizing the history field trip next week."

I looked at Becky's door and sighed. I really wanted to talk to her about Caleb.

"Anything I can help with, or maybe Dean?"

Dean Horowitz was the Vice Principal and taught Science and, while a decent sort of guy, I wasn't sure he was the right person to talk to. He was a pretty black and white type of person from what I'd observed. Maybe that was the scientist in him, but that meant he'd probably tell me that unless we had some sort of proof something was wrong, then we should leave well enough alone as far as Caleb was concerned. The issue I had with that was that I tended to go on gut instinct in most things, and my gut was telling me that something wasn't right with Caleb Tremaine

"No, it's fine thanks, Vicky. It'll wait."

"Okay then," Vicky said brightly and moved past me, down the corridor.

As she disappeared around the corner, I decided that I'd speak to Jemma later and get her thoughts. She'd know what to do.

At the end of the day, I was packing everything up, when I got a text message from Jemma.

Jemma: *Hey baby, got a meeting with a parent. Could be a while. Do you want to go home and I'll come out to the ranch to you?*

Jemma actively wanting to go out to my family home made me smile and the warm and fuzzies came over me again. Shit, I was becoming a real pussy, but I fucking loved it.

Garratt: *Okay. I'll cook and you can thank me by staying over and letting me relax you in my own special way. How's that sound?*

All I got back was a thumbs up, a smiley face, and a heart, but it was enough to make me feel some excitement for the night to come. All I had to do now was go and buy some groceries to make dinner.

I was just putting everything I'd bought into the trunk of my rental, when I noticed the door that led to Caleb's apartment open. He appeared on the stoop, dropped a waste bag into the trash, then slipped back inside, none of which looked particularly strange, but what did, and what proved I'd been right, was the black eye that the poor kid was sporting. Locking my car, I walked over to Caleb's door and pressed the buzzer. After a few seconds, I heard a crackle and then Caleb's muffled voice came out.

"H-hello."

"Hey, Caleb, it's Mr. Connor. You going to open up for me?"

There was a pause and then he coughed. "I'm n-not too good, Sir," he stammered. "I don't think you should have any contact with me. I don't want you catching anything."

His voice was shaky and I knew beyond a doubt that the poor kid was struggling with something, and it was most definitely not the shits.

"Caleb, just open the door, dude. I saw the eye and I think it'd be better for you to explain it to me than Social Services."

I knew it was a cheap shot, but I needed to check on him and make sure he was safe. As I waited for him to respond, the door was pulled open and

Caleb appeared, peering around it.

"Seriously, Mr. Connor, I'm fine. Please don't call Social Services." His eyes were bright with unshed tears, and the knuckles of his hand gripping the door were white. He was holding onto it for dear life, and it was evident that he didn't want me to get into that apartment.

"Come on, Caleb, don't bullshit me. I know that," I said, pointing a finger at his eye, "wasn't the result of you being bullied at school, or fighting with some other kid."

"It is," he snapped, grasping on to my comment. "I did it fighting with a guy at school."

"Really," I replied, with a burst of laughter. "Okay, which guy and I'll make sure he gets sent to Miss. Turnbull."

Caleb shook his head. "N-no, I meant a kid from another school."

"Okay, which school? Knightingale High? Because I'm sure Miss. Turnbull will speak to the principal, Mr. Drake."

"No, not Knightingale."

He was perspiring on his brow and I kind of felt bad for the kid, but not enough to let it drop.

"Well, which one, Caleb?"

We stared at each other and as his shoulders sagged, I knew I'd won this small battle. I stepped forward, putting my flat palm on the door and pushing it. I'd expected to have to shove it hard, but he held little resistance and as the door moved, he stood aside to let me into the hallway.

"Please, Mr. Connor," he said, looking at me with beseeching eyes. "I can handle this. He's just having a difficult time. Since Mom left, it's been hard on him…"

Caleb must have seen the anger on my face, because as I fisted my hands, his voice petered off, not finishing the excuse he was going to spew out.

"Please tell me that your old man did not do that, Caleb."

He stared at me, his lip quivering, and my heart constricted for him. He was a good kid, who was desperate to better himself; he had a future, but he also had a shit of a father who beat on him. How often he did that, I had no clue, but once was too fucking much.

"Is he up there?" I raged, pushing past Caleb. "'Cause I think I need to talk to him."

"Mr. Connor," Caleb cried, chasing after me up the stairs. "He isn't here, he's working. He won't be home for a while."

I got to the top of the stairs and pushed on the door that was slightly ajar. It brought me into a living room that was sparsely furnished and what furniture was in there was old and threadbare. There was a small couch and winged back chair at one end and a small table with a *Formica* top and two mismatched chairs at the other end. An archway led to a small kitchen, with cupboards painted in a sickly pea green and cream. There were another couple of doors leading off the main room and I remembered from my time dating Rick Hannigan's niece that that's where the bathroom and bedrooms were.

"Mr. Tremaine," I shouted. "If you're in here, we need to talk. *NOW!*"

Caleb came up behind me and grabbed hold of my arm. "Mr. Connor, I swear he isn't here."

I turned to face him and sighed. His black eye, up close and personal, was a lot worse than it had seemed in the dim light of the hallway.

"What was that for?" I asked.

Caleb's face reddened and he took in a breath. "Going on the field trip when he said I couldn't go."

"Shit," I cursed, knowing that I was responsible for the poor kid getting a beating. "I'm so sorry, Caleb. That's all on me. I'll explain to him, but that does not mean that eye is damn well acceptable. I can't let that go and I will be speaking to him about it."

"Please don't, Mr. Connor. He'll think I came to you. He won't believe you came here."

My anger boiled as I thought about what Caleb was evidently going through. How could a man lay a finger on his child in anger like that? Jesse and I had a whupping or two as kids, but usually it was my mom after we'd done something real bad, and it didn't hurt that much. Dad only ever had to look at us and we'd shit our pants - he'd certainly never raised a finger to us.

"Caleb," I said, softly, laying both hands on his shoulders. "This cannot happen again. He needs to be spoken to. Now tell me, has it happened before?"

Caleb's head dropped, and as he looked down at the ground, he let out a pained cry. Not thinking about teacher/student guidelines, I pulled him into a hug. As I wrapped my arms around him, he winced under my touch. I let him go and held him at arm's length.

"How bad?" I asked.

He shook his head and whimpered.

"Please, Caleb, tell me."

"He doesn't mean it, Mr. Connor. It's been really hard since my mom left, he only does it when he drinks."

"And how often is that?" I stormed.

Caleb didn't answer, but dropped his gaze to his feet.

"We need to call Social Services," I said, moving away from Caleb and pulling my cell from my pocket.

Caleb rushed at me and pulled at my arm.

"No, don't, please. Please, Mr. Connor," he sobbed. "Don't call them, please. He's my dad."

He was sobbing uncontrollably and tugging hard at my arm - desperate to get hold of my cell. I tried to pull my arm away, but he was determined, and as he struggled with me, and got more anxious, his breathing became erratic until he was gulping for breath.

"Caleb, stop," I shouted, dropping my phone to the couch. "Look, I've dropped it, I'm not going to call them. Please, calm down."

I took hold of his biceps and stooped slightly to look him in the eye, as at six-two I had at least a couple of inches on him.

"Come on, take a deep breath and calm down. Breath with me, nice and slow"

As Caleb mirrored my breathing pattern, he slowly started to calm himself down, until finally his chest was moving in a regular pattern.

"Please, don't call them," he finally whispered, wiping at his face with his palms. "He never used to be like this. He just works so hard and then drinks to help relax."

"But it's not relaxing him, buddy. He's getting angry and taking it out on you." I blew out a long breath, wishing I had a damn clue what to do. "You can't stay here, you know that right?"

Caleb looked up at me and, with his lip quivering, he nodded slowly. "I know that, sir. I have four weeks until I'm eighteen. I can leave then. I'll find somewhere to go for the last few weeks of school, somewhere until I go to college."

He was pleading with me, both with his voice and his hands, but I couldn't allow him to stay. One heavy blow from his dad and one night might be too long, never mind four weeks.

I shook my head, telling him no, I couldn't ignore this.

"Mr. Connor, please don't-."

"Caleb, hey, calm down. I won't call Social Services, but you cannot stay here. I would never forgive myself if he hit you again. Especially if something real bad happened."

"But I have nowhere to go," he cried, more tears springing against his lashes.

"I do. Have somewhere you can go, I mean."

I ran a hand through my hair, wondering if I was actually going mad, and also knowing I'd be paying off the debt to my brother from now to eternity. Jesse and Millie could help out and Mom and Dad would be back in a week, then hopefully they'd be willing to take Caleb in. I just knew I couldn't have him stay in the house with me. Even by placing Caleb with my brother, I was probably committing professional suicide, and I hadn't even started in my new profession yet.

"Go pack a bag," I said to Caleb, leaning forward to pick my cell up from the couch.

He wary gaze darted to the phone in my hand.

"I swear, Caleb. I'm not calling them."

He stared at me for a few seconds and then nodded before walking away towards one of the doors off the main area.

I moved into the kitchen, trying to put some distance between us, in case Jesse said no and I had to beg. I didn't want Caleb thinking he was a burden. The kitchen was dark as it had no window, so I flicked on the light, but nothing happened. I thought maybe the light bulb was out, so shrugged it off, but as I got to the sink, I saw it was full of cold water and a carton of milk and a bottle of soda stood in it. I turned to the refrigerator and opened it up. It was warm inside, empty of any food or drink, and no light came on. I opened up the cupboard doors and all I found was a box of Lucky Charms. Realization made my anger spike.

"Fuck," I growled, slamming the door shut.

The poor kid had no fucking food or electricity, that was why he stayed late to do homework, or sat under the streetlamp outside the diner to read. Mr. Tremaine appeared to be one loser of a dad who could only provide his son with damn punches. If he'd stepped in front of me at that moment, I'd have given him some fucking punches of his own.

Stabbing my finger on Jesse's thumbnail, I decided I'd fuck the consequences if he said no. Caleb would stay at Mom and Dad's with me; he certainly wasn't staying here.

After a couple of rings, my brother answered.

"Hey, douche canoe, what can I do for you?"

"Jess, I'm sorry brother, but I need the biggest fucking favor of my life."

thirty-two
Jemma

As I made my way to my car, I opened my phone up to read the text message that Garratt had sent to me. He'd sent it while I was chatting to the parents of one of my students, and this had been my first opportunity to read it.

Garratt: *Hey gorgeous, something happened with Caleb Tremaine. Will explain when you get to the ranch. Will be at Jesse's house so go there first.*

My stomach lurched, wondering what the hell had been going on in the hour and a half since school had finished. I knew Caleb was off sick today, as he hadn't turned up for the study group I was supervising after lunch, so I hoped he wasn't seriously ill. Whatever it was, though, it was worrying, especially as Garratt had appeared to get himself involved in Caleb's problems once again.

Driving just within the speed limit, I made my way to the Connor ranch, with all sorts of thoughts running around in my head. Caleb definitely had some sadness in his life, you could see it in his eyes, but I hated to think what was bad enough that Garratt had become involved and had in turn involved Jesse and Millie, seeing as he was at their house.

When I pulled up, the front door swung open and Garratt came out looking tired and disheveled. His shirt was untucked from his dress pants on one side, his tie had been loosened, and his hair stood on end.

"Hi," I said, meeting him halfway on the steps up to the house. "What's going on?"

"I don't want you to freak out," he replied, stroking a finger down my cheek, "but, Caleb is going to be staying here for a while, at least until Mom and Dad get back next week."

"What? What do you mean he's staying here? He can't, you're his teacher." My eyes were practically on stalks as I watched Garratt's shoulders slump.

"I know all that, but his dad had been beating on him," he explained. "I couldn't leave him there, Jem."

"Oh shit," I gasped. My hand went to my mouth. "You've called Social Services?"

Garratt winced and shook his head.

"Garratt! You have to."

"He begged me not to." Garratt let out a long sigh. "I tried, but he got so upset, Jem. He was hyperventilating and crying and so I just couldn't. And think of his college dreams. Going into the system, for even a short time, could really fuck that up for him."

I dropped my bag to the step and grabbed at my hair, pulling it away from my face. "You do realize that you may well have just ended your career before it's even started? Oh my God, this could be my career, too."

Garratt reached out and pulled at one of my hands, bringing it to his lips. He kissed it and then squeezed it tightly.

"No one needs to know," he said. "As far as we're concerned, he's staying here because he's working for Jesse. Becky already agreed that would be good for him. We just say it was easier for him to stay out here so he can help before school and in the evening."

I shook my head. "You can't be serious."

"Yes, I can and I am," Garratt said, tugging at my hand to reinforce his statement. "It's perfectly feasible. Then when my mom and dad get home, Dad will speak to Child Welfare and offer to be his guardian until he gets to eighteen, which is just a few weeks away."

"And you've asked your parents this, have you?" I asked, astonished.

Garratt grimaced. "Not as such."

"What does that mean? *Not as such*."

"I tried to call and got no reply, so sent him a text but haven't heard anything back yet. I think it's the middle of the night where they are - wherever that is."

"So, really, you have no damn idea whether they'll go for your stupid as shit plan?" I scoffed. "You idiot."

"Hey, gorgeous, come on," he said, letting go of me. "Don't tell me you wouldn't have got the kid out of there."

"Of course I would, but I'd have gone through the correct channels."

I heaved out a sigh, and placed my hands on my hips. He'd obviously made his mind up about this stupid, idiotic plan and there was no way I was going to persuade him otherwise. I could see by the grim look of determination on his face, he was not going to be swayed.

"What's he doing now?" I asked, with what I knew was an air of resignation that I was not going to win.

Garratt knew, too, because he let out a long sigh of relief. "He's on his second bowl of Millie's chilli, the poor kid has only eaten breakfast cereal for the last four days."

"What?" My heart thudded and nausea rolled around in my stomach.

"Yeah, his dad is rarely home and when he is, the only thing he buys is booze. He doesn't buy the kid food, or pay the damn electricity bill. There was no fucking power, gorgeous. He had milk and soda sitting in a sink full of cold water."

Garratt's face paled as he recalled what he'd seen, and I could see it had affected him badly. I reached up and brushed a hand though his hair, and then down his neck, caressing it gently.

"I just don't want you to get into trouble for this, baby," I whispered, moving closer to him. "I don't want to get into trouble, either, but, more importantly, I don't want Caleb to suffer anymore. So, while I don't totally agree with this, I understand."

"Thank you," he replied and kissed me softly. "If you saw how upset he was at the thought of going into the system, you'd have made the same decision. He was so scared and inconsolable. I just couldn't do it to him."

I nodded and stooped to pick up my bag. "Okay, but when your parents get back, if they say no, we call Social Services. We can use the work excuse for a week, but any longer and we become culpable of not following our duty of care as his teachers, he's still a minor."

Garratt nodded in ascension. "Okay, but I know my mom and dad, and I know they'll help. Dad used to sit on the local council and has a couple of friends that work for the education department, so I'm hoping he'll be able to pull some strings."

"This could still come back and bite you on the bum," I said, giving him a weak smile.

"My ass you mean," he replied with a short laugh. "But yeah, I do know, gorgeous. But if we stick to the story that Caleb didn't tell us what was going on at home until it was time for him to leave, then maybe we'll get away with it. I just know I can't let the poor kid go back there."

"Isn't his his dad likely to want to know where he is?" I asked, still worried this was totally the wrong thing to do.

Garratt shook his head. "He works long hours at a garage in Knightingale, so Caleb says he sleeps there a lot of the time, on a cot in the office. He only comes home during the weekends usually, but came home last night because he'd called Caleb's cell and it was dead; the bill hadn't been paid, apparently."

"So he does have some conscious then. Wanting to check up on his son, I mean."

"Yeah, I guess, although it would have been better for Caleb if he hadn't had an attack of guilt about leaving his son alone without any way of contacting him."

"What happened then? Why did he hit him?"

"Because Caleb let slip he'd been on the field trip." Garratt's head dropped and I knew he would be feeling guilt at his own involvement in that scenario.

"Hey, you did what you thought was right, baby." I put my hand at the back of his neck and pulled him to me for a soft kiss. "You weren't to know."

"He told me he'd called his dad at work. I should have insisted that I call him. I just didn't know his dad had said he couldn't go. He said it was because he couldn't afford the gear."

"And that was evidently true," I stressed. "You weren't to know he was going against his father's wishes, as well."

"I should have checked," Garratt cried.

"He'd handed in a permission slip, so why would you? He told you he'd let his dad know, and you trusted him." I kissed him again and then cupped his face with my hand. "Forget that now, what's done is done and I'm guessing it wasn't the first time his dad has hit him."

"No, it wasn't," Garratt replied, with a pained look in his eyes. "The kid is covered in bruises, Jemma. Millie has rubbed some *Arnica* oil into his back, she says it'll help to heal them."

"Oh God, the poor boy."

It was then that I became totally on board with Garratt's plan. Caleb didn't deserve a life of misery. He seemed like a nice boy and putting him into the system certainly wouldn't help his studies and his aim to get to college.

"Okay," I said with determination. "Let's get in there and see what we can do to help."

As I moved a couple of steps above him, Garratt grabbed my hand and pulled me to a stop. Reaching up, he kissed my forehead, my nose, and then finally my mouth.

"I fucking love you," he whispered against my mouth. "Don't ever forget that."

"I won't," I replied. "Never."

At around midnight, Garratt and I finally fell into bed. Millie and Jesse had moved Clemmie in with Addy, and had gladly given Caleb the little girl's Unicorn themed room, for as long as it was needed. I had marveled at the ease by which they'd taken Caleb in. When I got there, Millie was fussing over him, pushing a dish of apple pie and cream in front of him, while Jesse was stalking around the room suggesting what he'd like to do to Mr. Tremaine with the use of a baseball bat. And while all that was going on, Addy was gazing adoringly at their new house guest.

Once Caleb had gone up to bed, the four of us sat and drank a couple of beers discussing what needed to be done. Thankfully, Millie agreed with me, that as hard as it would be, Social Services needed to be advised at some point. So, after much arguing from Garratt and a little from Jesse, we agreed to wait until their parents were back and let Ted, their dad, make the call. Another thing to be grateful for had been the text message from Ted. He'd been adamant that they were in on the plan and not to let Caleb go back home under any circumstances. Garratt then called his dad back, and after both he and Jesse had spoken to him, I saw the relief hit Garratt. He might have been a grown man, but he evidently still had respect for his father's opinion and so for him to agree that Garratt had done the right thing, was huge to his youngest son.

"Shit, what a night," Garratt said as he pulled me to him and threaded his leg in between mine.

"Poor Caleb," I sighed. "I hope he's okay. You know, doesn't feel too upset being away from his home."

"I doubt that," Garratt replied, dropping a kiss to my shoulder blade. "Jesse said he couldn't thank him enough when he showed him his room - despite the damn rainbow striped wallpaper and unicorns everywhere. Think it helps that Jesse is a little bit of a hero to him."

I giggled. "Ah, and you're the one that saved him. Poor baby, not getting any credit."

"Always the way, gorgeous," he sighed. "I run in like the White Knight, and Jesse gets the credit because it's his fucking horse and sword that I used to kill the dragon."

Garratt's petulant tone made me giggle. "Well, you're my hero," I said with a yawn.

"Yeah?"

"Oh yeah. You're just like Superman."

"Yeah?"

"Definitely."

"I need my own super hero name," he said, letting out a yawn of his own. "What should it be?"

"No, you don't. You don't need to be Superman or anything else. Garratt suits you just fine." I replied sleepily.

"No, I have to have one."

"Okay," I sighed, too tired to even think. "What about White Knight?"

"Nope, too wishy washy." He snuggled closer, his arm tightening around my waist. "Oh wait, I have it."

"What? Tell me." My eyes were growing heavy, and the love and warmth around me was dragging me into sleep.

"Captain Big Dong."

We both laughed quietly and, despite everything that was possibly coming our way, I'd never fallen asleep feeling as happy or as grateful in all my life.

thirty-three

Garratt

When I drove myself and Caleb into school, I could sense that he was feeling nervous. If he wasn't twisting his fingers together, then he was picking at the seam of his jeans. His silence was only broken by the odd intake of breath, followed by a shuddering exhale.

"Hey, buddy," I said as we turned into the school car park. "What's going on in that head of yours?"

Caleb's eyes stayed firmly on the windshield as he spoke.

"I don't want to get you or Ms. Reynolds into trouble, Mr. Connor. And if my dad finds out-"

"Let me stop you there," I interrupted. "For one, Ms. Reynolds won't get into trouble. If this turns to shit, it's all on me. And, for two, we have a plan and we're going to stick to that plan. You're staying at the ranch because it's easier for you to help out that way."

"But my dad might come back early. I know he said he was working overtime, so wouldn't be home this weekend, but I didn't expect him to come home a couple of nights ago, and he did."

I turned in my seat and laid a hand on Caleb's shoulder. The poor kid was shaking, and I wished someone was here to give him a hug - after all, I couldn't, especially not on school property, alone in my car with him.

"Caleb, you said your dad agreed you could work for Jesse. Or was that a lie, too?"

Caleb shook his head. "No, sir. He definitely agreed to that. I think more because of the money that I would be earning, but he definitely agreed."

"Okay, so if he turns up while you're still at the ranch, before my mom and dad get home, he'll find the note that you left."

We'd stopped off at his apartment on the way to school, so that Caleb could leave the note. Millie had suggested it, just in case Mr. Tremaine came home and wondered where his son was. While we were there, I'd also got Caleb to pack up most of his stuff, enough to keep him going for a while, but not too much that would cause his dad to wonder if he did come home before we could bring Child Welfare into the picture.

Telling Caleb at breakfast that we were going to have to involve them had been difficult. But, props to him, he'd taken it like a champ and agreed it was for the best. I was sure they'd go for Mom and Dad taking care of him, until he was eighteen. It meant the department wouldn't have the worry of placing him and it would be little or no disruption to his education.

"Thank you, Mr. Connor," he said quietly. "I know you're right, but I'm real worried he'll be mad, get you into trouble, and then I'll have to go into some home."

"Not going to happen," I said, shaking my head. "None of it. Now get yourself out of this car before the rest of the school sees you and gives you shit for getting a ride with your nerdy math teacher."

Caleb grinned and opened the door.

"You're not nerdy, Mr. Connor. And you do know half the girls in school are in love with you, right?"

I dropped my head back and let out a laugh.

"I won't tell Ms. Reynolds, though," he said, still grinning widely.

That stopped my laughter. While he had to wonder why Jemma had been at the ranch with me, we hadn't given any indication that we were together. She'd even left before breakfast so he wouldn't see her car parked outside Mom and Dad's house.

"I'm not sure I get you," I replied, hoping I sounded suitably confused.

"It's pretty obvious, sir. The way you look at each other."

"We're friends is all." I gave him a smile, so wide that it probably didn't look particularly genuine.

Caleb's cheeks colored and his eyes turned down. "I saw her getting in her car this morning, outside your house."

As he looked back up at me, my mouth dropped open; I wanted to deny everything, but I couldn't. Caleb seeing Jemma get into her car meant he'd also seen me, dressed only in sleep shorts, kissing the damn life out of her up against her driver's door.

"I wasn't spying," he insisted. "I woke up when I heard Jesse go to work, and I didn't want to get up and wake the kids, so was just looking through the window. Looking at the ranch, the sunrise, I swear, Mr. Connor."

I gave a little chuckle. We'd been busted, no point denying it. "It's fine, Caleb, really it is. Just do me a favor, buddy."

"Anything, anything at all."

"Don't tell anyone else in school - not even Matty."

Caleb shook his head and looked at me with unblinking eyes. "I won't, I promise."

I knew he wouldn't. The poor kid wouldn't do anything to risk the safety and security that I believed he was beginning to feel.

"Okay, good man. Now, about those girls."

"Yeah," he said, grinning.

"I think you're right, best not tell Ms. Reynolds."

"Yes, sir."

He gave me another huge smile and then exited the car, running across the lot to the students entrance. Just when I thought he was going to go inside, he turned and waved and shit if my heart didn't do a great big tumble.

"You're sure about this, Garratt?" my boss, Grayson, asked on the other end of the line.

"Yes, sir. Yes I am."

"There'll be other transfers. You just need to wait it out."

Grayson had called me to say that the transfer I'd been hoping for wasn't possible. The loans manager position at the Knightingale branch was being filled internally; one of their cashiers was getting a promotion. I could go there as a cashier, but it wasn't what I wanted. Being in the bank, period, wasn't what I wanted any more. I'd had a taste of teaching and knew it was for me. Plus, I needed to be wherever Jemma was, either in Bridge Vale or the UK, and being six hours away, even for a short time, wasn't happening. Okay, so maybe I was nailing my balls to the wall, *yet again*, but we'd already wasted seven years and I wasn't wasting a minute more.

"I've made my mind up, Grayson. So, take this as my resignation."

Grayson sighed. "I'll be sorry to see you go, the bank will be sorry to see you go, but if you're sure?"

"Yes, positive." I was adamant, he was not swaying me and my tone told him that.

"Okay, well you'll need to put it in writing, too. I guess asking you to come back and work your notice is going to be pointless."

I laughed softly. He knew me too well, and I was glad he was a decent boss who also knew which battles to choose, and this wasn't one of them.

"I have another week of vacation I could take and maybe some sick days, if that makes your life easier," I offered.

"No, it's fine, Garratt," Grayson replied. "I can cover for you. Andrea can step up, see it as a trial period for the role, now that she's qualified."

I breathed a sigh of relief. I knew he wouldn't force me to go back, but if it had put Grayson in a spot, I would have felt guilty. Not guilty enough to go back, but it would have still eaten away at me.

"Thanks, Grayson."

"Yes, well, I wouldn't do this for everyone. You've been a good employee and if it wasn't for you, Dustin would have failed math and not gotten into USC, so I guess I owe you."

Grayson's son, Dustin, had been one of the kids I tutored, and had been one of the hardest as he really was failing badly.

"Well I appreciate everything, Grayson." And I really did. After just two years, he'd promoted me to loans manager when I was just twenty-three. He'd had faith in me and trusted me to do a good job, which I had, but now that phase of my life was over.

Grayson and I said our goodbyes and then I went to find Jemma to give her the news. I knew she was worried about me quitting the bank, after all there was no guarantee I'd get a teaching post at Bridge Vale High. Shit, the only ones might be hours away, so I'd be back to square one, but for now that wasn't my worry. My immediate worry was Jemma and her results and my need to be there for her. I had to admit, I also had Caleb on my list of concerns. I wanted to make sure he was safe and settled, and leaving to go back to the city in a few days wasn't conducive with that.

I found Jemma eating her lunch on one of the picnic tables. Thankfully, as I got there, Vicky and Marlene, the Home Ec' teacher, were leaving. They both smiled at me as I approached the table and I was sure I heard Marlene giggle; maybe mine and Jemma's relationship wasn't as secret as I thought.

"She just giggled at me," I said, as I sat on the bench opposite to Jemma.

Jemma rolled her eyes. "She has a crush on you."

"Marlene? No way," I hissed. "She's got to be forty."

"You don't become dead from the waist down when you hit forty, Garratt," Jemma scolded with a tsk. "I think even Gladys has a little soft spot for you."

"Ugh," I groaned, screwing up my face. "That's just wrong. She was my teacher."

Jemma started to giggle. "She was talking about you in her sleep, when we went on the field trip."

"Fuck off, that is not funny. Take it back, you little witch."

Jemma was full on laughing now, holding her sides.

"Well, for that, I'm not giving you my news." I was pouting as I unwrapped my sandwich.

"I'm sorry," she said around a quiet laugh. "I was joking. Now tell me."

I looked at her mouth as she chewed on her lip and saw her big eyes pleading softly with me, and I gave up any idea of stringing her along for a while. Yep, she made me fucking mush.

"I gave my notice at the bank," I blurted out before taking a bite of my tuna on rye.

"What?"

"You heard me," I said around a mouthful of lunch. "I gave my notice and I'm not going back. Well I'll need to go and pack up my apartment, but aside from that, I'm here to stay."

"But, Garratt…" she gasped. "It's your…what are you going to do if you can't get a teaching post here?"

I shrugged my shoulders and took another bite of my sandwich.

"What does that mean?" she asked, copying my shrug.

"Exactly that. I don't know what I'll do, but I'm feeling confident that I'll get a job here."

"But what if..." she paused and leaned closer to me, lowering her voice. "But what if you get into trouble with the Caleb situation? What if they stop you from teaching?"

"I won't, and they won't. We all stick to the story and if they do find out, which they won't, I'll find something else to do."

And for me, it was that simple. I would do something else. Even working on the ranch with Jesse didn't seem so bad these days. When I was twenty, all I'd wanted to do was get away and live a life in the city. Now, after six years of city life, I was ready to come home and help my big brother if he wanted or needed me to. Seeing him daily, over the last week, and how he was with Millie and the kids, made me want some of the same. It also made me realize how lucky we were to live on such a beautiful piece of land in such an amazing part of the country. I'd taken it for granted for too long. Caleb had lived a version of my ranch life at one time, when his parents had the farm. Now he was living in a tiny, two-bedroomed apartment, with a dad who could give two shits about him. When I'd been just a little older than him, I thought I knew it all and that ranch life was boring. Well, I'd experienced the excitement of the city and it wasn't all-fucking-that. I wanted a life with Jemma and I wanted it here. I wanted to raise my family alongside my family.

"Jemma, when we have kids, I don't want them growing up anywhere else," I said. "So if I have to clean up cattle and horse shit for the rest of my life for that to happen, then so be it."

Jemma's face paled and I knew I'd said something to spook her. I'd seen that look before, at the campsite when I'd pretty much told her I wanted her to be my forever.

"Don't you dare fucking run away," I said quietly as I reached over the table and took hold of her wrist. "Tell me what's wrong."

Her eyes filled with tears as she drew in a breath and shook her head. "I can't talk about this here," she whispered.

I looked around and saw that the other two tables were no longer occupied, aside for Zak the Science Lab technician, and he had his head in a book while wearing a huge pair of white *Beats* on his ears.

"Yes, you can. No one else can hear. So, tell me."

Jemma looked around nervously and then leaned forward. "What if the test is positive?"

"You have the surgery," I replied, shrugging with confusion.

"Yes, but if I have it then the chances are, if I had children...I can't..." she trailed off and shook her head. "I'm sorry, I can't do this now or here, Garratt. Not when I've got classes in twenty minutes. We can talk about it later."

She stood up and started to gather together the wrapping from her lunch.

"Jemma-" I started.

"No, Garratt," she snapped. "I can't, not now."

Without another word, she picked up her bag and stalked away on her high heels.

"What the..." I muttered.

Then it struck me. If she had the gene, chances were her children would have the gene. That would mean *my* children would have the gene. Children who I was now desperate to have.

thirty-four

Jemma

My day just went from bad to even shittier. Once I'd escaped from Garratt, and the possibility that I was about to cut all his dreams to shreds, I was faced with a freshman class who had as much interest in Arthur Conan Doyle as I had in NASCAR, that being, none at all. They made it pretty clear, too. If I wasn't dealing with girls passing notes, it was two boys arguing over one of the girls passing the notes, and then finally, one of the students, James, had an enormous meltdown because I'd made him change desks with one of the arguing boys so that I could split them up. No one had told me that he had *Asperger's* and sat at the same desk, in every classroom, for every lesson.

By the time I threw my bag and jacket onto the couch when I got home, I was ready for a large glass of wine. I knew Garratt would be around, as soon as he'd finished helping Benjie with basketball practice, and I knew we'd have to have the discussion that we hadn't finished at lunch. That was playing on my mind and had been all afternoon. How the hell was I going to tell him that the family he so wanted, probably wasn't going to happen with me? I was mulling it over, my bare feet resting on the coffee table, when my phone rang. I looked at the screen and sighed. It was my mum.

Knowing that I'd avoided her long enough, I swiped the screen to answer.

"Hey, Mum," I said, trying to sound as bright as possible.

"Jemma, why the hell haven't you been answering my calls?" she asked impatiently. "I've been trying you for almost three weeks. I've been so worried."

"I've sent you a couple of texts and I called when I first got here." I winced, knowing that one text since I'd come back to the US was by no means enough contact. My parents had already lost one daughter, so avoiding them wasn't fair.

"Not good enough," she snapped. "Not good enough, at all. Anyway, I know you're avoiding me."

"Mum, I'm-."

"Don't even pretend you're not, Jemma." She knew me too well and I couldn't deny it. "I know you think I'll ask about the test."

"Well, are you going to?" I asked, petulantly.

"Of course I am. You need to have it. You *have* to have it. I can't lose you, too." Her voice wavered and I realized how selfish I'd been.

"Mum, please don't get upset," I soothed. "I've had it done. I was going to call you once I got the results."

That was a lie, because I hadn't actually made my mind up about that. I'd been thinking if it was bad news then I'd keep it from them - at least until I had no other choice. Another part of me wanted to tell her, even if it was the worst result. That way if it was bad news, I'd be able to talk to her about it, after all she'd gone through the same thing.

"You have?" she gasped. "Oh, Jemma, I'm so glad. What made you change your mind, was it the letter from Dr. Monroe?"

"No, not really."

"What then?"

I took a deep breath and couldn't help the smile that came to my lips.

"You remember the boy I met in college, when I was studying here?" I asked, as I absentmindedly picked at thread on my blouse.

"Yes," Mum replied. "Gary, wasn't it?"

"Garratt." I corrected her with a smile. "Well, we met up again."

"And?"

"And," I sighed, "he's kind of turned my life upside down."

I talked to my mum for another half hour, and then had a quick chat with my dad. He wasn't one for talking and was eager, as usual, to get back to his garden. I ended the call promising to keep them informed of the results, but still not sure it was a promise that I could keep. I was just about to go and start some dinner, when Garratt's familiar knock resounded against the door.

"Round two," I muttered to myself as I let him in.

Garratt gave me a quick kiss to my forehead and then walked past me into the lounge and flopped down onto the couch.

"Okay," he said, patting the seat next to him. "Sit and talk."

I rolled my eyes and sighed.

"Now, Jemma."

He didn't sound as though he was going to stand any argument, so I rounded the couch and sat next to him. He looked at me expectantly, so I gave him the same look back, giving him some attitude with the tilt of my head.

"Jemma," he warned.

For all my bravado, I was dreading this conversation. I was scared that this would be the thing that *would* make him run. The thought of me being scarred hadn't deterred him, but not giving him children might just be the one thing he wouldn't be able to cope with. This wasn't something he was going to be able to talk me around about. It wasn't something that I would change my mind about after some of his sexy moves. *This* I *was* adamant about.

"If the test comes back with the news that I have the gene," I said, staring him straight in the eye, so that he knew that I was serious. "Then I'm going to ask to be sterilized."

I paused, knowing he'd have something to say.

"You're saying if you have the gene, kids are a no-no for you?"

"Yes," I said, nodding my head. "I cannot and will not pass this on to any of my children."

I held my breath, trying to abate the cry of anguish I wanted to let out. This wasn't just Garratt's dreams I was shattering, but my own, too. I'd love nothing more than to build a family with this beautiful man. Have him cradle my babies to sleep at night. To teach my children how to ride a horse. Protect my daughter with his life. Show my son how to be a great man. But none of that could happen when I might pass on a death sentence to them.

The only sound in the room was the ticking of the clock on the shelf. The quiet tick-tock was strangely comforting as I waited to hear how my little bubble of happiness was to be popped.

Garratt took in a breath through his nose and then slowly let it out through his mouth. I waited for him to stand and leave my apartment; leave my life. It was going to kill me, but I would never blame him.

"Okay," he finally said. "We can adopt. I'm good with that, and to be honest, after seeing what Caleb is going through, even if you don't have the gene I'd like to do that anyway. If we can give a child a better life than the one that poor kid is suffering, then that's what I'd like to do. Mix it up a bit, some kids of our own and maybe adopt a couple. Right, that's all fixed, so what's for dinner, or shall we go to Rowdy's or maybe the diner?"

"Garratt," I gasped, tears burning my eyes. "Did you hear what I said?"

"Yeah, gorgeous, I did. I get it. It's fine and, like I said, we'll adopt. Hey, you are okay with that, aren't you?" He reached for my hand and pulled me closer to him. "I mean, if you don't want to adopt, yeah it's a huge thing for me, but we can talk about it and come to some sort of agreement."

"Oh my God," I cried, the tears now careering down my cheeks. "You are the most amazing man I have ever met."

I launched myself at him, and clung to him like a limpet to a rock. I was never, ever letting him go. My arms went around his neck and my legs moved to either side of him, so that I was straddling his waist. Squeezing him as tightly as I could, I let out a huge sob.

"I love you, so much," I said against the shell of his ear. "I was so scared you'd run away."

"Hey, hey," he replied, gently rubbing my back. "I'd never do that, even if you said no to adoption. I'd be pissed, but I wouldn't run. Like I said, we'd talk it through. You do want to adopt, don't you?"

I nodded my head, my nose still nuzzled against his neck.

"Yes, more than anything," I sobbed. "I thought I'd never have children, couldn't see it if I couldn't give birth to them. But, seeing Millie with Addy just showed me how easy it is to love a child that isn't your own. So, yes I want to adopt."

Garratt chuckled softly. "So stop crying, baby. It's all going to be okay, I promise."

"You mean so much to me, and I couldn't stand the thought of you leaving me."

Garratt put his hands under my arms, and held me away from his body. He leaned forward and kissed me softly and then brushed a thumb under my eyes, wiping away my tears.

"I love you," he said, followed by another gentle kiss. "I love you so damn much, I have no fucking idea how I survived before you came back into my life. It's like everything I've done this last seven years has just been me filling in time until you came back. I didn't know it, but I've just been messing around, waiting for you. Now you're here I can breathe again. Life isn't just something I do until I die. Life now is precious and good, and I only want to do it with you, so no, baby, I'm not going anywhere."

I felt as though my heart had expanded too much, and was too big for my chest. It was so full of love for the beautiful man in front of me; the beautiful boy that I'd been starting to fall in love with all those years ago.

"Now," he said with a grin. "I know what I'd like to eat, but that would mean a late dinner. Is that okay with you?"

I looked at him quizzically and then realized what he'd said.

"Garratt!" I scolded.

"What?" He started to laugh. "It works for me, gorgeous."

As I kissed him with as much love and passion that I could, I knew that it would work for me, too.

thirty-five

Garratt

When I woke, my dick was hard and throbbing and my balls were aching. It didn't matter that we'd had great sex the night before, I was addicted to Jemma. Turning on to my side, I watched as she slept. Her lips were parted and pouty, her hands resting on the pillow above her head, and her beautiful tits were on display. God, she was beautiful and she was mine. I looked at the clock, seeing it was just after eight. I grinned to myself, loving the idea of Saturday morning sex with a sleepy Jemma.

I crawled over the top of her, and kissed at the corner of her mouth, causing her to stir.

"Garratt," she whispered, in a husky, sleepy, breath.

"Hey, gorgeous."

"I'm so tired," she replied, running her fingers through my hair.

If her nipples hadn't hardened, I'd have moved away and let her sleep, but I knew it wouldn't take much to get her interested. She and I were so in tune with each other, two sides of the same coin, both knowing and understanding what the other needed and wanted. And I knew that she wanted and needed this, right now.

I slithered down her body, and with my hands at her waist, pulled her down the bed. Then, with my hands on her knees, I opened her legs. Whether it was instinct or desire, I had no idea, but Jemma bent her knees and lay her feet flat on the mattress.

"Not so sleepy then?" I asked as I started to kiss up the inside of her thigh.

"Uh huh," she moaned, grabbing hold of the sheet. "Hmm, that's so nice."

Nipping at her soft skin, I reached a hand up and started to play with her nipple. I pinched it and drew circles around it, while all the time I continued to lick and suck on the inside of her thigh. Jemma's hand came down to her pussy and she started to rub at her clit, making the most erotic noises as she moaned with desire.

Kissing up her thigh, I prized her fingers away and replaced them with my mouth, taking a long lick from the center of her delicious pussy, right up to her clit.

"Oh my God," she cried, and grabbed hold of her breasts, pushing them together.

I repeated the stroke of my tongue, only this time I ended it by sucking on the tiny, throbbing peak. As Jemma's groans got louder, I pushed her legs wider and inserted two fingers inside her, pushing them in and pulling them out with a steady rhythm.

"Garratt." Her voice was breathy and anxious - worried I was going to stop.

I moved my mouth from her clit, and kissed along her pubic bone, up her stomach, and between the valley of her breasts, finally reaching her mouth.

"You taste fucking amazing," I said, pushing my tongue inside her mouth so she could taste it, too.

My fingers continued to work inside Jemma, then when I felt her start to tremble, I removed them and sat up on my haunches, looking down on her.

"Touch yourself, gorgeous," I gasped, taking my hard cock in my hand.

"Make yourself come while I jack myself off all over that amazing body of yours."

Jemma's whiskey colored eyes looked up at me and they were full of lust, of sex, desire, and love. I started to pump my cock, squeezing it on each upward stroke and watched as Jemma dipped a finger inside herself and then pulled it out, spreading her desire over and around her clit as her fingers rubbed in a circle around it.

"Fuuck," I groaned.

She looked amazing, thrusting her hips in time to the tempo of her own fingers masturbating. Her eyes were hooded and her bottom lip was caught in her teeth as her body became shrouded in pleasure. Watching her, I knew I would never love anyone as much as her; no one would ever make me as happy as she did. That thought had me pulling harder at my dick with one hand, and wincing at the mixture of pleasure and pain at the pull on my balls.

"Jemma, I'm gonna come," I gasped.

She looked up at me, with a mixture of love and yearning, and dipped her fingers into her pussy once more and started to ride them. Fuck, if it wasn't the greatest sight that I'd ever seen. I angled my body towards Jemma's, and with one more pull and squeeze, I was done, coming all over her stomach.

I gave a guttural roar as I continued to empty myself all over her, and just as I was finished, Jemma started to tremble. Her hips moved faster as one of her hands squeezed one of her breasts. I dropped my head down to her pussy, and licked her clit. That was all she needed, to come with a scream of my name, her fingers continuing their push and pull and her hips keeping pace.

"Morning, gorgeous," I said as her hands flopped onto the mattress and she let out a heavy exhale.

"Morning," she gasped, breathlessly. "Oh shit, that was...I have no words."

"I do," I replied. "Sexy as fucking fuck."

After taking a shower together and another round of sex, I was watching the sports news on the TV while Jemma was looking over some essays from her freshman class.

"Any good" I asked.

She screwed up her nose and shook her head. "No, not really. I have no idea what they were taught last semester, but it certainly wasn't punctuation."

"Yeah, but is the content any good?"

"So-so. None of them have understood the real meaning behind *Animal Farm*. They really do think it's about a farm with animals that can talk."

I let out a laugh seeing the disappointment written all over her face.

"Looks like you've got your work cut out for you." I leaned into her and dropped a kissed to her temple. "I'm sure you'll think of something."

As Jemma turned to me with an 'I'm not so sure' kind of look, her cell started to ring. She reached for it and frowned.

"Who is it?"

She turned the screen to me. "It says it's Millie. I don't remember programming her number into my phone."

"You didn't, I did. She said she might give you a call." I nodded at the cell, still ringing in her hand. "Are you going to answer it?"

"Oh shit, yes."

Jemma quickly swiped at the screen and started to chat to my sister-in-law, who I already knew was inviting her along to a shopping trip with herself and her best friend, Sarah. Watching Jemma's face light up as she agreed to go, made me happy beyond belief. Not that I was happy to be spending the day away from her, but because I knew Millie and Sarah would keep her mind off things. We were told it could be months before Jemma's test results were back, and every minute was going to be torture.

"I'm going shopping," Jemma said excitedly as she put her cell down on the table. "Is that okay with you?"

"Yeah, sure," I replied. "Go have fun with Millie."

"But we were going to spend the day together."

She reached for my hand and took it in her own; tiny, delicate fingers, giving it a squeeze.

"It's fine, baby. I'm not going back to the city, so we'll have plenty of time to spend together.

"About that-."

"No argument." I shook my head. "I'm not going back. Decision made."

Jemma sighed and then gave me the brightest of smiles. "Okay." She reached forward and kissed me. "I'd better go and get ready."

I watched as she excitedly skipped off and then pulled out my cell to check if Jesse fancied some company while looking after the kids. I couldn't help the grin that spread across my face as I waited for him to answer, because this was what I wanted for always; spending time with my family, Jemma spending time with my family. It was how my life was meant to be.

"So, she's the one?" Jesse asked as he patted Hunter's freshly changed, diapered ass to send him on his way.

"Yeah," I replied, watching Hunter join his youngest sister on the lawn. "I know it seems fast, but I can't imagine feeling this way about anyone else, ever."

"You were probably a little bit in love with her seven years ago, bro. So, no, it's not that fast. Pretty fucking slow, actually."

"I guess so," I agreed with a laugh. "It's going to be tough going, if the test comes back with bad news, but we'll get through it."

I'd told Jesse everything, mainly because I'd needed some guidance. I'd realized that Jemma was worried about passing the gene on to her kids, and knowing Jemma as I did, I also knew that would be something she would struggle in her heart with. She'd pretty much said that kids weren't an option, if not with her words but the look of pain and terror in her eyes. She didn't know, but I'd begged off from helping Benjie with basketball practice and sought out my brother instead.

Jesse had given it to me straight.

"Garr, you're one of the best men I know, and you think she's pretty wonderful, so if you think that then she probably is, and any kid would be lucky to have her for their mom. If she's worried about having her own kids then adoption would be a great fit for you both. So, stop worrying and bleating about what isn't going to happen and doing something positive about what could."

It was then that I went over to Jemma's place and, when she told me what I already guessed, I told her that we were going to adopt. Yeah, I know, bossy as usual, but I think she kind of loved that about me.

"Love isn't easy," Jesse said, bringing me back to the present. "Shit, me and Millie are testament to that."

"But when it works, it's great, right?"

"Oh yeah, bro, most definitely."

Jesse gave me a grin and I knew dirty thoughts were going through his mind.

"Please, don't. I have enough images in my head of you two from before I moved out."

"Can't help being a sex God, Garr." Jesse winked at me and went over to the edge of the deck. "Clemmie, baby, come get some more sunscreen on."

"Okay, Daddy," she called back, giving him the most beautiful smile.

Jesse came back and sat down in the Adirondack chair next to me.

"Where's Addy, by the way?" I asked.

Jesse grumbled and shook his head. "In her room, surfing the web for 'essentials for school'. Fucking stupid ass school."

"Daddy!" Clemmie cried, standing hands on hips. "You said a bad word."

"Oh shi-shoot, baby, pretend you didn't hear that."

I couldn't help but laugh at Jesse's wide-eyed look of shock. He knew that Millie was going to kick his ass when she found out. His language in front of the kids was a war she had yet to win.

"Hah, you are in so much trouble," I said, slapping Jesse's back.

He turned and gave me the stink eye. "She won't find out, will she?" he asked Clemmie pointedly.

Clemmie looked at him with a glint in her eye, and put a tiny finger to her lips.

"What's it worth?" she asked.

I bust out laughing and Jesse groaned.

"Sheesh, Clemmie. This has to stop. I bought you a new dolly last time."

Jesse's hands went to his hips in exasperation.

"Well, you shouldn't cuss then, should you?" Clemmie tilted her head to one side and wagged a finger at my brother.

"She has a point, Jess," I added.

"And you can be quiet."

"I think I'd like a new pair of sneakers, please, Daddy." Clemmie grinned at him.

"And what do I tell your momma?" Jesse asked. "How do I explain that you're getting new sneakers, and your brother and sister aren't?"

"Well," she said, shaking her head. "I guess you'll have to buy them some, too. That's a real expensive cuss word."

She then held her arms out straight in front of her.

"Okay, I'm ready for my sunscreen now, Daddy."

As Jesse covered her up, I couldn't help but continue to laugh. He'd been tied up in knots by a six-year-old. Once he'd finished and sent Clemmie on her way, I could see a smile twitching at his lips.

"She's fucking amazing," he whispered, watching his youngest daughter. "She's just like her momma."

"Yep, she is," I said, handing him a can of soda. "Anyway, how's Caleb doing? I haven't seen him around."

Jesse popped the can and sat back in his seat. "He's doing great. An absolute natural with the horses."

"Really?" I asked with a huge smile.

"Yep, he really is. He's calm and patient with them and knows exactly when to show them who is the boss and when to give them their head."

That was praise indeed coming from my brother, who was revered by many and was inundated with requests by folks from all over the country to work with their horses.

"I've got him working on a mare for a guy from Colorado. He paid a hell of a lot of money for it, but can't get within four feet of it without it kicking up dust and bucking itself into exhaustion."

"Shit," I groaned. "Is it safe for Caleb to be working with her?"

Jesse gave me a narrow-eyed stare. "I wouldn't risk him getting hurt, Garr. I thought you knew me better than that."

"I do, but it sounds pretty dangerous"

"Not anymore, she's not. Caleb's been helping me the last two nights, after school. She's not bucking anymore, but she's still a little spooked at having a saddle on her. He's doing some bareback work with her this morning."

I glanced anxiously in the direction of the training paddock, not that I could see anything with the barn and a line of trees in the way.

"The situation is tricky enough as it is," I said. "I don't want to have to explain to Becky that he's broken a bone, or worse, been kicked in the head while we have him unlawfully living with you."

Jesse leaned forward and slapped my back. "He'll be good, bro. Don't you worry about it. I've told him to only work with her until lunchtime anyway, so he'll be along soon."

I nodded and took a large gulp of my drink, hoping that when Caleb appeared around the corner he'd be all in one piece.

We sat in silence for a few minutes, watching the kids play, when finally Jesse spoke.

"I'm proud of you, Garratt," he said, without taking his eyes off his children. "You're a good man and you're going to ace teaching."

The emotion hit me like a thunderbolt. Jesse and I weren't ones to hide our feelings, but to hear my brother, the man I respected most after my dad, say something like that, filled me with more pride and hope than I'd ever felt before.

"Thanks, Jess," I said, clearing my throat. "I appreciate it."

He didn't say anything else, but tapped his soda can against mine and then sat back in his chair, watching over his beloved family, and I was more determined than ever to make sure Jemma and I had the same peace in our future.

thirty-six

Jemma

It was Garratt's last day of teaching practice and, bizarrely, I couldn't shake off the sadness that the day brought with it. I knew it was totally stupid feeling that way, he was staying in Bridge Vale, but somehow it felt like the end of something. Maybe it was the thought of him going back to the city for a few days the following week, to pack up his apartment and say goodbye to his friends and colleagues. Whatever it was, I couldn't muster even the faintest of smiles when Becky was thanking him during the staff meeting after school finished.

"You've done a great job," she said, toasting him with a glass of cheap, sparkling wine. "And I'm sure you'll go on to have a great career…maybe back here, you never know."

She smiled at Garratt, who grinned at me. A grin that said 'I told you we'd get away with the Caleb situation'. Of course, he'd been right. Becky had accepted that Caleb was staying at the ranch to make it easier for him when working, and his father hadn't even realized that he wasn't at home.

Eight days he'd been there and not once had his dad called him; if he'd been home and seen the note that Caleb had left, we had no idea. That was why a couple of nights earlier, Caleb had called his dad at work. I'd insisted on it, if only to cover Garratt's back, but Mr. Tremaine had bawled his son out for pestering him at work, without even listening to what Caleb had to say. Caleb had looked totally crestfallen when he'd ended the call, but as soon as his eyes lifted up to see me and Garratt watching him, he lifted his chin, smiled, and went out to tend to the horses.

"So," Becky continued. "Thanks again, Garratt, for all your hard work, and here's to your future."

Everyone raised their glasses and said their own cheers, as Garratt smiled and nodded, and I could see he was taken aback by their good wishes and the pile of cards and gifts from the kids that were on a chair next to him.

"You still driving yourself to the ranch?" Garratt asked me, as everyone started to gather their things together and leave.

"Yes," I replied, suddenly feeling nauseous.

His parents would be home in a few hours, and I was feeling anxious about meeting them. Simply the thought of it had my palms sweating and my stomach roiling.

"Seriously, gorgeous, they're going to love you. I promise."

I looked at his bright blue eyes, searching for uncertainty in them, but there was none. He was positive our meeting was going to be, in his words, 'epic'. As usual, Garratt had enough positivity to power a whole town if necessary. He was never anything but confident and I shouldn't have expected anything less from him.

"I hope they do," I said, chewing at the corner of my mouth nervously. "I left you once before, they might hate me for it."

"Come on, Jem," he retorted, bumping shoulders with me. "You know they don't. You left for Lauren."

I took in a sharp breath and held a hand to my stomach, wondering when the mention of my sister's name would bring a smile to my face, rather than a deep embedded sadness.

"You're going to stay over?" he asked.

My eyes widened. "No. Not with your mum and dad at home, no I'm not."

Garratt chuckled quietly and dropped a hand to sneakily pinch my bottom.

"We'll see."

"No, Garratt," I scolded, moving a pace away from him. "I won't. It seems disrespectful."

"They know I have sex, gorgeous. In fact, if I remember correctly, my mom caught me in the barn, in the middle of that very act, with Trudie Daniels on my nineteenth birthday."

I rolled my eyes at him. "Whatever, but I still don't want to sit down to breakfast with them in the morning, wondering whether they heard you give me an orgasm the night before."

"Just the one?" he asked, with a wink. "Now, baby, you know that it would be multiple."

I rolled my eyes again and, shaking my head, walked away to speak to Becky, leaving Garratt laughing to himself.

"They're going to hate me, aren't they?"

Millie laughed and pulled me into a side hug. "No, they're not. They'll love you because Garratt loves you and you make him happy."

I really hoped that she was right about Garratt's parents, but I couldn't help thinking that once they knew about all the baggage I was bringing with me, plus the fact I wouldn't be giving them grandchildren, they'd be telling Garratt to run back to the city as fast as he could.

I looked over to Garratt, who was talking with Jesse and Caleb, and I knew that even if they did hate me, I wasn't going anywhere. I loved him.

"Momma, how long now?" Addy asked, wrapping her arms around Millie's waist.

"Not long, baby. They'll be here before you know it."

Millie kissed the crown of Addy's blonde head and closed her eyes as she inhaled and squeezed her daughter tight. Her obvious love for Addy only reinforced how easy the possibility was to love a child unconditionally, even when they weren't your own, your blood. Millie and Addy had a very special bond and it filled me with hope that maybe one day I'd get that. The thought of possibly getting cancer had weighted me down so heavily that I'd pushed the fact that I was going to be childless to the back of my mind. It was a pain that I'd always thought I'd think about on another day. Now, I had hope and Garratt had given that to me. His stubbornness and unadulterated confidence had pushed me into a tunnel with a glowing light at the end of it.

As excitement for the future gave a little nudge at my belly, we all heard a car pull up outside the house. Addy let go of Millie and ran to the door, flinging it open.

"Granma, Grandpa, you're home!" she squealed excitedly as she skipped down the porch steps.

At the bottom, the two older Connors and their granddaughter hugged and exchanged kisses, while we all watched from the doorway.

"Granma," Clemmie called, and not wanting to be left out, pushed past our legs and ran at full pelt to join them.

"Gangan," Hunter cried, flailing his arms around as he tottered towards the steps.

"Oh my goodness," Bonnie, Garratt's mum gasped. "What a welcome."

"We've only been gone three weeks," his father said, his deep baritone rumbling through the air.

Looking at his parents, I could see where Jesse and Garratt got their good looks from. Bonnie was blonde and petite and extremely pretty, while Ted was a big, imposing man, who still had a great body and was ruggedly handsome. His hair was dark and had a peppering of grey at the temples, and Garratt was the image of him. Jesse was a mixture of both his parents, different to Garratt in many ways, yet they were so obviously brothers. It was scary the amount of good looking genes there were in one family.

"Let Granma and Grandpa come inside," Jesse said with a chuckle. "They haven't even had time to breathe."

The girls let go of their grandparents and, grabbing hold of their hands, pulled them towards the house. As Bonnie and Ted stepped onto the steps, they looked up at all of us and my heart plummeted; I was so scared that they would hate me. As Bonnie reached the porch, the first person she pulled into a hug was me, and as she squeezed me tight, I felt the anxiety drain from every pore of my body.

"You must be Jemma," she said, stretching her arms out to look at me. "I'm so glad you're here, honey. I've heard an awful lot about you."

Before I had chance to respond, she pulled me back into a quick hug before letting me go and moving onto Millie, finally hauling Hunter up into her embrace.

"Shit, Mom," Jesse grumbled. "What about us, your sons? Shouldn't we be the first with the hugs?"

"You know your momma, son," Ted said. "She likes to prioritize properly."

As everyone laughed, Jesse led us back into the house. Bonnie and Ted's house was a similar style to that of Jesse and Millie's across the paddock, but a much smaller version. Inside was markedly different, though. Where the big house was modern and stylish, this one had a much more traditional feel to it. The couch was big and chunky in a rich ox-blood colored leather, while at the other end of the room was an oval dining table with chairs in the same ox-blood red. At the windows were pretty flowered drapes that matched the scattered pillows on the couch and winged back chair, and on the highly polished, wooden floor were large rugs with patterns of dark green and deep red. I'd only seen the bedroom that Garratt slept in, but it was of a similar style, with a dark green checkered comforter and curtains, and dark green towels in the adjoining bathroom, that was painted in white.

"We have gifts for everyone," Bonnie, said as she flopped down onto the couch. "But they'll have to wait until tomorrow, sorry. I'm pooped and they're in the bottom of one of the cases."

"So," Ted said, looking between me and Caleb. "You are the two new members of our little clan."

Caleb blushed and held out his hand. "Good to meet you, sir."

"Same here, young man. We'll chat in a few about your situation and what we need to do. But, be assured, you aint going back there, no matter what the damn department says. Okay?"

Caleb drew in a breath, and I could see he was trying to hold it together. Ted evidently did, too. He placed a large hand on Caleb's shoulder and gave it a squeeze.

"It's going to be fine, son. Don't you go fretting about it."

It was at that point I fell a little bit in love with Ted Connor. I was guessing his youngest son was a lot like him in temperament, so it would be hard not to.

"Now, young lady," Ted said. "I'm guessing that you're the one we have to thank for my youngest boy's smile and for getting him to come home to us."

"Yes, I suppose I am," I replied, my eyes nervously darting to Garratt who was standing with an arm around his mum.

"Well, welcome, sweetheart. You've made me and Bonnie happier than you'll know." He turned and looked at his wife, who gave him a huge smile that crinkled her eyes. "Now, before we do anything else, let's get this shit storm with young Caleb here sorted."

Almost two hours, and numerous phone calls later, and Ted and Bonnie were unofficially - until the forms were signed to make it official - Caleb's guardians until he hit eighteen. Ted had steadfastly argued with the Child Welfare department, telling them in no uncertain terms that Caleb wasn't going anywhere; certainly not back to his father. According to Ted, at first they were adamant that he had to go into the system and stay with a foster family, pending investigation, but he'd been determined. At one point I thought Caleb was going to get up and run, he looked petrified as we waited for Ted to emerge from his office, but Garratt sat next to him and laid a flat palm on the crown of Caleb's head, visibly calming him down. Finally, Ted rejoined us with a huge smile on his face.

"Looks like you're staying here, son," he said to Caleb.

Caleb let out a huge sigh of relief that was on the point of becoming a sob, it was so expansive.

"Thank you, Mr. Connor," he said, pushing up from his seat. "Thank you so much. Thank you all, for everything. My dad, he's not a bad man, he's just having a real bad time."

"Doesn't give him a right to hit you, Caleb," Jesse growled, scrubbing a hand down his face.

Caleb's head dropped and his shoulder slumped.

"What did they say, honey?" Bonnie asked.

"They're going to come around tomorrow and fill out all the paperwork with us, and they'll need to speak to you, Caleb."

Caleb's head shot up and he gasped.

"It's okay, nothing to worry about. They just want to know the details and check out your injuries. Bonnie and I will be with you the whole time. Once they've done that, well," he sighed. "Well, then they'll go see your dad."

The bruising on Caleb's back and around his eye was all yellowing now, but there was no doubt how bad his injuries had been. Luckily, he also had some photographs, as Caleb had had the foresight to take some on his cell. The pictures of him in his bathroom mirror sporting a collage of black, blue, and yellow over his back had brought myself and Millie to tears.

Jesse moved over to Caleb and ruffled his hair. "Welcome to the family, Caleb."

"Thank you, Jesse," Caleb replied, his awe of Jesse still evident in his eyes.

"Okay, I'm going to go back over to the house and check on Millie and the kids before I sort out the horses. You want to meet me at the stables in thirty-minutes? And then, I guess you should stay here tonight, your new home."

Caleb grinned and nodded. "Yes, sir."

"Good. See you then. Night everyone, see you tomorrow." Jesse kissed his mum and then left to go home to Millie, who'd left with the kids once the conversation about Caleb had started. They were far too young to have to hear about what the poor boy had gone through.

Garratt took my hand. "I'll go and stay at Jemma's place tonight."

"You don't need to do that," I said. "Stay here with your mum and dad. They haven't seen you for weeks. Catch up with them."

Bonnie smiled at me and put a hand to her chest. "Oh, you sweet girl, but it's fine as long as you're both back here for breakfast at eight."

Garratt groaned. "Mom, eight? Really?"

"You heard your mom, son," Ted chided. "She wants to spend some time with you. You and Jemma."

"But I'll be here all the time after next week," Garratt replied.

Ted looked at him with arched brows. "Just once you think you could do as we ask?"

"Okay, eight it is," he sighed, sounding like a teenage boy.

"Eight is great," I added and turned my body to Bonnie. "Is there anything you need me to bring?"

"Oh no, honey, just my son."

"Once we've eaten breakfast, you can help bring Caleb's stuff over here," Ted added, smirking at his son. "Might as well put you to work while I can."

"I can do it, Mr. Connor," Caleb said. "I don't have much."

"That's fine, Caleb, but I reckon you'll need a desk in your room and maybe a TV. You know the usual stuff you teenagers want. Garratt can help make all that happen. You okay with that, Garr?"

I looked at Garratt whose eyes were bright with emotion.

"Yeah, Dad. I'm more than on board with that."

I couldn't help but be grateful for the Connors. They truly were a wonderful family, and by the huge smile on Caleb's face, I knew he also realized how lucky he was.

thirty-seven

Garratt

3 months later

Time had flown by, with summer on its way out, and the cooler air of fall biting at our lungs. Addy had gone off to school, and while it had been traumatic for Jesse and Millie, their daughter was thriving. She was still super excited to be home every weekend, which I knew Jesse was relieved about, but she was also full of stories of what she'd been doing in class and the new friends she'd made. She was still our beautiful, sweet Addy, though, and we were all grateful for that.

It had been crap, but necessary that I'd spent her last week at home, back in the city. I hadn't been able to get out of my lease on my apartment, without it costing me a shit load of money, so I was still the official tenant when a water pipe burst and flooded the place. So, if I wanted to get my deposit check back, it was up to me to go and clean the place up; after all, I'd been the dumb fuck who'd left the water on in an empty apartment. It had taken a lot longer than I expected, so I was there for two weeks, solidly cleaning and painting. Thankfully, as school was out for the summer, Jemma came with me. She'd help me during the day, then at night we visited restaurants and bars or the comedy store, and enjoyed a little bit of city life.

I had to admit, when we came back, I was worried that Jemma would miss the buzz and noise, but as we attended a party to celebrate Addy's first week at school, she sighed and told me she was glad to be home. My relief was immense and I could breathe easily, knowing I'd made the right decision.

I'd applied for a teaching position, covering maternity leave for a year, at a high school in Jericho which was just thirty miles east of Bridge Vale. I was waiting to hear from them, but with my usual confidence, I was pretty sure that I was a shoe in. Unfortunately, Jim Taylor came back from his travels, having '*found himself*' sufficiently enough to want to fit back in to Bridge Vale High. However, Jemma was pretty sure he'd be off again soon, as Becky had already had to reprimand him about taking his stress levels out on the kids. Old Jimbob was therefore considering his future. He needed to get his skates on though, as I would be starting in Jericho in just under a month if I got the job. Okay, *when* I got the job. In the meantime, I was helping Jesse on the ranch, mainly with the horses as Caleb was now at college.

The kid had worked hard, both on the ranch and at school, and got the GPA he needed, along with a scholarship. The day he left for college, Mom cried as though he were her own son. In fact, I don't think she cried that much when *I* left for college. Addy shed a little tear, too; she had a real crush on that boy and I think that while he'd miss him, Jesse was kind of glad that Caleb wouldn't be around on the weekends when Addy was home. As for Mr. Tremaine, well, he'd moved permanently to Knightingale. Social Services paid him a little visit and he denied everything; said Caleb was a liar who was always getting into fights with other kids. Of course, we all vouched for Caleb, and it was agreed he was better off with my parents. When he reached eighteen, Caleb made his own decision to cut his dad off. That had been because he'd been to see him at his workplace, to talk and see if they could sort things out, but Mr. Tremaine had back-handed his son, cutting his lip. Luckily for Caleb, but unluckily for his dad, Jesse was waiting outside and had heard the shouting. Two of Mr. Tremaine's work colleagues had had to hold Jesse back from pummeling the man to death. Caleb then decided that enough was enough and hadn't seen his father since.

As for Jemma and I, we were just going from strength to strength; happy as sows in shit. The only thing marring our blissful happiness was the ongoing wait for the gene test results. We'd been told it could take months, but it didn't make the wait any easier. One thing that helped was that I'd pretty much moved into her apartment - which wasn't ideal when I had to be back at the ranch at six-thirty every morning, but it was preferable to spending nights apart. Jemma was still feeling shady about having sex under Mom and Dad's roof, so early nights and mornings became our routine. There were benefits with the early nights of course, and I made sure my woman reaped those benefits pretty much every night.

Jesse knew how important family time was, so had insisted that, like him, I take the weekends off. In his words, 'I'm the fucking boss, Garr. I can pay someone to do weekends, so stop stressing'. So, who was I to argue with my big brother? Which was why Jemma and I were enjoying a late Saturday morning breakfast after some lazy Saturday morning sex; something that had become a spectacularly, amazing norm for us. And, as was usual, she was grading the kids work while I read the newspaper.

"What is it this week, gorgeous?" I asked, taking a sip of my coffee.

"Shakespeare." She grinned at me, knowing how much I hated the bearded guy and his fancy words. "The kids are actually loving it."

"Seriously? Did you whack them all over the head or something?"

"No. But I did let them watch Romeo and Juliet with Leonardo DiCaprio and Claire Danes."

"Yeah, well, you gotta admit old Leo does it for most teenage girls, even now."

"Twenty-eight year old girls, too," Jemma replied, with a sexy little glint in her eye.

"Huh," I huffed. "You don't need Leo when you have me. An Oscar he might have, but does he have a magic dick? No, I don't think so."

Jemma laughed and the beautiful, tinkling sound hit me right in the chest. Every time she laughed meant that I was doing all the right things. I was keeping her safe. She was feeling loved. Cancer hadn't touched our life. Yet.

"Is my baby jealous?" she asked, leaning across the table to give me a quick kiss.

"Nope," I replied, pulling her back to me with a hand at her neck. "Nothing to be jealous about. LD may have the money, the Oscar, the cars, the private jet, but I have a magic dick and I have you."

As we kissed, Jemma sighed and smiled against my lips.

"I love you," she whispered. "You're so bloody romantic, it's unreal."

"I know, it's a gift."

We kissed again, this time our breaths getting a little heavier, my fingers holding on tighter, and hers tangling in my hair a little bit deeper. It was all getting hot and heavy when Jemma's phone chimed.

"Seriously?" she said on a long sigh as she pulled away from me.

Reluctantly, I let her go. At least it wasn't her mom's ringtone; those calls could last for fucking hours now that they were back in regular contact. I'd spoken to her parents a couple of times, and they seemed happy that I was looking after their girl and were grateful that I'd persuaded her to take the test, so all was good on that front.

"Garratt," Jemma gasped, breaking me from my thoughts. "It's the Cancer Center."

I felt the color drain from my face and watched as Jemma's did the same.

"Answer it," I replied, grabbing her free hand.

This was it, this was when we found out her fate. I was never a man to pray, but I had prayed to God every damn night in the last three months since she'd taken the test. I'd prayed that my beautiful girl was given a break and she wasn't going to go through hell.

As bile rose to the huge lump in my throat, I watched Jemma swipe the screen with shaking hands and hold the cell to her ear. My stomach felt as though it was holding some sort of sea battle, it was churning so wildly.

"Hello. J-Jemma Reynolds speaking," she said hesitantly and then paused. "Yes, my p-password is Angel."

I took a huge swallow and watched as Jemma listened. She didn't speak, simply nodding even though the person on the other end of the phone couldn't see her. The silence became a terrifying wait to hear whether her life, our lives, might be about to erupt into one full of uncertainty and pain. Finally, after what seemed an eternity, she cleared her throat.

"Okay, thank you…yes, I will. T-thank you."

She dropped her cell onto the table and turned to look at me with wary eyes that were shining brightly with unshed tears. As her bottom lip trembled, her hand went to her left breast and I knew. The pain in my chest was strong enough to make me double over, and I had to fight with myself to stay upright.

"Baby," I whispered.

She nodded and her face crumpled. "I have them both, Garratt. They found that I have a known harmful mutation of both genes."

I had no idea what that actually meant, but I knew it wasn't good news. Without any further hesitation, I got up and went to her side of the table. I pulled Jemma up, took her seat, and then pulled her onto my lap and against my chest. I clung to her, allowing my tears to silently crawl down my face and into her hair. I knew I was holding her too tight, but I couldn't let go. My brain was telling me that if I loosened my grip by even the minutest amount, she would slip away from me; I would lose her and I could not and would not let that happen.

We stayed fused together, with no space between us, for an indefinite time. I had no idea how short or long it was, just that Jemma being in my arms was the only thing that made sense. The fact that she had the chance of getting cancer, made fuck all sense to me. She was good, kind, and beautiful. She'd already lost her sister and gone through the same torment with her mom. She didn't deserve this.

Long after my tears had stopped and her sobs had quieted, Jemma gently eased away from me and looked up at me with red, rimmed eyes.

"I'm so scared, Garratt," she whispered, her voice shaky and unsure.

"I know, gorgeous," I replied, holding her hair from her face with both my hands. "But we will get through this. I swear we will."

She bit on her bottom lip and nodded before resting her forehead against my shoulder. I kissed the crown of her head and took a deep breath.

"What exactly did they tell you?" I asked.

"Just that they found both the genes, and that once I've had time to process it I should call and make an appointment to see Dr. Kruger to discuss my options," she replied, her head staying down.

"Okay." I rubbed my hands up and down her back, not knowing how else to soothe her, because I had no fucking words that would do the job.

"The nurse said I should consider having some counseling, too."

Jemma's hands moved to my waist and reached under my tee, where her smooth fingertips cooled the heat of my skin. As she silently wept, I cradled her like a baby.

"I'm so sorry," she murmured against my chest.

"Hey, what are you sorry for?" I asked.

"For putting you through this. You don't need this, to be worried about me. I should never have told you."

"We've talked about this." I lifted her chin with my index finger so that she was looking at me. "I'm all in, I'm not going anywhere, and I'm glad I know. Like I said, knowing means I actually get to look after you."

"But, you don't need to. You shouldn't have to," she protested.

That caused me to let out a hollow laugh. "I do need to, and I want to, it's not a case of *having* to. And let's be clear, if it was then there's nothing wrong with that. Any guy that loves his woman does *have* to look after her, there's no choice. The only reason I wouldn't *have* to look after you would be because I have no damn idea what's going on in your life and that you need looking after. And that just isn't something I can even comprehend, gorgeous, because *that* would mean you weren't *in* my fucking life."

Jemma kissed me gently, with soft, slightly parted lips. It wasn't a kiss that was going to lead anywhere, it wasn't full of lust or desire. It was sweet and heartfelt and told me she loved me more than any other kiss that we'd shared before had.

"I love you."

I smiled, pleased with myself at being able to understand her, at having the ability to know her so well.

"I love you, too," I replied, and returned the kiss with one that I hoped was equally as meaningful.

"I guess we need to talk about things," Jemma said with a sigh.

I shook my head. "Nuh uh, baby. They told you to process it first, and today is a beautiful, warm, sunny day and is not a day for processing."

"It's not?" she asked, with a quiet giggle. "What's it a day for?"

"It's a day for having fun. A day for me to take my beautiful girlfriend on a date."

Her smile was watery, but thankfully it met her eyes, so I knew that she was on board.

"Okay, go get changed into a pair of those tight jeans of yours that show off your ass." I tapped said ass and grinned.

She nodded. "Okay."

"Good, so go."

Jemma slid off my lap and stood in front of me, running a hand through my hair.

"I don't know what I'd do without you."

"You won't ever have to, so stop the chatter, Jemma, and go get changed. Oh, and maybe a tight, little tee would look good, too."

"Why? Where are we going?"

I shrugged. "I have no fucking idea, but you in skin tight jeans and a top that shows off your tits can only make the day better..."

As soon as the words left my mouth, I really wanted to cut my fucking tongue out.

"Jemma-."

"Hey," she said, cupping my face. "Don't ever stop with that dirty mind and mouth of yours. It makes everything feel normal, and I just need normal today. Okay?"

I took in a long breath and once I saw the truth in her eyes, I slowly let it out.

"Okay," I said with a nod. "And make sure you wear the purple underwear - they're my favorite."

With a giggle that made my heart race, she turned and left the kitchen, with an extra wiggle to that fine ass of hers. Once she'd disappeared, I slapped a hand over my mouth and let out the sob of pain that I'd been holding. I couldn't lose her and would do everything in my power to make sure that this fucking shit storm she was about to enter didn't swallow her up whole.

thirty-eight

Jemma

As we walked out of the Cancer Center, the tension between Garratt and I was as thick as glue. I knew he was seething with pent up anger, trying hard not to let it loose just in case he could persuade me that my 'stupid ass decision' was wrong. He could barely look at me, and hadn't been able to since I'd told Dr. Kruger I didn't think I was going to have the mastectomy.

"That's the most stupid ass decision I ever heard," he growled. "You damn well will have it."

"I think that's my choice. Isn't that right, Dr. Kruger?"

I pulled my hand away from Garratt's grip and crossed my arms over my waist. I knew I was being a total bitch about it; he loved me and wanted what was best for me, whatever would keep me alive. I, on the other hand, decided I hated everyone and everything at that moment. Life fucking sucked hairy balls and I was going to do whatever I wanted to do, fuck to anyone else.

"It is, Jemma," Dr. Kruger replied, leaning forward on her leather topped desk. "But I would strongly suggest that a mastectomy is something you should think seriously about."

"I could have regular checkups, though. Yearly ones to ensure that if I do get it, it'll be caught early."

Garratt made a sound beside me that told me he was close to losing it.

"Yes, you could. However, when you consider how aggressive your sister's cancer was, and according to her notes, she got it checked out as soon as she found the lump-"

"It's a stupid damn decision not to have it," Garratt said, interrupting Dr. Kruger.

Dr. Kruger smiled at him, and I could see the sympathy in her eyes. She thought, as he did, that I was making the wrong choice.

"Garratt's right in that my recommendation would be that you have the procedure, but you're also right," she sighed. "It is your decision."

"This is fucking bullshit," Garratt cursed and pushed up from his chair. "You can't be serious, Jemma."

I couldn't look at him, because I knew if I did and saw his pain, it would break my heart into thousands of tiny shards. This was what I wanted. I did not want to be ashamed of my body, or hide away from the man I loved because I was scared he'd be turned sick to his stomach by my scars.

"Listen," Dr. Kruger said. "Why don't you take some time to think about it? There's no real urgency, but I wouldn't suggest that means we leave it for months. You could take a couple of weeks."

"No need," I replied shaking my head. "My mind is made up."

That was when I heard the door slam behind Garratt.

He'd been waiting for me outside Dr. Kruger's office, but hadn't spoken a single word as we made our way to the car. Not a word was spoken in the car on the way back to my apartment, or as we walked up the stairs, or even when we went inside and he threw his jacket onto the couch. Then he finally let it rip.

"Please tell me all that bullshit in the doctor's office was exactly that - fucking bullshit."

I shook my head. "No. I don't want it done."

"You do realize having it done will save your fucking life right?"

"Yes, but so will regular checkups."

Garratt shook his head and put his hands to his hips. "You were listening to what she said, about your sister's cancer being aggressive? Because if you were, I know you're intelligent enough to know that regular checkups would not have saved her."

"Don't even talk about her," I cried, hot tears stinging my eyes. "This is not about her."

"Like fuck, it isn't." Garratt grabbed hold of my shoulders and stooped down to look me in the eye. "Jemma, you have to have this procedure, otherwise, if you get cancer it could be too damn late."

"I might be lucky," I said, not really believing it myself. "I might not even get cancer."

"Why take the fucking risk?" he asked, exasperation lacing his tone.

Garratt's gaze was pinned to my face as he watched me carefully. He must have seen that I wasn't changing my mind, because he shook his head and let me go, moving a few steps back from me.

"Does what we have mean nothing to you?" he asked.

"This is not about us," I sobbed, my face wet with tears. "This is about me. What I want or don't want."

"So you don't want us? Because you not doing something that could save your life, pretty much tells me that you don't."

"Of course, I want us," I cried, my voice breaking. "Not having the procedure doesn't mean we can't be together. I just have to be extra vigilant, that's all."

Garratt dropped his head into his hands and let out a thunderous growl.

"There isn't any point in being extra vigilant," he said. "Not if you get an aggressive cancer. Did you not hear what the doctor said?"

"I heard her," I screamed, slapping a palm at my chest. "But *I* don't want it."

"You heard her, but you won't fucking listen, will you?"

Garratt moved closer to me and gently cupped my face with his cold hand. I shivered at his touch and leaned into it.

"Gorgeous," he whispered. "I love you more than I can comprehend, more than I can explain to you. All I want, for the rest of my life, is you, us, living a life that we both deserve. I know I'll shrivel up into nothing without you. I won't believe able to breathe-"

"Garratt?" My heart beat was so fast I was sure I was going to have a seizure. "What are you saying?"

Garratt looked at me with tears in his eyes and the pain etched on his face was savage. What I was doing to him was brutal and cruel, but it had to be my choice. I just couldn't find it in myself to make this easier for him.

"I can't be here, waiting for you to wake up one day and find a lump. I can't carry on with my life watching and waiting for the fucking bomb to go off, Jemma. It'll kill me to be without you, but my demise will be far more vicious having to sit and count the clock, waiting for that day."

"Baby." The word came out as a shuddering, desperate plea. "It doesn't mean-."

"Yeah, Jemma, it does. It means I'm not enough for you. If I was, you'd have the procedure. If I'm not enough for you, then I can't put my life on hold waiting for us to end. What's the point of me clinging on, if you don't even want to?"

I reached out a shaky hand to him, but it was too late. He snatched up his jacket and stormed out of my apartment, slamming the door behind him.

"Garratt!" I cried.

I ran to the door and pulled it open. Running onto the breezeway, I leaned over the wall and shouted for him again as he walked across the small parking lot to his car.

"Please, Garratt."

He didn't even falter, but got into his car and drove away, leaving me to collapse onto the cold, hard concrete, crying until I thought my lungs would give way and my heart would stop.

thirty-nine

Garratt

How the fuck I managed to drive back to the ranch, I had no idea. The Monday evening traffic was busy with people on their way home from places like Knightingale, Missington, and Jericho, but I drove like an idiot, taking risks to overtake them, my fury blinding me of any sensibility.

I didn't care what happened to me or, selfishly, to anyone else. My life was fucked the minute Jemma said she wasn't having the mastectomy; the minute I left her alone in her apartment. But, more by luck than judgement, I finally screeched to a halt in front of Mom and Dad's house, dirt and stones flying up around my car.

"What the hell, son?" Dad asked, popping up from the side of his truck. "What you doing here looking as crazy as a wounded bull? I thought you'd pretty much moved out."

"Yeah, well, things change," I snapped, slamming my car door and starting towards the house.

"You and Jemma had a bust up?" He stepped in front of me, wiping his hands on an oily rag. "'Cause if you have, I reckon her apartment is where you need to be if you're gonna sort it out."

"Leave it, Dad," I growled and moved to go past him. He moved, too, barring my way.

"Want to talk to me about it?"

"Nope," I snapped. "Now, can I get past?"

"Not until you tell me what's wrong, no."

"Dad!" I warned.

"Garratt, I've already had one son almost lose himself because he wouldn't talk to me or your mom. I'll be damned if I'll let that happen again. Now, sit down and tell me what the hell is going on."

I sighed and shook my head. "Do I get a fucking choice?"

"Nope." He pointed to the steps leading up to the porch. "Sit and spill it, son."

A half hour later, I'd told him everything that had gone down at the doctor's office and my freak out and storming out on Jemma.

"Have you fallen out of love with her since this morning?" Dad asked.

I frowned and shook my head. "No."

"So what the hell is your problem?"

"I think that's pretty obvious," I replied. "I can't be with her just waiting for her to die."

"Yep, that sounds as though it'd be a pretty shit thing to have to do. But, don't you think being apart and waiting for her to die would be even worse? And in any case, who said she's going to die? Yeah, the doc' said it's likely her cancer, *if* she got it, could be aggressive like her sisters. But she didn't say it was probable."

"So?" I asked, wondering why I was even having this conversation with him when all I wanted to do was go inside and drink a bottle of bourbon and wake up with a storming hangover in, say, ten years.

"So, if she doesn't get cancer you will have missed out on having a good and happy life with her for nothing. You know, some other guy might just step up to the plate for you. He might just sweep on in there and replace you as the one who takes care of her and supports her through each day of uncertainty."

That thought made the blood in my veins boil and my heart clench painfully.

"No fucking way," I snarled.

Dad shook his head. "You can't stop him if you ain't there, son. And to be honest, if I was Jemma's dad, I'd be welcoming that guy with open arms."

"Why the fuck...?"

"Ain't it obvious? Because he'd be willing to be there for her. He'd have the guts to stand by her and support her decision, no matter how shit it made him feel or how it would break his damn heart."

Dad gave me a small smile and then looked out across the paddock as we heard a high-pitched squeal of delight. My eyes followed his and saw Clemmie running through the long grass, waving at us.

"Uncle Garratt," she cried as she reached the driveway. "I've been waiting all week for you to come around."

"Hey, baby," I said as she flung herself into my arms. "What's so important that got you this excited to see me?"

Clemmie hugged me tightly and kissed my cheek before stepping back and watching me, her little chest heaving up and down as she tried to catch her breath.

"Addy gave me something," she finally said, a huge smile enveloping her face.

"Okay, and what's that got to do with me?"

"Oh, hey Grandpa." Having just realized she'd ignored my dad, Clemmie reached forward and kissed him.

"Hey, baby girl." Dad shook his head and chuckled at the brown haired cherub in front of us. She was so like Millie, I could envisage exactly what my sister-in-law would have been like as a kid.

"Okay," she said, turning back to me. "So, Addy gave me something real important."

"Okay." I nodded, urging her to continue.

"She gave me her box of hearts." Clemmie straightened her shoulders and stood a little taller, her pride evident.

Since she'd been a little girl, Addy had a box full of hearts of all types;

paper hearts, hearts made of twine or material. All of them had a name on them, and when Addy thought the time was right, she would give out the hearts to people that she knew needed to give them to someone they loved. Just as Jesse gave his to Millie, and she in turn hers to Jesse, Tommy Kincaid from town had given his to Cynthia from the diner and they were now married with a bruiser of a three-year-old boy. I think there was even a heart in there with my name on it. So, it appeared that Bridge Vale's very own matchmaker had passed on the role to her little sister.

"That's a real important job you got there," my dad said.

"I know, Grandpa," Clemmie said excitedly. "Addy said I have to be real sure before I give the hearts out. I was going to give Benjie his, because Daddy said he was sweet on the principal at his school, but I haven't seen him. And I kinda need to see it for myself." She nodded earnestly. "I mean, just because Daddy said, doesn't mean it's true love, right?"

Dad and I nodded, exchanging amused glances.

"So, how can I help?" I asked. "You want me to bring Benjie and Principal Turnbull over so you can check it out for yourself?"

"No, silly," Clemmie gave a hearty laugh and waved a hand at me. "I'll see them soon enough."

"Well if that's not it, I'm a bit stumped as to what you want, baby."

Clemmie frowned and dug her hand inside the pocket of the denim skirt she was wearing with a lemon tee that said "My Daddy is Awesome" on the front of it.

"Here," she said, thrusting her hand at me. "This is for you to give to Jemma."

She placed a heart shaped eraser in my hand and tried to wink at me, which to be honest was more of a slow blink.

"It's time, Uncle Garratt."

I looked down at the red, white, and blue eraser with my name written on it in black ink, and sighed.

"I think she has a point, Garr," my dad said.

I looked at him and then at my beautiful niece. They were right, it was time. Time I stopped being a selfish, pig-headed, dick brain and go and support my gorgeous girlfriend.

"Yeah, I think she does," I replied, getting to my feet.

"Are you going to give it to her now?" Clemmie's eyes were as wide as saucers as she jumped up and down, clapping her little hands.

"Yeah, baby, I am."

I stooped down and kissed the top of her head.

"Oh my goodness, that's my first one, Grandpa."

"Is that so? Well that's just great, honey. Who's getting the next one?"

"Jemma of course," she said as a matter of fact. "Next time she comes over. I'm going to give it to her and then she can give it to Uncle Garratt."

My only hope was that she accepted mine first, because if she didn't, it was my own stupid fault.

forty

Jemma

My eyes were raw from crying and my chest ached from trying to breathe through the fear of how I was going to survive without Garratt. It was impossible to even consider it, yet it still didn't make me decide to pick up my phone to call him and say I'd changed my mind. So, maybe I didn't actually deserve him. I didn't want him enough, just like he'd said, so if I didn't want him enough then it was right that I shouldn't have him. But, I did want him, so badly. He was my life, my air, my light, my…everything. I just couldn't bring myself to go ahead with the mastectomy.

I lay on my bed, listening to the silence, knowing that I'd have to get used to it and wondering whether I should stay in Bridge Vale. Thinking that maybe I should go home, but knowing that I'd be faced with the same arguments there. Maybe I could get a transfer to a school in a different state, or even take a page out of Jim Taylor's book and go overseas and do some teaching. All those thoughts ran around in my head, but it always came back to the same thing-I couldn't stand the thought of not being with my beautiful boy, my beautiful Garratt.

My eyes had started to get heavy, when I heard a key in the front door. My heart stalled. Garratt. I scrambled to get off the bed and ran out into the hall. He was standing in the doorway, his blue eyes full of intensity as he watched me skid to a halt. My heartbeat increased to a rapid beat, and all I could hear was the thudding pump of my pulse as I watched him with one hand on the key still in the door, the other hanging loosely at his side. We were both frozen, waiting for the other to move, neither of us daring to break whatever spell it was that we'd managed to cast. I held my breath, not wanting to do anything that would make him leave again. Stupid, when I knew that there was one thing that would make him stay, yet I couldn't give that to him. Emotion clawed at my throat as I looked at my beautiful boy and saw the hurt and despair on his face. I sucked in a breath, trying to hold back the tears but there was no stopping them. It was too much, I couldn't let him leave. I'd beg, on my knees, if I had to. As I took a step towards him, Garratt let go of the door and rushed towards me. My own pace picked up and I ran until our bodies collided and he took my face in his hands and covered my mouth with his.

"I'm so sorry," Garratt gasped in between kisses. "I was being selfish. I shouldn't have stormed out."

"No," I whispered my reply, pushing up on my toes to get his mouth back on mine. "I understand, just don't leave me again."

My tears continued to roll down my cheeks as Garratt's kisses rained over my face and we clung to each other, desperately holding on.

"I'm never leaving you," Garratt said. "It's your decision, and whatever you decide, I'm all in."

I nodded as my sobs got heavier and held on even tighter. I needed him more than anything or anyone I had ever needed before and I was so grateful that he'd come back to me. Grateful that he was letting me make my own choices.

"I love you." We both said at the same time and then crashed our mouths together, trying to forget the pain around us. Garratt put his hands under my ass, and urged me up his body. With my legs wrapped tightly around his waist, and our mouths still fused together, he carried me back to the bedroom where we apologized and loved each other.

It had been two days since our fight, and while things were back to normal, I wouldn't have said we'd managed to steer through the stormy waters just yet. There was still the huge iceberg that we needed to discuss; my mastectomy, or rather my choice not to have it. We'd touched on the edge of the subject, mainly Garratt telling me he'd support any decision I made, but I knew that if I changed my mind he'd be much happier.

We had made one positive decision, though, and that was to move in together, properly. Garratt had been offered the job at Jericho High and being nearer to town and the main road to Jericho would be much easier for him. That wasn't the only reason, the main being we hated being apart, but his job was the shove we needed. So, we were at the ranch picking up any of his things that he needed that would actually fit into my small apartment.

"We'll buy a house when I get a permanent job," Garratt said as he threw clothes into a suitcase.

"We could start looking now," I replied, wanting him to know that I was determined to be here for a while. I might not be having the procedure, but I was going to do everything in my power to ensure I had a long and happy life with him.

"We could, but I'm not sure how much the bank would loan us, with me only having a temporary contract." He stopped what he was doing and snagged me around the waist, pulling me into his arms. "I can't wait, though, until we have a house. Somewhere with a yard where all our kids can play safely until the sun goes down."

I giggled against his chest, giving his bicep a squeeze. "I think they'll probably need to be in bed long before the sun goes down when they're little."

"Ah, who cares what time they go to bed? As long as they grow up having fun and knowing that they're loved." He gave me a quick kiss and then turned back to the case of clothes. "You got room in your closet for my gear?"

"Yeah, I've moved my summer clothes into boxes under the bed, so you might have to do the same."

"No problem. Sounds like a good idea."

"What else do you need me to pack into this box?" I asked, pointing at the container on his bed.

"Everything that's on the chair has to go," he replied, nodding towards the chair. "The rest of my stuff, Mom said I can leave here and just get it as and when I need it."

"Did I hear my name?" Bonnie came into the room carrying a mug of something hot. "Here you go, sweetheart, this is for you."

She passed the mug of coffee to me and then turned to Garratt.

"Yours is downstairs. Your dad wants some help with his printer. Everything he's printing has a big black stripe through it."

Garratt sighed and rolled his eyes. "I've told him before about making sure the ink heads are always clean. Okay, I'll be back soon, gorgeous."

"No worries, I think I'll manage."

As he left, Bonnie started to laugh. "I should go down and referee them, but I just don't have the energy."

"They're really close, aren't they," I said, moving to the pile of Garratt's stuff on the chair.

"Oh yes, they bicker, as do Ted and Jesse, but the boys adore him and he adores them."

I looked at her and sighed. "I'm sorry I'm not going to be able to give that to Garratt."

"Oh, sweetheart, of course you will. Garratt told me that you're thinking when the time is right you'll adopt. And if I know my son, his love for that child will be fierce."

"You think? He's not just saying he's happy to adopt to appease me?"

Bonnie shook her head. "No way. He loves you, and a life with you means more to him than anything. Kids are a gift in a marriage, they're by no means a given. I was lucky, I fell pretty quickly with both the boys, and I feel desperate for anyone who can't have them, I really do, but it doesn't mean your life, or your love, is going to be any less."

"I suppose not. I just so desperately wanted to be a mum."

"And you will be, honey," Bonnie said, cupping my face. "You'll just go about it a different way. Just remember Garratt adores you, no matter what life may bring."

I knew she was right, and the fact that he'd acquiesced to my decision about the mastectomy proved that.

As Bonnie busied herself folding Garratt's clothes and putting them into the suitcase, I moved over to the pile on the chair. The first thing I picked up was the ugliest looking soft toy I had ever seen. It was a neon green and yellow striped animal of some kind, with a huge purple nose. It had one eye missing and its tail appeared to have been singed and was all crusty and brown.

"What the hell is this?" I asked, holding it up to Bonnie.

She giggled and took it from my hands. "That is Woodrow, Garratt's toy from when he was a baby. I could never get him to sleep without it."

"Really?" I asked, incredulously. "It's ugly."

"I know, but not to Garratt. I remember once we went on vacation and we forgot to take it with us."

"What did you do?"

"We bought him a gorgeous, soft, grey bear with the cutest little face, but Garratt hated it. He wouldn't have a bar of it and kept throwing it away." Bonnie smiled at the memory and passed Woodrow back to me.

"I guess you didn't get much sleep that holiday."

"Oh, we did," she replied, folding a shirt. "Ted pretty much mutilated the bear. He cut one arm off and scorched some of the fur by holding it over a match. I sewed up the stump where the arm had been, with some real rough stitches and did some crazy darning over one of the eyes. It was real ugly by the time we'd finished but Garratt loved him. He wouldn't put it down until he got home and he found Woodrow."

"What happened to the bear?" I asked, giggling.

"I do believe Addy has it. She's just like Garratt in so many ways. A beautiful kind soul. Just like Garratt, looks mean nothing to her, they both see more in people than what their face is like. If Garratt and Addy love someone then you know they're good people inside."

We continued to pack up Garratt's stuff in silence, although the thoughts in my head were loud and clear.

"You okay, gorgeous?" Garratt asked as I slipped into bed. "You're not already wishing I hadn't moved in, are you?"

"God, no," I replied, lifting a hand and running my fingers through his hair. "I've just been thinking."

"You've been pretty quiet since we left Mom and Dad's."

"Just something your mum said." I turned on my side to look at Garratt, laying a flat palm on his chest.

"She upset you?"

Garratt moved to sit up, but I pushed him back down.

"No, not at all. Your mum is adorable and you're right," I giggled. "She loves me."

"Yeah, she does. So, what gives? What did she say?"

I reached up and kissed him softly on his stubble and then the corner of his mouth.

"I'm going to have the mastectomy," I said, moving back to get a better look at his face.

I was rewarded with a look of shock, followed by the most beautiful smile.

"You're joking?"

"No, baby. I'm going to speak to Dr. Kruger tomorrow. I'm going to get it done and ask for the reconstruction, too, using muscle from my back."

"You sure?" he asked around shallow, excited breaths. "It's what you want, you're not just doing this because you think I'll leave again? Because I swear to God, Jemma, I won't. I had two hours when I thought we were over and it was too fucking long."

"I know," I stressed. "I know that you're not going to leave me, and I'm not going to leave you. I can't even breathe thinking of you living without me. The idea that our lives together could be cut short because I'm too scared that you'll hate my body when-"

"Hey, wait a minute." Garratt interrupted me. "Is that what it was about, you thinking I'd hate the sight of your scars?"

I nodded as I chewed on my lip.

"Jemma, you know that's not going to happen. I told you, I'd rather have you here with scars than looking at photographs to remember you, or recalling images in my head. You're who I want, not your damn breasts." Garratt's hands cradled my face. "I adore you, your soul, your goodness, your kindness. The body is just an added fucking bonus."

"But you call me gorgeous," I protested.

"Yeah, because you are, inside and out. You have a beautiful face, but it doesn't define who you are." He kissed my nose and pulled me against his chest; my favorite place in the whole world. "Are you sure that this is what you want?"

I nodded. "Most definitely. I've already left a message with Dr. Kruger's messaging service."

Garratt let out a huge sigh of relief that quavered with emotion and, as his arms wrapped tighter around me, I knew I'd made the right choice, and that choice was Garratt Connor.

forty-one

Garratt

I felt like a total dick for doing what I had, but Jemma was my main priority. I couldn't give teaching my all while she was having a major operation, and then recuperating for almost six weeks. So, just three weeks before I was due to start, I had to decline the offer of the job at Jericho High. I was lucky that the principal had a sister who'd gone through the same thing - shit, if you call that lucky - so he totally understood what I was going through and accepted why I couldn't take the position.

I knew I couldn't have been there for her every day if I'd gotten a full-time, permanent job, but I didn't so was taking advantage of my current position and spending the time with her. Jemma's mom and dad had insisted on coming out to be with her, but after many telephone conversations and Skype calls, they'd finally agreed that Mom and I would be adequate substitutes. Yeah, my mom was an absolute angel and had offered to help look after Jemma. We agreed that we'd move back to the house for the first few weeks, so that I could work on the ranch, but the last couple of weeks I'd do it alone, and Jemma and I would move back to the apartment.

To be honest, I'd have rather taken care of Jemma by myself for the whole time she needed someone, but Mom insisted and I needed to earn some money. I had savings, but they wouldn't last forever and I'd made my mind up, we were getting a house sooner rather than later; and there was the subject of a diamond ring I wanted to buy.

Jemma had been real nervous as she'd waited to go down to surgery, and I couldn't help but feel guilty at putting her through it.

"Hey, gorgeous, if you want to pull out of this, you can," I said, kissing the knuckles of her cold hand. "I hate seeing you like this, so if you don't want this-"

"No," she said, with a wobble of her chin. "I want to do this. It's just a little scary, that's all."

"You're amazing, you know that?"

"No, I'm not. There's nothing amazing about crying because you're scared you might die on the operating table."

Big, fat tears now rolled from the corners of her eyes onto the pillow. Her little chin and bottom lip were quivering and she looked tiny and fragile.

"You're not going to die," I whispered. "Not if I have anything to do with it."

Jemma sniffed. "Maybe it's a good thing that I'm scared of dying."

"How so?"

"Because it means I've made the right decision. This will save my life," she stated, wiping at her face. "So to answer your question again, no, I don't want to pull out of this."

It was at that moment a nurse pushed through the door. She smiled widely at us both.

"Ready to go, Jemma?" she asked.

Jemma nodded and turned to me. "I love you, remember that."

"I love you, too, gorgeous, and I'll see you in a few hours."

I leaned down to kiss her and whispered my love to her once more before she was wheeled away, leaving me alone in the stark white room, in a hospital two hours from home. I was alone, with nothing but a chair and the smell of antiseptic.

The next room I ended up in was the pale blue waiting room, with Mom beside me, passing the time worrying about how Jemma was doing in surgery. It was going to be a long haul, sitting on the hard grey sofas, because not only was Jemma having the mastectomy, but she was having the reconstruction done at the same time.

"You okay, honey?" Mom asked, rubbing a soothing hand down my back.

"Yeah, just wondering how she's doing in there."

"She'll be doing great, I just know it." Mom stood up and went to look through the window. "It's looking like a storm is coming."

"Not a bad one, I hope."

I really didn't give a shit about the storm, but tedious chit-chat was just about all I could manage. Better to talk about the weather than how Jemma was going to cope after the operation, or whether she'd need counseling, or if she would get infections. No, the weather was a much better option at this stage.

"The boys may want to get the cattle to the run-in shed, though," Mom replied. "It looks real dark over to the east, and I guess it's going their way."

I muttered an answer and dropped my head into my hands.

"I'm sorry, honey. I'll shut up. You don't want to hear about the weather or if the cattle are going to be okay."

I looked up at Mom and gave her a weak smile. "It's fine, Mom. It takes my mind off things."

As we lapsed into silence, my cell went off. I reached into my pocket, took it out, and answered it, not bothering to check who it was.

"Hey, bro," Jesse's deep voice sounded over the line. "How you doing?"

"Feel a little like shit, but I'll be fine."

"She's going to be okay."

"I know," I replied with a sigh. "It's just the waiting and not knowing. The nurse said someone would come and update us once the mastectomy had been done, so I'll feel better when I know she got through that okay. Everything okay on your end?"

"Yeah, it's all good here. We're just about to get the cattle to the run-in shed. There's a big storm coming."

I let out a laugh and looked at Mom. "Mom just said that exact same thing."

"Yeah? Well, just shows you she's a damn good rancher's wife."

"It does." I reached for my mom's hand, threading my fingers through hers. "Damn good mom, too."

"Sure is," Jesse replied. "Oh, and by the way, Jemma's principal called."

"She did?

"Yep, wanted to check everything was going ahead and to pass on her thoughts."

"That's nice of her," I said, looking up at the clock. "I'll call her tomorrow."

"Whatever, bro. You just worry about Jemma for now, okay?"

"I will."

"Good. Give Mom my love and I'll see you in a few days. If Jemma isn't home by this weekend, Sarah has offered to have the kids so Millie and I can come visit."

"Jess, you're busy," I protested. "You don't need to do that."

Jesse grunted and I knew he'd be rolling his eyes at me. "You're my brother and Jemma is my future sister-in-law, so yes, I do."

"I haven't asked her the question yet," I replied, smiling, knowing I would be very soon.

"Ah, like she's going to say no," he scoffed. "For some reason she fucking loves you. Of course she'll say yes."

We said our goodbyes and I slipped my cell back into my pocket.

"Everything okay?" Mom asked. "Your dad hasn't burnt the house down?"

I shook my head. "Nope, not yet."

"That's good."

"Mom, thanks for this." I leaned into her and kissed her cheek. "Staying here with me. I know the ranch is busy, so I appreciate you leaving it for a couple of days."

"It'll survive without me, but I wasn't sure my little boy would."

I cuddled to her side, and as if I was that little boy she talked about, I let her stroke my head, comforting me during the most frightening experience of my life.

forty-two
Jemma

To say I felt as though I'd been run over by a truck, was an understatement. This truck had run me over and then backed up to have another go. The ache was constant, dull, and thudding. Added to that, I was prone to burst into tears at any given moment. No one had hardly dare speak to me for the last week, in fear of me sobbing great big, fat tears over the slightest thing. Only a few days before, poor Clemmie had given me a lace heart, with my name on it, and explained the story behind it and I burst into tears, spluttering about the fact that Garratt hadn't given his to me. Clemmie ran downstairs for Bonnie, who also couldn't console me. It was only when they called Garratt back from mending some fence posts that I finally stopped. When I explained what was wrong, he laughed and placed his heart, a red, white, and blue eraser, in the palm of my hand and said he'd been waiting until we got home, back to the apartment. So, yes, I started crying again.

Dr. Kruger had said I might get emotional, or even depressed, with a sense of mourning, but I didn't believe her. I was strong, I'd known what to expect and I'd been mentally prepared. I was wrong. I felt as though I wasn't a proper woman any longer and was petrified at how my breasts were going to look. Would I look like a freak? Dr. Carter, my surgeon, told me that everything had gone really well. The scars on my back, where they'd taken muscle for the reconstruction, would gradually fade, and he'd been able to construct nipples for me, too. In his words, 'those boobs are gonna be round and perky, sugar'. Apparently, he was one of the best reconstruction surgeons in the country, but the fact that he wore a Stetson on his rounds did make me wonder. However, Dr. Kruger couldn't speak highly enough of him, so I had to take Dr. Carter's word that he'd given me amazing new boobs.

"Hey, gorgeous," Garratt said, coming into the room. "How you feeling?"

I wasn't sure I was supposed to feel hot and bothered by him just a week after major surgery and while feeling so much discomfort, but I did. Working on the ranch suited him. He looked gorgeous in a suit, but in jeans, a plaid shirt with the sleeves rolled up, cowboy boots, and a Stetson pushed to the back of his head, I really wasn't sure which version of Garratt was my favorite.

"Okay," I sighed, putting my Kindle down on the side table next to my chair. "Getting a little stir crazy being stuck in here."

"I know, but you need to rest. Maybe in a few days you can go over and see Millie and the kids. You just need to be careful."

"I know."

I pouted but knew it would get me nowhere. Garratt had listened intently to Dr. Carter's instruction on my after care, and had even written it all down in a note book.

"You done your stretching exercises?" he asked, pulling up a foot stool and perching on it.

"Yes," I groaned, mentally reliving the pain my shoulder rolls, elbow circles, and overhead reaches had caused. "And your mum has emptied my drainage tubes."

"Everything look okay?" Garratt asked, concern etched on his face.

I nodded. "Yep, and not as much as yesterday, so hopefully I won't have them for much longer."

Garratt gave me a small smile and pulled his hat off, laying it on the floor. His head was sweaty and his hair was at all angles, especially after he ran a hand through it.

"You look tired, baby," I said, holding my hand out for his.

Garratt took it and leaned forward to kiss it. "I'm fine. Just got out of the habit of manual work, is all."

Tears pricked my eyes and my throat got scratchy. "If it wasn't for me you'd be teaching."

"Hey, come on," he cajoled, taking my hand to his lips once more. "We talked about this; even if I'd been teaching, I'd have taken some unpaid vacation time to be with you."

"But you're not teaching. You turned down a job to look after me and you're having to spend your days working like a Trojan instead."

As was the norm, I started to cry.

"Jemma, sweetheart," Garratt whispered. "I was working on this ranch from just thirteen-years-old. This is nothing that I haven't done before. While it's not what I want to do long-term, I'm loving it. Working with Jesse and the boys, it's hard, but it's like a fucking 'Boys Own Adventure' story every damn day."

"You sure you're not just saying that?" I asked, wiping my nose with the back of my hand.

"I'm sure, but I have to say, gorgeous, you keep wiping your boogers on the back of your hand I might have to spank your ass."

I started to giggle and was rewarded with a beautiful smile from my beautiful boy.

"Now," he said, scooting forwards on the stool. "Tell me again how perky those tits are going to be."

The next few weeks became a daily routine of exercises, drainage tubes being emptied, medication, and checkups. Once the drains were removed, I was allowed to do a little bit more than sit in a chair and be waited on by Bonnie all day, so I spent a lot of time with Millie and Hunter while Clemmie was at school. I had to be honest, I loved it. Hunter was an amazing and boisterous child who laughed at absolutely everything. Being around him, though, made me yearn even more for a family of my own. The trouble with that, was Garratt hadn't mentioned adoption, not since I'd had my mastectomy. In fact, if I thought about it, he'd never, ever mentioned marriage. Yes, he'd said he wanted to spend the rest of his life with me and for us to have a family, but never anything about me being his wife. Not that I was particularly bothered. I wasn't religious or had any particular moral views on living together and having kids out of wedlock, but I was surprised at Garratt, coming from the background that he did, living in the town that he did. Bridge Vale wasn't exactly an avant garde metropolis.

"How did Jesse propose to you?" I asked Millie as she placed a blanket over Hunter, who had dropped onto the rug in front of the fire and fallen asleep.

She sighed dreamily. "At the airport. I was on my way home, running away from him because I thought he didn't want me."

"What?" I exclaimed. "I cannot imagine Jesse *ever* giving that impression. He's absolutely crazy about you."

"Yes, well, he wasn't always so open with his emotions," she replied as she flopped down onto the couch next to me. "Let's say he was consumed with guilt over his first wife."

"Garratt told me all about that. He said Jesse didn't cope well."

"No, he didn't. But, the main thing is we got through it."

She shook her head, and I could sense that it was something that she wasn't comfortable talking about.

"So, did he follow you to the airport?" I asked, moving the conversation back to safer grounds.

"He did. He brought Addy with him and they both asked me to marry them, in a packed departure lounge."

"Oh my God, that's so romantic."

Millie hugged herself, obviously in full agreement.

"Did you ever consider having the kids before you got married?" I asked. "Just living together, I mean?"

Millie looked at me quizzically and shook her head. "No, we didn't think about it. Once we were married we decided we wanted a baby together. Why do you ask?"

"It's just that Garratt and I have talked about adopting, but never marriage."

"Well, I'm sure he's thinking that's all part of the plan," she replied, leaning forward to move Hunter's blanket further up his body. "So, it's the big reveal tomorrow. The bandages come off."

I nodded and smiled, a little bit surprised in the sudden change in subject; Millie always loved to swap stories about Jesse and Garratt, it was pretty much our favorite topic, just not today apparently.

"Yeah," I replied. "Tomorrow is the day."

And I was scared beyond belief about it.

forty-three
Garratt

Jemma stood in front of me, and my heart broke for the agony she was going through. She'd been scared to take the bandages off and see what her body was going to look like but had asked for me to be here. However, I could see that she was torn; she needed my support, but didn't want to risk that I'd hate what I was about to see.

That wasn't going to happen. I'd told her on numerous occasions it wasn't her body I loved, it was her. I couldn't see how I wouldn't like what I saw anyways. Dr. Carter had included us both in his consultation, discussing size and shape. Ultimately, that had been Jemma's decision, but she'd asked my opinion.

"You ready?" she asked, her hand shaking against the hospital gown that she was holding against her.

Dr. Carter had removed the bandages and dressings, and had then ushered me into the consulting room before leaving us alone.

"I'm ready." I smiled widely, trying to give her confidence, but I knew it would take a lot more than a flash of my teeth to do that.

"Okay," Jemma said and, swallowing hard, she dropped the gown.

I kept my eyes on hers as I felt the cotton fall into the space between us.

"I love you. More than anything in this world. Okay?"

Jemma nodded and gave me the tiniest of smiles. "Just look, Garratt. Please."

Slowly, I lowered my gaze, bracing myself to be shocked, preparing myself to hide it, but when my eyes moved from her slim shoulders down to her breasts, I was astonished. Yes, there was an angry, red, horizontal scar across each one, and her nipples weren't exactly like real nipples, but they were…amazing.

"You hate them, don't you?" she asked.

"God, no. They're fucking great. They look so real."

I continued to stare at them in wonderment and reached out a tentative hand.

"Can I touch them?" I asked, my eyes darting up to Jemma's face.

She nodded. "I won't be able to feel much. They're going to be pretty insensitive," she sighed.

My heart dropped for her. My woman loved having her nipples sucked. It was her favorite part of our foreplay, and that, too, had been taken from her.

"I'm sorry," I whispered.

"It's fine." She forced a smile. "Go on, touch them."

My hand shook as it stretched out towards her right breast, and as my palm cupped it gently, I took in a deep breath.

"Shit, they're good," I said, grinning like a teenager getting to second base for the first time.

"Really?"

"Oh my God, yeah. Turn around, let me see your back."

Jemma gritted her teeth and slowly twirled around to show me the neat, diagonal scars under her shoulder blades.

"They're not as bad as I expected," I said, running a finger down one of them. "He's damn good."

Jemma turned back to face me, her hazel eyes questioning me. "Are you sure?"

I pulled her into my arms, being careful not to squash her against my chest too tightly, and kissed her forehead.

"They look great, gorgeous. I swear to you."

It was then that I felt her sag in my arms. The relief seeping from her.

"Oh, thank God. I was really pleased with them," she said, her voice high with excitement. "But I wanted you to like them, too."

"Told you before, it's you I love, but that said, that's one of the best pair of tits I've ever seen, and your real ones were freaking awesome."

Jemma started to laugh and gently pulled away from my hold. "Well, thank you, but I'd better get dressed now."

I kissed her quickly on the mouth and moved back. "I'll wait outside."

"Okay. Hey, do you think we could go shopping and then grab some lunch somewhere before we go home?" Jemma's face was bright with anticipation.

I quickly looked at my watch, it was just after ten. Thank God Dr. Carter had offered to see us at Knightingale Hospital. I groaned inwardly, knowing I was going to have to spoil her good mood. I had stuff to do.

"Sorry, gorgeous. I really need to get back."

"Oh, okay, no worries."

Her little face fell and I felt like a total dickwad.

"Maybe dinner?" she asked, hopefully.

Fuck. "Sorry, no can do. I'm going to be out all day with Jesse looking at cattle and then we thought we might stop off at Rowdy's for dinner; Thursday is chili night. Maybe tomorrow?"

Sucking on her bottom lip, Jemma nodded and turned away from me. I could see by the stoop of her shoulders that she was upset, but I couldn't change my plans. I just hoped that she understood when she found out what I'd actually be doing.

"You good to go?" Jesse asked as I met him by the side of his truck a half hour after getting back from the hospital.

"Yep. You got everything fixed?"

He rolled his eyes and got inside the truck, muttering to himself.

"I'm just checking," I said as I buckled myself in. "This is important, Jess."

"I know that, *Garr*. So just fucking trust me."

"Well that's more than Jemma does of me at the moment," I growled. "It was like a fucking episode of *Jeopardy* she was asking so many damn questions. Where were we going, who would be there, what time would I be back. I almost congratulated her on winning a thousand dollars."

Jesse snorted out a laugh. "You are such a dick sometimes."

"Yeah, and my girlfriend seems to think so, too."

"It'll be fine. This time tomorrow she'll forgive you."

"I fucking hope so, bro, because without putting too fine a point on it, if this all goes wrong I'll be lucky if I get my hands on those new tits *ever*."

Jesse groaned, smacked me around the back of the head, and put the truck into drive.

forty-four

Jemma

I felt sick to my stomach with fear, dread, and uncertainty swilling around in there and fighting with each other.

Garratt hadn't got home until almost one in the morning after going out with Jesse. I knew he'd gone out with his brother, but when he got home there was no stench of beer or alcohol of any kind. I knew that should be a good thing, but Jesse was driving, so why hadn't Garratt had a drink at Rowdy's? And why did I hear Jesse's truck just after midnight, and only one door slam shut?

I couldn't bring myself to ask Garratt, because I was too scared that I'd see through a lie. Call me cowardly, but what I didn't know couldn't hurt me, right?

"What you doing today?" Garratt asked, swigging down the last of his coffee. "Any plans?"

"Nothing, why?" I looked at him expectantly, hoping he was going to suggest lunch or something.

"No reason. I'll be back a little late tonight. Jesse wants me to check on some cattle that a guy in Missington has for sale."

"More cattle." I smiled, but felt miserable. "Okay."

"Mom should be back from the bunkhouse in about a half hour. She's changing the linens. You be okay until then?"

"Yes, fine."

Garratt stooped down and gave me a perfunctory kiss on the top of my head and then left the house. As the door banged shut, I jolted and felt tears prick my eyes. I had a feeling that after everything, I was losing him and I wasn't sure I'd survive if I did.

"Hey, you," Millie greeted me as she came into the lounge. "How do you fancy getting dressed up and you and I go out for a drive?"

I shrugged, not feeling any enthusiasm to do anything but stuff my face with chocolate and watching reruns of *One Tree Hill*.

"I don't think I'm really up for company," I said, trying to offer up a smile. "I don't have much to wear anyway. I've only got a few loose fitting tops with me, nothing really nice."

"I have lots of stuff that I never get chance to wear," Millie said. "It'll be great. Bonnie is having the kids, Jesse has gone to look at some cattle with Garratt, and you and I could go into Knightingale and get cocktails. We could get an Uber back."

On hearing Jesse had gone with Garratt, my nerves eased a little; he hadn't been lying about that. I looked up at Millie, who looked so excited, and it *would* do me good to get out.

"I'll have to drink virgin cocktails, because of my medication, so I could drive," I said hesitantly, still not sure I was feeling in the mood.

Millie waved a dismissive hand at me. "Ah, phooey. A couple of drinks won't hurt you. Seriously, Jem, you deserve to let your hair down a little."

I looked outside and the bright, autumn sunshine *was* pretty inviting.

"Okay, but seriously I have nothing to wear."

"Come with me then," Millie giggled, holding out her hand for me. "I can easily find something."

I doubted it, she was at least three inches shorter than me and had the most curvaceous bottom I'd ever seen, whereas mine was just average. Not wanting to disappoint her, I nodded and followed her out of the house.

"Where's Bonnie taken the kids?" I asked as Millie messed around with my hair with a curling iron.

"Oh, erm. Not sure. The cinema maybe, or the library? I can't remember what she said."

I frowned, as either of those places with Hunter was hazardous.

"It's really good of her, seeing as it's wash day for the bunk house." I'd got used to Bonnie's routine over the last four weeks and knew how frazzled she got when new linens were put on the beds as well as washing all the towels and cleaning the bunk house.

"Yeah, I think she's asked Bella to help."

Bella was Trent the foreman's wife, but she had a job at Hannigan's food market, so didn't usually help out on the ranch, so it was surprising.

"All done," Millie said, standing back to look at her handiwork.

I had to admit she'd done a great job, but it was a little fancy for virgin cocktails on a Friday afternoon. Somehow, she'd managed to tame my wild curls into loose, silky, spirals.

"Wow. It's lovely, Millie. Thank you."

"My pleasure." She clapped her hands. "Now for the dress."

She ran over to her closet and without even looking at anything else, pulled out a cream colored, lace dress and held it out for me to look at.

"Oh my God, it's beautiful," I gasped, because it was. "I can't wear that. It looks brand new."

I touched the delicate lace of the dress that had the tiniest pearls sewn under the bust and along the v-shaped neckline, but other than that there was no adornment. It was simple, sophisticated, and just what I would have bought.

"Go and try it on," Millie urged, "and I'll see if I have any shoes to match."

"I'm not really wearing nice enough underwear for this," I said, moving towards the bathroom.

"Oh, take these." Millie threw some ivory colored panties at me.

"They're new, too."

"Millie!" I grumbled.

"Oh stop complaining and go get changed." She grinned at me and turned her back, searching through the bottom of her closet.

Half an hour later and we were getting into Bobby's Uber, both of us looking fabulous, even if I did say so myself. Aside from finding me the most gorgeous pair of bronze sandals to wear, Millie had produced an elegant, dusky pink dress for herself and a pair of silver sandals that matched the ones I was wearing. The dress was also similar to the one that I was wearing, but was shorter and didn't have the pearls inlaid.

"We look like we're going to a wedding," I giggled. "Not drinks in Knightingale."

Millie's face suddenly paled and she leaned forward, tapping Bobby on the shoulder.

"Bobby, you think we could have some AC back here, please?"

"Sure thing, Millie."

As the cold air blasted us, I began to wonder if maybe drinks were a bad idea, because I was pretty sure Millie was pregnant again.

forty-five

Garratt

"I feel sick, bro," I said to Jesse as I smoothed out the pants of my suit. "What if she doesn't come, or gets spooked and runs away when she sees me?"

Jesse let his head drop back and let out a loud belly laugh.

"Fuck me, Mr. Confident is feeling his ass twitch for the first time ever."

"Because this is fucking important, you douche."

This was *the* most important day of my life. This was the day I was marrying the love of my life - if she didn't run away faster than a turkey on Thanksgiving.

I'd spent the last two weeks planning everything. Every idea that had come to mind while I'd been sitting at her bedside after her operation. Every little thing that Jemma had told me she liked; pink peonies, fairy lights and candles, me in my charcoal grey suit, fish and chips, some fancy ass drink called *Pimms,* and her mom and dad. I'd organized it all, got every damn thing I thought she'd want at her wedding. And it hadn't been easy, believe me, especially the damn fish and chips.

"Garratt, sweetheart," my mom said, "Jemma's folks are here."

I breathed a sigh of relief. The only flight we'd been able to get them on had been cutting it fine, so when Barry, her dad, called me to say it was delayed by an hour, I was fucking shitting my pants.

I turned to see them both rushing down the makeshift aisle in the corn field where we were hopefully going to be married; another of her wishes. I knew I was a country boy, but who the fuck got married in a field at the start of autumn? Yep, me, if it was what my girl wanted.

"Barry, Patsy, I'm so glad you're here."

"Oh, Garratt, we were so worried," Patsy cried, throwing her arms around me. "I'd have hated to have missed it."

"She hasn't said yes yet," my brother joked.

"Not funny, dickhead." I practically snarled at him and then turned back to my future in-laws. "There's a tent set up over there for you to change in."

Barry grabbed my hand and shook it vigorously. "You're a good man, Garratt. Thank you for doing this for Jemma. You have no idea how happy it makes us to know you're looking after her."

"Forever and a day, Barry," I sighed. "Forever and a day."

"Showtime," Jesse said with a chuckle. "She's here."

I felt as though I was going to throw up, but getting married with puke down my tie was not on the top of my to-do list. I nodded at Jesse.

"Millie has this covered, right?"

Jesse slapped me on the back. "My baby got her here, didn't she?"

"Yep," I breathed out. "Now she just has to persuade her to marry me."

"Erm, Millie," I said, poking her in the side. "What's going on?"

As I looked through the car window, the most beautiful sight met my eyes. Bobby was parking up in front of a corn field that had a circular clearing cut into it, and down the middle was what could only be described as an aisle, plotted out with candles inside jars. Around the circle were tall poles and hanging from them were more jars with candles inside, and strung from pole to pole were beautiful, sparkly, fairy lights.

"What does it look like?" Millie asked, the color now back in her cheeks.

I looked out at the clearing, at the lights and candles, and at the white, wooden chairs either side of the 'aisle'.

"It looks like a church of sorts." I looked at Millie. "Like somewhere a wedding is taking place."

As Millie cupped my cheek with a cool palm, I looked down at my dress, at Millie's dress, and then it registered that Bobby was wearing a sports' jacket, cream chinos, and a shirt and tie.

"Oh my God, I'm so stupid. Is this…am I…? "

"You need to watch this before I answer that question," Millie said, passing me her phone.

A video was ready to play, and on the screen I could see Garratt's smiling face. With a shaky finger, I pressed play.

"Hey, gorgeous," he said, waving a hand at me. "I'm thinking you've guessed where you are by now. Sorry I've been a bit secretive these last few weeks, but I wanted this to be the best thing you'll ever experience in your life, if you say yes, of course. Everything you love under one sky, in one place. But, no pressure, don't let me guilt you into agreeing to marry me today."

I started to silently cry as my heartbeat increased, already wanting to say yes and not bother with the rest of the video. Millie passed me a tissue that I took and dabbed under my eyes.

"Aside from all of this," Garratt said on the video. "There are lots of other reasons why you should marry me. So, here goes." He cleared his throat and sat up straighter, making me giggle through my tears. "Firstly, no other man will love you like I do. Well, he might say he does, but he won't. He won't know that after sex, before you go to sleep, you like to have your back rubbed. Well, he might work that out, but fuck, gorgeous, his back rubs won't be a patch on mine. He might figure out that your favorite band is Oasis, but will he realize that when it's ready for the laundry, that damn tee of yours has to be washed and dried the same day otherwise, again, you can't sleep?"

I gasped, because he was right. I'd never told him that, but it had been Lauren's t-shirt, and somehow it made me feel closer to her. Taking in a breath, I carried on watching.

"You know what," he said, flapping a dismissive hand. "He might actually figure out a lot of things about you, Jemma with a J, but I can guarantee he will never love you and cherish you like I do. You see, I thought I was going to lose you, and that changes a man, when he thinks the love of his life might die before they've even had chance to live, or start to build a future together. It changed me. It made me realize that life isn't easy and I can't be a cocky, confident shit about everything. Sometimes things are beyond my control, but I'll still work my ass off to get what I want.

"So, that, gorgeous, is why you should marry me today, because even if you say no, I will not stop asking you. I'll keep organizing shit like this, until one day you turn to me and say 'shit Garratt, stop being a pain in the ass. I'll marry you'. So, just do us both a favor, save us some time, and say yes. Plus, you're Jemma with a J and I'm Garratt with a magic dick; we're meant to be together."

The video ended and I was a sniveling wreck. Millie sighed beside me and clicked open her purse.

"Good job I came prepared," she laughed, pulling a powder and lipstick out. "That boy, he really knows how to be romantic. It's a good job I'm already pregnant, because while it kind of freaks me out to think it about Garratt, he just made my ovaries explode."

"I knew it," I cried around a sniffle.

Millie laughed and put a finger to her lips. "Ssh, it's our secret. I'm only twelve weeks, so we've not told anyone else yet. Anyway, I take it those are happy tears and we have a wedding to go to?"

I nodded. "Yes, it does."

"Excellent. Bobby, get the flowers and give Ted the signal."

Bobby pressed his horn twice and then got out of the car and opened the trunk. As he came to the door and opened it for me, I saw Ted striding towards us with Addy and Clemmie holding his hands. Both were dressed in pretty, cream dresses, with dusky pink flowers on them, and both were holding a small bouquet of cream colored peonies, my favorite flower.

Ted came to the door and held out his hand. "I do believe you're here to marry my son, sweetheart."

I nodded and smiled down at the girls. "You look so pretty."

"So do you, Aunt Jemma," Addy replied. "Uncle Garratt is going to be so happy."

Bobby came to me and handed me a larger bouquet than the girls held, in a gorgeous dusky pink that matched Millie's dress. Everything was perfect.

"Did he do all of this?" I asked Millie, who was clutching a cream colored bouquet.

She nodded. "He was quite clear on everything. Even that."

She nodded to right of us and there, parked up and adorned with fairy lights, was a real English fish and chip van.

"What the hell it is, I have no idea," Ted said. "But he was adamant that he find one. He went all the way to Bulmarch yesterday to get him."

I looked at Millie. "It's a five hour drive," she explained. "Garratt and Jesse took a low loader down there to bring it back, because the guy didn't think the van could travel that far."

"Oh my God," I gasped. "Is that where they went yesterday? Is that why he came home later than Jesse?"

"Jesse left Garratt at Zak's place, that's where the van guy stayed last night," Millie said. "Garratt walked back once he got him settled."

"I thought…" I let my words drift off, it didn't matter what I thought anymore.

"Oh, hey, one last surprise," Ted said and pointed over his shoulder.

I squealed with delight, as walking towards me were my mum and dad.

"Mum, Dad," I gasped and ran to them, pulling them both into a hug. "I can't believe you're here."

"Well, we are," Dad replied. "Now I do believe there's a young man waiting to marry you."

As I stood at the top of the aisle, the opening bars of Oasis' Don't Go

Away started and as I looked forward, Garratt turned to face me. He didn't care about superstition, he wanted to watch as I walked towards him. As I walked towards our life together. Our beginning.

"You ready?" Dad asked.

I nodded, and as I took my first step, a single white feather floated down in front of me, and landed on my flowers.

"Lauren would have loved to be here," Dad said, his voice breaking.

I turned and kissed his cheek. "She is Dad. She is. Now, let's do this."

e p i l o g u e

Garratt

"Hey, baby," I whispered against Jemma's ear. "Stop worrying. It's going to be fine."

Jemma bit on her bottom lip and eyed me with tears in her eyes.

"What if she doesn't settle, or she hates me?" she whispered.

"She will settle and she doesn't hate you."

Today was the day that the beautiful, eighteen-month-old girl that we'd adopted came to live with us permanently. We'd had home visits for the past few months, and everything had gone well, bar a couple of curves in the road. They had tended to be at bedtime when Nell, the gorgeous blonde haired, brown eyed toddler that we'd fallen instantly in love with, was confused that her foster mom, Annie, wasn't putting her to bed. After the fourth sleepover, though, we'd pretty much cracked it and had a good routine in place.

"Garratt," Jemma whispered, snuggling into my side as we watched through the window. "What if her mum changes her mind?"

"She won't, and even if she did, she can't have her back. She's going to be in jail for the next five years at least. She left that baby alone for two days while she sold herself for drugs. You really think they'll let her have her back? She'll be ours officially by law soon."

Jemma nodded and reached up to kiss my cheek. "I know, I'm just panicking. It's like a dream come true, and I keep having to remind myself it's all real."

I kind of had to agree with her, our life from now on would be complete. Nell would be the final piece of our jigsaw, and if we weren't able to adopt any more kids in the future, then it wouldn't matter. We would have our much wanted child.

About six months after we married, Jemma and I bought a house on the same road out of town as Jesse's place. We were real lucky as property rarely came up for sale in Bridge Vale and I was worried that we'd have to move to Knightingale, or stay in Jemma's tiny apartment forever. Jesse did say that he'd build us something on the ranch before he'd let that happen. Jemma was up for that, she was real close to Millie and loved the kids, but we were only a mile up the road and our small piece of land backed onto the ranch land. That meant that the kids could safely visit us whenever they wanted to, which, when we weren't working, was a lot of the time. Speaking of work, Jim Taylor finally caved and quit his job at Bridge Vale High. It was halfway through a semester, and as I was still working on the ranch, yours truly kindly offered to step in and fill the void. Becky had shown her gratitude by recommending me to the school board and the education department. So, at the beginning of the next semester, I officially became the math teacher at Bridge Vale High School.

The house we got had belonged to old man Jenkins, and was pretty run down when we bought it, but Jesse worked his magic and renovated it for us. Typical of my big brother, the only money he would take from us was for the materials; all the costs of the guys doing the labor, and his design time, he took on board. He said he was just glad we were still Bridge Valians.

Once we were settled into the house, we started the adoption process, and so almost two years later, here we were waiting for our little girl.

As I ran calming strokes down Jemma's arm, the doorbell chimed.

"Oh God, she's here," Jemma gasped, looking at me with saucer like eyes. "Garratt, she's here."

I kissed the side of her head and then stood up, pulling her with me.

"You ready for this, gorgeous?"

Jemma nodded. "I think so," she said, taking in a deep breath.

We both walked through to the foyer and clasped hands as I opened the door. Standing in front of us was Tamra, our social worker, holding our daughter.

"Hey, guys," Tamra said, with a huge smile. "You good?"

We both nodded.

"Hi, Nell," Jemma cooed and tickled the beautiful child under her chin.

"Mamma."

Nell held out her arms to Jemma and my whole world fell into place. My heart jammed against my breastbone and the air rushed from my lungs.

This was everything to me. My wife, my daughter, they filled my soul with warmth and happiness. Times might be rough along the way, but we were going to make it. We'd been through so much, traversed so many troubled waters, that bringing this beautiful child up would be an honor and a pleasure that we'd relish, no matter what it brought.

Her eyes shining with unshed tears, Jemma tentatively took Nell from Tamra's arms and hugged her close to her chest.

"She's home, baby," she whispered to me as Nell touched her cheeks.

"I know, I know."

I drew in a shuddering breath and pulled my wife and daughter into my embrace. My whole world was in my arms, and as I looked up to the sky in thanks, a single white feather floated down and landed on Nell's nose. She giggled and with her chubby little fingers, she handed it to me.

"Dadda."

"Yes, sweetheart," I said, my voice breaking with emotion. "That's a kiss from your aunt Lauren. An angel's kiss for daddy's angel."

With the feather held gently between my fingers, I placed a kiss on the forehead of each of my girls and with a final look up to the sky, silently thanked Lauren for being with us every step of the way.

The End

Please read the author's note on the next page.

Author's note

When I start writing a book, I never set out to send any message, my main aim is that you enjoy it, you smile, maybe laugh and go away from it with a warm feeling. So, while the subject matter of this book is extremely emotive, my aim is the same – although this time, there is something else I'd like you to do. I want you to read this book and then make a determined effort to check your breasts regularly and go to your cervical screening test when it's due. I want you all here enjoying life for a long time to come. If nothing else, please take that away with you.

As for the story, some of you may be a little disappointed that there isn't a major catastrophe at 75%. Something that rocks yours, or Garratt and Jemma's world - there isn't, there was never going to be.

This book was always going to be a love story. A story about two people who have something terrible to face, but are determined to do it together. It's about a man who adores his woman and will do anything to be with her and keep her safe. There is no love triangle, no cheating and no break up. The reason is because, just as life doesn't always have a happy ending, it isn't always full of heartbreak either. I wanted to show that if you're strong together, you can face anything.

If you did enjoy Angels' Kisses, that makes me extremely happy and, as usual, my appreciation knows no bounds. You will never know how much your support means to me.

Be safe ladies, don't forget to check yourselves and keep a look out for the final story in the Connor's Series - Secret Wishes, Caleb and Lorelai's story, coming in 2018.

nikki ♥
ashton